THE PRICE
OF
WATER

By
Ross Adams

PREFACE

I've always wanted to be an author, but more "serious" things always got in the way. I've had lots of story ideas over the years, but never the opportunity to seriously pursue them. *The Price of Water* arose from an unexpected opportunity presented by the demise of my then law firm, time on my hands as a result and an intellectual property perspective, IP being a large part of my law practice. Then I found my writing method randomly online. The next thing I knew, I had what I call the "textbook" draft. I got busy again with a new law firm so "the book" took a back seat again. Finally, this year, five years after the textbook version, I met someone who helped me across the finish line and became a friend.

We face many challenges today and tomorrow. Water is but one of them. Perhaps coming sooner rather than later. Water is a precious commodity today. I wanted to tell a story of how it could be viewed in the near future and the consequences of that view. I hope you enjoy it.

ACKNOWLEDGEMENTS

First, I would like to thank my friend and colleague in writing, Gene Hsu, who's advice and mentorship helped me restart and finish the book. Next, my editor, Holly Atkinson, who opened my eyes to certain themes I did not realize were there and making it a better story. To my friends, Eric Katzfey and David Brodess, thank you for reading early versions of this book and encouraging me to keep going. And, finally, to my wife, Kasia, and our kids, Victor and Sabina, for the constant support, late-night conversations, and belief in this project when it was just an idea.

Table of Contents

1. INTRODUCTION   7

2. ILSE   17

3. POWER   25

4. HOME   90

5. RUN   106

6. DESCENT   138

7. HOPE   177

8. SHANGHAI   209

9. BETRAYAL   235

10. NINGBO   253

11. ATYRAU   268

12. THE PLAN   293

13. SURVIVAL   308

14. JUSTICE   330

15. EPILOGUE   345

INTRODUCTION

Ross Adams is a reader and a writer his whole life. He's been captivated by the power of narrative since he was a kid and started his journey to becoming a published author in 2019. He combines his love of history and futurism into his novels. With his unique writing style, Ross approaches each project as an opportunity to push the boundaries, experiment with genres, and craft stories that will resonate with readers. His work often explores the intersection of the present and the future, making you feel and think. Inspired by personal experiences and a desire for knowledge. Ross seeks to write stories that will entertain and stay with you. Whether through possible futures or rich historical settings, his stories will transport you to new worlds.

Chapter 1
RIOTS

Despite the oppressive heat, the man wore a ski mask, odd among the peaceful demonstrators marching through the Center of Cape Town. The front end of the crowd passed through the expensive shopping district in the city center chanting "Water is Life! We need Water! We will have Water!"

Feeling the rising emotion of the people around him, the man with the mask angled through the protesters toward a row of retail shops lined up neatly along a city block now deep within the passing throng. Standing in front of a posh liquor store, he raised a cricket bat and shouted, "They will never give it to us! Water is a human right! The only way is to take what is ours."

He lifted the cricket bat and smashed the plate glass window before him. "Let's go!" he shouted and ran into the liquor store, followed by a wave of demonstrators who began looting and drinking the store's wares.

A block away, another masked man clubbed the window of a high-end furniture store. The glass fell as a solid sheet before shattering at his feet on the sideway. "Water is life! Not for profit! Follow me!" He motioned to the crowd that had gathered in front of the store. They all rushed in.

* * *

A helicopter circled the waterworks in Ulaanbaatar, Mongolia, surrounded by thousands of tribal clan members on horseback. The well-fortified facility withstood the rocks and other projectiles the clansmen hurled at it. The pilot could see the mechanized national army coming through the nearby streets.

"It won't be long now." The pilot grinned.

As the first soldiers rounded the corner to the street on which the water works facility stood, the clansman closest to them shouted to his fellows. As one, the horses turned to face the marching soldiers. As the last of the troops rounded the corner, the clansmen let out a war cry and galloped towards the soldiers. The soldiers opened fire. Horses and men dropped in heaps on the street. The surviving riders crashed into the soldiers.

* * *

Half a world away, on the streets of Lima, another man donned a ski mask and picked up the wooden club he'd just set down. He joined a large stream of people wearing masks of all sorts marching in a demonstration over the price of water in the drought-stricken city. The front of the crowd reached the government seat built on the central plaza in and around the city's most exclusive shopping district.

The masked man fought his way through the crowd across the plaza to an expensive jewelry store. He lifted the heavy wooden club from his side, and without hesitating, smashed the large plate glass window in one smooth swing. As the glass dropped, he shouted, "Water is life! Not for profit! They will never give it to us. We must take what is ours! Come on!"

He led a small group masked as he was into the jewelry store followed by a larger group of protestors eager to find an object for their rage. He smiled under this mask, watching display cases smashed and jewelry stolen. He was not surprised. He emerged from the jewelry store into a maelstrom of people shouting and running in all directions. Crashing sounds came from all the stores around the plaza. An angry roar rose from a corner of the plaza where a bank was on fire. The crowd was hot and unhappy.

"Stop! What are you doing?" screamed a woman carrying a sign in Spanish. The masked man seemed to stand guard outside the plundered store. He pointed at the woman. Immediately, two men in similar masks came from behind, grabbed her, and abruptly hustled her away, her scream cut off by a hand clamped over her mouth.

On the far side of the plaza, a Lima police captain stood out from a line of police clad in riot gear protecting the government buildings.

"This demonstration is over. Disburse immediately. Disobedience will not be tolerated," he shouted through a powerful voice amplifier.

The defiant crowd chanted back, "We need water! Water for life! Not for profit!"

The police captain heard breaking glass toward the back of the crowd. He could see smoke pouring out of several high-end stores.

"This is your last warning," the police captain was done. "We will arrest anyone stealing or damaging property. Go home!"

* * *

"What's going on back there?" asked a worried man near the front of the crowd carrying his young son on his shoulders. "This was supposed to be a peaceful rally.'

"I have no idea," said the woman next to him. They both heard shouts and breaking glass behind them. As the echo of the police captain's final warning died away, the Lima police in front of them raised their riot shields, drew their batons, and prepared to advance. The man frantically brought his son into his arms and joined many other protesters searching for an escape. They were hemmed in between the police and the rioters towards the back. There was nowhere to go.

The woman shouted, "Look out! Tear gas! No!"

Several canisters flew over their heads, some as far as the back of the crowd, the others just behind the protestors caught in the front. They exploded. All hell broke loose as the police advanced into the crowd, batons swinging.

* * *

"Our agents are in place?" Ivan Damsky spoke to the air. His personal communication device, or PCD, picked up his words.

"Yes, General."

"Good," replied the former Russian General. "Stand by."

From his perch above the demonstration in Lima, Damsky and his small group of operatives watched the protestors make their way through the heart of the shopping district in Lima. He was a large, fit man of forty-one years. An air of command surrounded him. As the crowd reached the government buildings and the waiting police, he decided.

"Now," Damsky gave the order, his voice calm.

He heard the sound of smashing windows and excited shouts echoing up from strategically chosen places around the large crowd now entirely in the plaza.

After a few minutes, Devang Sen appeared on his right side, "All agents reporting mission accomplished, Sir."

"Thank you, Sen," Damsky appreciated the big Indian's no-nonsense approach.

"All in a day's work, Sir," Devang responded.

Damsky watched the riot grow as protestors tore into the stores his agents had conveniently opened with their clubs. Fires broke out in several places around the plaza. Those near the back of the crowd hurried away, arms full and pockets bulging. Smoke rose.
"Stop looting at once . . ." The police captain's voice was overwhelmed by the mob's noise. The big Russian remained in his perch to record the events himself.

You can never be too careful. Gezi should be pleased. Cape Town, now Lima. We didn't have to do much of anything in Mongolia to get those savages going.

Fights broke out between demonstrators. He watched tear gas canisters launch into the crowd. The police, much like one of his former army units, marched into the crowd with shields and clubs held high. It was time.

"Withdraw," Damsky ordered, pleased with the progress. He continued recording.

* * *

Bjorn Langstrom stood motionless in his lab coat before the holographic image. He was focused on an odd-colored rock slowly rotating in the air, with the experimental results on its expansive properties written below the image as part of the display. He also watched the three-dimensional video images at the end of a small funnel of light and color across the room a foot above his desk. The news feed caught his attention.

"Welcome to this edition of World News, brought to you by the Greater European Water Company. "It is Monday, August 7, 2041. And now the headlines."

"Riots broke out in several cities across the globe over the weekend as protests demanding lower water prices, intended to be peaceful, turned unexpectedly violent. Lima, Peru, Cape Town, South Africa, and Ulaanbaatar, Mongolia, historically parched and draught-prone areas, were the first places to explode on Saturday, while many other cities saw violence on Sunday. Chronic shortages of fresh water have plagued these cities for over a decade. The controversial privatizations of water sourcing and distribution saw prices for water rise steadily worldwide, particularly hurting drought-prone nations. The protesters claim that private water companies are earning unreasonably high profits and control a necessity of life. Here's how Lars Kunta, President and CEO of the South African Water Company, responded to the allegations."

A handsome, well-dressed man with a **warm, golden complexion that seemed to catch the light just right,** appeared in the hologram behind a podium. Bjorn did not like his smug look as he took in his audience. Lars Kunta delivered his message.

'First, I want to offer my sympathy to the owners of the property that was damaged and destroyed in the riots over the weekend. There is no excuse for violence. As to the price of water, as you all know, we are highly regulated. Too much, we think. Without us, there'd not be enough fresh water to go around. We are entitled to make a profit if we can deliver. We do. We are saddened by the violence and will do all we can to help repair the damage. We always place the public's interest first in everything we do.'
The news anchor concluded, "Let's hope so. And now, here is a word from our sponsor."

CHAPTER 2
ILSE

Ilse Langstrom was in the lab working late again. She enjoyed the quiet. Everyone else was gone, and she was alone. She liked being alone.

Do I really? Like being alone?

Well, she had her experiments and chemicals to keep her company. She thought of them as soldiers marching into a battle to purify water. The world was dying of thirst. She needed to find a way to quench it. After five years of research and double that in dedication, she was on the verge of a breakthrough.

Always on the verge.

Frustrated, she looked up from her microscope and caught sight of her reflection in the large windows. Unconsciously, she reached up to adjust her long, silky dark hair piled high to keep it out of the way. Her gaze lingered on the image before her. The small details of her face were obscure, but her large, almond-shaped eyes above high cheekbones regarded her thoughtfully. She considered that day's distraction.

"It is so annoying," she said to her reflection.

That day, at lunch, she and her best friend and co-worker had noticed a creepy guy staring at them.

"Do you see that man across the street under the traffic light?" Natalie Roche asked, moving her expressive blue eyes toward the intersection.

"I do," answered Ilse. "He's not that creepy At least he's not old. I just don't get your paranoia."

"I don't get your naivete. I hope you never do understand," Natalie said with a sigh. A heartbeat later, Natalie decided. "It's time to go. The creep hasn't moved and keeps staring. I'm going back."

Ilse had agreed, Natalie's mood infecting her. The young women had returned to the lab.

Her eyes refocused past her likeness to trees blowing in the wind.

A storm was coming.

She shook her head and returned to work. As she adjusted her microscope, the small white circle came into focus, revealing the remaining impurities that stubbornly resisted her protein soldiers—the failed results of her latest experiment.

"How do I get you out of there?" she said aloud.

A sharp snap down the hall startled her. She glanced toward the lab's open door just as a gust of wind sent the branch of a small tree tapping against a window. She didn't think it was the same sound.

"Let's just go and check this out, shall we?" she said aloud to her reflection, sighing at the interruption. Pushing her lab chair back from the bench, she got up and went to the door. She peered down the hall for several long seconds.

"As I suspected, just the wind," she continued the conversation with herself but was not convinced.

She liked speaking aloud to herself when alone at night in the lab. It helped clarify her thoughts. As a child, she picked up the habit of watching her father, Bjorn, working in his lab.

"Speaking things aloud helps me think them through," he would say with a smile and a wink. She was very proud of him. He was a world-renowned chemist and professor. Her mentor. Her idol.

She peered down the hall for a few seconds more, but seeing and hearing nothing, she returned to her work. Her work. It was what got her up each morning. She loved it.

Because of her father.

* * *

"What do you say we go on an adventure into the Sahara Dessert?" Bjorn Langstrom asked his wife and daughter with a big smile as they lounged poolside at the Tunis resort. He took in the Mediterranean Sea just a short distance across the sandy beach. "It would be a nice break from all this hard work," he joked.

"What kind of adventure, Father?" thirteen-year-old Ilse asked.

"I'm thinking we do an overnight excursion to Nefta, an ancient oasis at the northern edge of the desert," he answered. "There is a large Salt Lake and ancient ruins from the Carthaginian Period. Very interesting."

Ann Langstrom rolled her eyes. "Interesting to whom, Bjorn? We are quite comfortable here at the resort."

Ilse saw the disappointment in her father's eyes and knew immediately how to make him feel better. She liked pleasing him.

"Father, I'll go. It sounds like a wonderful place." Ilse piped up with a bright smile, trying to sound excited.

Bjorn smiled, appreciating the indulgence of his luminous young daughter, already striking at a young age. A younger version of her mother.

"Enough, you two," said Ann. "I'll go too. But Ilse, you need to be prepared for this trip. We may see some ugly things there. Nefta used to be an oasis, but this part of Africa has depleted nearly all its freshwater resources. This year, there have been demonstrations protesting the cost of water and riots all around the world, including here in Tunisia. I don't know what we'll find at Nefta."

"And that is exactly why it will be an adventure," Bjorn happily concluded, his big smile returning. "I'll go make the arrangements."

✴ ✴ ✴

"We're here, Ilse," Bjorn bent past Ile to look out the window. "Not a bad ride, huh?

The Mercedes electric tour bus arrived at midday on the outskirts of Nefta.

"I did enjoy most of it. The Tunisian countryside was amazing. Kind of empty but mostly beautiful," Ilse piped up.

"Nice try, Ilse," Ann said. "Don't think I didn't see you playing the games on the seatback console."

"I know, Mom. But it was boring at times."

The bus made its way deeper into Nefta. Ilse saw burned-out cars along the road and several destroyed buildings. Cave-like empty spaces where shops should be. So many people just sitting or lying on the ground. Seemingly asleep. Hardly moving. Their world crumbled.

"What's going on here, Father?" Ilse asked, her face mirroring her father's pragmatic frown. "Why are these buildings empty or destroyed? What's wrong?"

"It's worse than I thought," Bjorn muttered. Then remembering her questions, he looked at her and asked, "You know how Daddy has to pay the water company every month so we have water at home?"

Ilse nodded.

"Well, here it seems they've just about run out of water. These people on the street are having a hard time getting water to drink. Imagine living with little or no water all the time."

"But there's a huge lake right there, Father," Ilse pointed across at the large Salt Lake filling the windows on the other side of the bus.

The Chott el Djerid, Dad had called it.

"Yes, dear. But that is a Salt Lake, so no one can drink its water. We're still trying to find an easy way to purify water from places like Chott el Dierid or the ocean. The problem is Getting all the harmful things out quickly and cheaply. A problem still not solved."

"I don't understand," Ilse looked confused. "It's a simple chemical formula. H2O. Why is it so difficult to change salt water so people can drink it?"

Bjorn looked again at Ilse, then at Ann, who gave him that "I told you so" look.

"Do you remember your school lessons about how water can dissolve anything over time?" he asked.

"Yes, Father," she said with a bit of exasperation. "Of course! But it seems such a simple problem. There must be a simple solution."

"Well, Ilse, it's much harder to take things out of water once they have dissolved," Bjorn explained. "All of this water is mixed with so many different things, both large and small, that scientists haven't been able to get the bad things out so people can drink it unless they use a lot of energy and special technology that is very expensive and takes a long time. Here, where people don't have much money, they just can't afford it."

"That's not fair, Father," Ilse felt angry, a feeling she did not experience frequently. "Why do we get fresh water when these people don't?"

His face became somber, and he said, "I don't know, Honey. The world can be a very unfair place. I wish it were different. It just isn't."

* * *

The obvious injustice of Nefta never left her. The solution should be simple.

How hard could it be to purify water?

On that bus in Tunisia, she decided then and there to find a new way to purify water.

How hard, indeed.

She was glad to be through the grind of getting her doctorate. She'd done it by the time she was twenty-two. For the past year, she pursued her quest by the graces of the Greater European Water Company. She recently got promoted to running one of their many research labs in Stockholm. The breakthrough always seemed just out of reach. But she was determined to find it.

That thought brought her back to her work, and she was lost deep within it in a few seconds. She did not hear the door softly open and close down the hall, nor the stealthy footsteps. Her attention was focused on updating her lab book. She felt a light draft of air and looked up just in time to see his reflection as he grabbed her from behind.

CHAPTER 3
POWER

Lars Kunta glanced at the time displayed on the vid screen inside the Peugeot limousine and sighed. An update on global water scarcity streamed beneath the time. He watched Lake Tahoe in the American West recede to a water line one hundred and fifty feet below its historic banks. The image changed to sand blowing through deserted streets of an abandoned city swallowed by the Sahara. Next was the Indus River riverbed, covered in grass, its bottom spotted with small pools connected by a slow-moving stream. The drone bringing the live feed of the Indus rose above the riverbed to show Indian and Pakistani forces on either side facing off in an uneasy truce.

"And now for our coverage of sports events," a new anchor intoned. The vid screen turned to a European futbol match between competitors in the Bundesliga.

"Incoming call, sir," intoned the limousine's operating system. "Will you take it?"

A welcome interruption, Lars watched his personal aid from Cape Towne materialize in miniature on the screen. "Yes, put him through."

"Mr. Kunta," said the clean-shaven face of a fit young man replacing the cricket match coverage. "I am informed that Messrs. Gezi and Gheel are already at the Club. I wanted to make sure you were prepared."

"Thank you, Dieter," Lars responded pleasantly. "It will be interesting to see whether they get along. If it had not been for the need for absolute secrecy, I would have preferred a holographic conference to avoid their being in the same room. Thank you for the warning."

"Is there anything else?" Lars asked after several beats of silence.

"No, Sir. Nothing more, Sir. I will be standing by if needed."

Lards ended the call with the press of a button on the armrest of the luxurious car.

Lars idly glanced out the window after ending the link and above through the roof windows of the self-driving limousine. It expertly navigated through mid-day traffic once off the autobahn that led from the airport to Brussels Centrum.

Gray skies.

The skies were always gray in Brussels. The weather almost always dreary. Rainy. He envied Europe. The weather here changed little despite the ravages of climate change elsewhere.

Water scarcity.

The phrase from the earlier broadcast stuck in his head. "Even here in Europe, fresh water is rationed." He looked down on Brussels's water-deprived areas below the raised highway.

If they only knew.

The vehicle slid to a smooth stop in front of a palatial three-story building.

"Open the door, please," Lars asked the vehicle's operating system.

"Of course, sir," the vehicle responded. "Watch your head when exiting. Have a nice day."

Lars expertly exited the limousine and through the open gate.

"Welcome to the Club von Lotharingen, sir," said the white-gloved attendant stationed at the front gate. "Can I help you with anything?"

"No, thank you. I know the way," Lars half-saluted as he began the walk from the front gate to the main entrance.

He enjoyed the walk up the driveway on the red carpet that covered the sidewalk from the arch in the gate to the main entrance. Spear-tipped wrought iron fences connected massive concrete pillars on all sides, speaking to the power housed in this palace since the Middle Ages. Large oaken doors opened for him as he approached as if on their own accord.

The Chief Butler stood to the side as Lars passed through.

"Welcome, sir," the butler smiled brightly. Her underbutler stood on the opposite side of the entrance.

"Thank you, Brigitte," Lars returned her smile. "It is nice to see you again. Which room are we in today?"

"The Salon Bosquet, sir," Brigitte said. "Your guests have arrived."

"Thank you again, Brigitte," Lars set off on the familiar walk to the conference room he knew well and liked.

Lars felt Brigitte's eyes linger on him. Their liaison was brief but enjoyable. He was always generous. She had been discrete.

He passed the gigantic wooden staircase dominating the front half of the building. The stairs ascended to two additional floors, which housed more meeting rooms and guest rooms. The administrative offices were tucked away at the far end of the third floor.

The arched corridor led into the internal courtyard, now entirely enclosed by the three-story rectangular stone edifice. On the far side of the courtyard was a glass elevator gliding up the palace wall opposite the main entrance.

"Third floor, please," Lars requested of the elevator bank. A few moments later, the elevator to his right opened, announcing, "Please watch your step as you enter." When it reached the third floor, it intoned, "Third Floor. Please watch your step as you exit."

Lars stepped out of the transparent cage into a familiar hall. He glanced at the directions to Salon Broquet on the wall opposite the elevator as he turned to his left and strode down the hall briskly.

He paused momentarily before entering the conference room to mentally prepare for the challenge of refereeing his two "partners" in their secret endeavor.

Omar Gezi and Bert Gheel, the Presidents of the North African and Greater European Water Companies, were the proverbial oil and water.

These two really test my superpower.

People consistently underestimate the power of persuasion. The world thought Lars' power came from his money and position. However, Lars' most remarkable talent was getting others to do things they usually would not do. So far, he'd kept Gezi and Gheel on track but was under no illusions. The two men loathed one another.

Lars strode into the room. Gezi and Gheel were sitting at opposite ends of an elongated oval table in front of the fireplace, directly beneath a massive crystal and gold chandelier. Both men studiously ignored each other.

Lars greeted the two in French. "Bon jour, Messieurs." The two men rose as one. Both stepped forward to greet him. Gezi, sitting closer, reached him first. Lars looked him in the eye as he shook the man's strong, callused hand.

"You are becoming more and more distinguished looking, my friend," Lars said warmly, addressing Gezi. "A touch grayer at the temples, I see."

Gezi returned Lars' look with piercing brown eyes, "We all can't have the good fortune of two beautiful races from which to draw," he joked awkwardly in English. Less tall than Lars but ruggedly built. Raised in Libya, he came from a world where mixed-race people were not tolerated. Lars knew Gezi was joking. It didn't bother him in the slightest.

Lars turned to Bert Gheel. Gheel's hand felt soft and small in Lars' own, so he recalibrated.

"How are things in Belgium, Bert?" Lars asked, knowing Gheel could rarely contain himself when talking about himself or Belgium, particularly Brussels.

"Things are quite good here, Lars," Gheel began. "I dare say quite a lot better than either North or South Africa. Of course, Europe has a wetter climate, but even Europe has been dryer than in previous years. The precipitation is moving farther north. But all in all, Europe is fine. "

As Gheel tried to continue, "Thank you, Bert," Lars smoothly interrupted before he got going. He wondered if Bert lived in the city he had just driven through. "That's enough for now. Thank you. Today, we are here to discuss technology directly in your area of expertise, Bert. I understand you have news for us."

"Yes, of course, Lars," Gheel hesitated and returned to his end of the table. "I am ready. Shall I begin?"

Lars casually pulled out a chair at the head of the conference table near where Bert retreated.

"Gezi, please join us at this end of the table," Lars motioned Gezi toward the seat opposite Bert. Gezi grumbled under this breadth but complied.

"There is no need for us to shout at each other across the room," Lars soothed.

The oddness of this uncomfortable alliance struck Lars, as it usually did when the three met in person: two Africans and a European. However, their paths had crossed many times prior to their first meeting for the purpose of acting in concert twelve years earlier. The world had just endured its first taste of real nuclear war, and by then, all three had gained control of their respective companies.

Once Gezi settled, Lars turned to Bert Gheel again and said, "The floor is yours."

"Thank you, Lars," Bert responded. "As you both know, to control all new water purification technology, one of my, er…our key strategies were to recruit patent examiners at WIPO, the World Intellectual Property Office, as information sources. Coupled with the sources within academia and government research laboratories, we have an unparalleled view of water technology to come. The challenge, of course, is separating the wheat from the chaff, so to speak."

"Come on, Bert," interjected Gezi. "Stop bragging about how brilliant your informants are. What have you discovered?"

Bert bristled at the interruption and then smirked, "Gezi, your patience is legendary. There are sensitivities here, which I'm sure you will appreciate once you have the full explanation. If not, perhaps you have a trusted representative who could stand in for you at these meetings?"

Lars watched the man's face flush as Bert mocked him and quickly interjected. "Patience, Gezi. Bert doesn't get to pontificate often in our meetings. Let's grant him the opportunity to wax eloquent on this one." And turning to Bert, "Do you really need to antagonize him? That accomplishes nothing. Gezi and his people are every bit as important to the success of our purpose as yours. Please continue and try to make it efficient."

Lars locked eyes with Bert who was not happy with Gezi's challenge or Lars's reprimand. Bert sat back looking out the window.

Lars quietly sighed. Neither man was used to others questioning them. That made these meetings difficult. Even after so many years and so much progress, ego still filled the room. They shared an insatiable need to dominate and control. That passion brought them to the top of the water industry.

Lars smiled at Bert, the gesture having the intended effect. Bert calmed noticeably, and Lars nodded, "Please continue, Bert."

Bert resumed his soliloquy, not realizing Lars' effect, "Alright then. Before I was so rudely," he paused and looked again at Gezi, "interrupted, I was explaining that some of my most fruitful resources are the patent examiners at WIPO. They recently reviewed a new technology coming out of Ghana. Ekow Aboah is the inventor's name, a chemistry professor from the capital city of Accra. He was a child prodigy invited by the Chinese to attend Shanghai University, where he completed his studies, culminating in a doctorate in organic chemistry. He returned to his home university, Ashesi University, to commercialize his invention. From there, he filed his initial patents, now under examination at WIPO."

Bert paused to wipe his glasses before he resumed. Lars could see Gezi's irritation rising.

"Professor Aboah has been attempting to license the technology, but so far, I've been able to thwart his efforts. But not for long. An essential term of each of the licensing deals he seeks is non-exclusivity. He is a do-gooder, wanting this technology to have maximum adoption worldwide. Exclusivity is the least of our worries, Gentlemen." Burt paused for dramatic effect, looking at his colleagues in turn. "The invention is game-changing. Perhaps revolutionary. We must have it, or we must destroy it. Gentlemen, the world as we know it has changed."

"Enough mystery! For God's sake, Bert, get on with it. What the hell is it?" snarled Gezi.

Now, it was Lars' turn to round on the big Libyan. "I never understood where your animosity comes from, Gezi," he said pointedly, letting his annoyance show through, "but this is neither the time nor the place. You're not dodging bullets anymore!" Turning back to Bert, "Bert, please explain what you've uncovered. I am intrigued."

CHAPTER 4
DISCOVERY

David Jacobs gazed out the large conference center windows down the valley towards Nice. The low mountains framed blue water in the distance. He enjoyed Sophia Antipolis, a sophisticated technology and business hub set on ten beautiful undulating acres' minutes from Nice.

"I think I can see waves breaking on the shore," David said to Ilse in a poor attempt at humor.

He watched her out of the corner of his eye as she glanced out the window, but she seemed preoccupied. She smiled sadly.

"What's wrong, Ilse?" David asked.

"I really don't like people staring, Uncle David," Ilse complained. "That's one of many reasons I avoid these meetings."

"Try not to let it bother you, Ilse," David inwardly cringed at the hollow advice. Her dark brown hair, almond-shaped brown eyes, and smooth skin made her celebrity-like. Something like a rare animal in the reserved halls of the water symposia world. He'd ensured his travel plans included a flight with her from Geneva to Nice after she agreed to attend. They arrived that morning.

"Thanks for the advice, Uncle David," she laughed.

He enjoyed being "Uncle" to Ilse. He reached up to fix his dark, salt-and-pepper hair that never seemed to remain in place.

His hazel/grey eyes were merry when he caught her blue ones. He knew she appreciated that he was trying to help. But he was not happy about the knowing looks from colleagues as they walked the hotel corridor together.

When they reached the conference center, their conference badges got them past security, where they joined a steady stream of attendees flowing towards the exhibit hall.

"Thank you, sir," David said to the security guard as he opened the door for them. David ushered Ilse ahead of him and into the exhibit hall. The guard's gaze lingered on Ilse as she walked by, sending a shiver up his spine. Water industry vendors lined the aisles of the crowded room. Holographic presentations assaulted David's eyes and ears. It took a moment to adjust. David watched a few heads turn to where Ilse stopped.

He took her arm and escorted her slowly down the central aisle. To bring them back to the reason for attending, he asked, "Do you see what I see, Ilse?" He swept his arm in a circle to encompass the room.

"I'm not sure what you mean, Uncle David."

"Well, look at the vendors in this room. All I see are variations on existing technology. Nothing really innovative. What's it been? Ten? Fifteen years since any real progress has been made. Especially in water purification. I just don't understand it."

"I guess some nuts are harder to crack," Ilse said carefully. "I'm sure there's something new here. It just may not be breakthrough technology."

"That explanation sounds too complacent," David continued in his professorial way. "With so many brilliant minds making important discoveries daily in other fields, no one in our industry seems to be getting us any closer to the needed solutions. Where are the Kozlowskis, the Quists, the Drakes? Why aren't they and others like them here with their new discoveries on display? Few are even on the delegate list."

He smiled as they passed by a booth where a pretty girl talked with a group of distracted potential customers until Ilse passed by. He heard the girl's confidence grow as he and Ilse moved on. The next booth wasn't manned, but marketing "keys," driven by artificial intelligence, provided video capabilities. The Key's motion sensors activated as they approached, projecting an impressive holographic advertorial. The voice came from the three-dimensional holograph of an attractive, friendly face of a woman now standing directly in their path next to the display table. In deep, important tones, she began:

"It's 2051. Potable water is the issue of our day. The Sahara Desert now covers a full third of the African continent. The Yellow River barely flows. Australia is parched. There simply isn't enough fresh water. And it's getting more and more expensive. We invite you to contact us, Pure Aqua, Inc., to learn more about the latest in efficient desalination technology . . ."

David walked them through the holographic projection and gestured toward the keys, "This is the exact problem," he said frowning. "I know this company and their desal tech. Twenty years ago, interesting discoveries were presented every year or two. These company's slight improvements just aren't the same thing. What have you seen, Ilse? As a patent examiner, you see new inventions all the time. Is there any hope?" He said this last with a hopeful smile.

"Come on, Uncle David," she mocked him. "You know everything I see is confidential. But I can say there are hundreds of thousands of filings yearly."

Seeing the disappointment on his face, she went on, "Don't act like you didn't know I can't speak of these things. Let's keep moving. I'm sure things will get going again. I do see amazing discoveries every day."

David looked at her sharply. "Really?" he was suddenly passionate, almost angry. "Then where are they, Ilse? What do you see we're not? Why aren't they being commercialized?" David said, "No, I can't believe what you see is that interesting. We monitor the WIPO publications. It feels like there's something weirdly off. It reminds me of the stories I heard from Michael Burry when I first joined the company. 'Look for anomalies in the marketplace' is something I remember him saying. 'Because that's where you find opportunity.' Or something like that. Well, the progress of our industry is a huge anomaly."

Ilse didn't know who Michael Burry was, but it seemed an excellent way to steer the conversation another way. As they reached the end of the aisle with the keys and turned into the virtual tunnel that led to the next one, she asked, "Who is Michael Burry?"

David's face changed noticeably. She knew he enjoyed pontificating on the history of the industry. They came to the end of the aisle and started down another, this one dedicated to software vendors.

"Michael Burry was a physician who left medicine for Wall Street in the early 2000s," David began. "He predicted the Great Recession of 2008 and cashed in for himself and those clients who stayed with him. Burry then turned his talents to the water industry. He predicted the commoditization of water."

"I remember him now," Ilse answered, genuinely interested. "He was an important figure in my studies. The Burry Prediction was right. He must have been a remarkable man."

Ilse relaxed as David embraced the topic. She aimlessly watched the nearest display tout the virtues of its water distribution management program.

"Yes, the Burry Prediction," David became slightly distracted as they continued to walk past the vendor booths. "I got to meet the man, actually. He was quite a character. A bit off socially but obviously brilliant. We need more people like him, Ilse. Otherwise, we're dependent on giant multinational water companies who control a necessity of life. Efficient water purification is the answer. We must get past the expensive and time-consuming current state of the art."

"You're right," she agreed, unable to keep the conversation off the topic. "What I'm seeing at the patent office just isn't revolutionary."

She lied and felt a pang of guilt. He was like an uncle to her. One of her father's best friends. She enjoyed his company. But she knew the real world. There was no such thing as fairness. The pang faded quickly. There was brutality. There was corruption. There was no right or wrong, just survival. It justified everything. She wished she'd not come to the conference. She felt exposed. Vulnerable again.

As they reached the end of the row, David sighed, "Even though everything on your desk isn't revolutionary, I envy you. You see new technology all the time."

He put down a gadget he'd picked up from one of the tables, a hand sanitizer designed to look like an iceberg. He looked at his watch rather than the clock over the entrance to the hall. An old habit.

"We should move on. There's a panel presentation I want to see. A Ghanaian chemistry professor is presenting his latest work. I heard from colleagues that it could be the first major breakthrough in water purification technology in years. Let's get out of this depressing exhibit hall and get a quick drink before the session starts. Then we'll see what all the fuss is about."

A Ghanaian?

Ilse vaguely recalled seeing a patent application involving water purification technology from Ghana in the last six months or so. It was reported to her supervisor as was the agreed procedure. After that, she didn't think much about it. Now, she was curious.

"Sounds interesting, Uncle David. It would be good to sit down. I'm not used to standing in heels for so long."

They walked out of the exhibit hall, turned right, and continued down the corridor deeper into the conference center. After about fifty feet, the corridor opened onto a spacious landing above a broad staircase leading down to the meeting rooms on the level below. They stopped in front of the large monitor on the far side of the staircase to find the correct meeting room.

Ilse found the listing:

Session 3; 10:30 to 11:45; Room A-1. Panel discussion on the state of water purification technology. Ekow Aboah, Jonathon Funch, Thomas Steeple, and Richard Grimes discuss Professor Aboah's latest discoveries and other developments.

Ekow Aboah. I know that name.

The unusual name reminded her of a patent application she recently reviewed disclosing promising water purification methodologies.

"This will be interesting," she said to no one in particular as they descended the stairs.

A few minutes later, David ushered Ilse to their seats just off-center in the fifth row from the front. They sat down carefully, drinks in hand, as the well-credentialed moderator described his own glowing contributions after which he introduced the speakers on the panel leaving Ekow Aboah for last.

"Ladies and Gentlemen, we have a real treat today. While he was the last to be introduced, he will be the first to speak today. Professor Ekow Aboah comes to us from Accra, the capital of Ghana, and Ashesi University's well-respected Chemistry Department. I'm going to take some liberties, which may embarrass Ekow somewhat, but it's important to know how special this man is."

Ekow's eyes widened as he looked pleadingly at the moderator to stop. He was ignored.

"At the tender age of fourteen, Professor Aboah received a scholarship to Shanghai University, where he began his career in chemistry and specifically in water purification. He received his doctorate at twenty-two. He then returned to Accra to join the fabled Department of Chemical Sciences at Ashesi University. It was at Ashesi University that he made his breakthrough for his remarkable discovery. Without further ado, one of the brightest young minds in our industry, Professor Ekow Aboah."

Relative to most fully tenured university professors, Ekow Aboah looked quite young to Ilse as he approached the podium. She had not pictured him this way. She imagined a tall, thin man with glasses in a white coat when she saw his name on the monitor. Like her father, she supposed. But Ekow was only five feet, six inches tall, with dark, almost black skin and a wiry build. He was clean-shaven, his hair short and neatly trimmed. He could easily be mistaken for a student.

Ilse liked his smile which he beamed at the audience as he reached the podium, clearly embarrassed by the glowing introduction. She felt a palpable effect and saw the same thing on several faces in the audience smiling back. She watched as he pulled something out of his coat pocket, mostly likely notes for his remarks, and began in his clipped but precise Ghanaian English accent.

"Thank you so much for inviting me to speak today. As you know, I come from a small country on the west coast of Africa. The land was blessed with many resources, including abundant fresh water. Sadly, like most societies, we Ghanaians took the water for granted. Now Ghana joins those countries with significant water scarcity issues, quality and quantity chief among them. From a very young age, I wanted to solve this problem. With my colleagues at Shanghai University, we completed theoretical research on a new reagent. It creates a simple chemical reaction. We call it the 'Waterfall Reagent' because it reacts with any substance in water that's not H_2O, causing pure water to virtually fall out of the chemical scaffolding. We can now purify as much water as is needed."

He delivered his last remark in such a matter-of-fact tone that it took a moment for the audience to react, but when it did, it became unruly. Everyone began speaking, several denying the possibility, others wanting to hear more. Some of the exchanges grew heated. The moderator came to the flustered Ekow's rescue.

"Ladies and gentlemen, please," he shouted over the growing growl. "Please return to your seats. Please quite down." After several attempts to restore order, and with the help of calmer members of the audience, the crowd quieted. "Professor, please continue."

"Thank you, sir. And my apologies to all of you. I did not expect to cause such a commotion," Ekow said. "Getting back to the Waterfall Reagent, I promise I will be brief. For the first time, we created a reagent that reacts with all the impurities in water, causing large clumps of inert precipitate to form, which are easy to remove. The reagent reacts with all poisonous impurities. We have yet to find an impurity that will not react with our reagent, making all non-potable water available. Last, the principate itself is minable, allowing us to reuse many of the valuable minerals captured within it. There are many interesting possible uses of the principate, which is our next area of research."

"But at what scale, Ilse?" David asked quietly, leaning toward her. "This is amazing technology, but without scale, it's useless."

As if hearing David's question, Ekow continued, "At Ashesi University, we devised manufacturing for the Waterfall Reagent at scale. The reagent should be able to purify enough fresh water to end drought on this planet. We have several strong patents pending and issued worldwide. We seek funding and cooperation to finish the job. Thus far, there has been no significant interest, which baffles us. We believe this could be the solution the world has been waiting for."

Stunned, David turned to Ilse. "How could I not know about this discovery? I've never heard of Ekow Aboah. I look for people like this! Something very strange is going on."

You have no idea, Uncle David.

Ilse leaned away from David slightly, becoming more and more uncomfortable as the magnitude of Ekow's discovery began to sink in. She turned to face the podium as Ekow continued.

"I had the great good fortune of being part of what some call the 'African Enlightenment.' The talent locked in perpetual, grinding poverty and tribal violence broke free. Water scarcity threatens that progress as it threatens the entire world, until now. We believe our discovery is the answer. Help me bring this discovery to the world."

Ekow's plea hung in the air for a moment. Then, a mild pandemonium broke out as the audience recovered, with hands shooting up and others simply shouting their questions, not waiting for the moderator.

Ilse was taken back to that fateful family trip to Tunisia ten years earlier. Her experience there had changed her life. The horror of a near-waterless existence had ignited a passion to seek an end to such suffering. Years later, the flame died.

She sat perfectly still, her face reddening, as she realized that she was complicit in the attempt to keep Ekow's discovery from the world.

David, charged with excitement, missed Ilse's reaction.

Ilse's embarrassment transformed into anger. Her long dormant passion reignited. Not since the trial of the bastard who had attacked her had she felt so determined. Not only did he get away with attacking her, her professional reputation had been ruined along with any chance at continuing as a scientist in the water industry. The hit job done on her to compromise her credibility to any trier of fact had been devasting. She watched the moderator join Ekow at the podium try to restore order.

"Please hold your questions until after the last speaker."

"Professor Aboah," a younger man in the front row addressed Ekow, ignoring the moderator. "Where have you and your discovery been? Surely your work at Shanghai University was published and widely distributed?"

"Professor, when do you think your Waterfall Reagent can be available commercially?" asked a woman from the far right of the stage.

"Professor Aboah, who have you approached so far in your efforts to license this technology?" asked a well-dressed, middle-aged man in the row just in front of Ilse. "I represent the Greater European Water Company and would like to speak with you."

Ekow looked at the moderator, sheepish. The moderator, clearly unhappy, said, "Okay. We'll allow a few questions but must move on to the next speaker. Five minutes is all we can spare. Professor Aboah will be here after the panel concludes for further questions." He looked at his watch and sat at the table with the other speakers, determined to manage his program to the end.

Ilse listened to the questions and answers. She felt the buzz in the room. Ekow Aboah had done it. For her, it was like a match igniting a smoking cinder of joy and pain in her mind. Vicariously, she felt the joy of his discovery, though tempered by the thought of all the harm she and her colleagues at WIPO may have caused. This incredible achievement was in danger of being hidden from the world. She felt a sudden stabbing pain and gasped.

> *I need to make this right,* she thought angrily.
> *Starting right here, right now.*

She turned to David, jealous of the bemusement on his face as he followed the questions and answers. She hated to interrupt, but this was too important.

"Uncle David," she began. "I need to speak with you in private right away."

It took a moment for him to register Ilse's demand. His smile faded, replaced by a look of concern.

Having seen the look too many times, Ilse added, "It's not what you think! Please can we go? Now?"

"Can it wait until after the discussion is done?"

"No. It cannot. Please, Uncle David."

She watched him reluctantly nod and follow her out of the room, wistfully trying to catch the answer to the last question.

CHAPTER 5
INVESTIGATION

Maya McCarthy loathed New York City. The frigid temperatures in the winter. The sauna-like days in the summer. It got worse every year. She made the mistake of taking the subway to Freedom Plaza. She cursed the leaders of her childhood for abdicating their responsibilities.

They could have acted. They had time.

She looked across the sunlit plaza, which shimmered in the June heat from inside the air-conditioned station, and then at her aide.

"Well, there's nothing for it," Maya said to her aide. "Open, you glass monster."

The glass doors slid open, and they were engulfed in an oppressive wave of humid air, along with the briny, slightly rotten smell of Hudson Bay. Her aide gasped as they stepped through the door. Today was particularly hot, even for June.

What was I thinking?

She was sweating freely once she was halfway across the plaza. By the time she was back inside the cool haven of the Freedom Tower lobby, she was drenched. And pissed.

"Remind me never to take the subway in summer again," she said to her aide, exasperated. She smiled to soften her harsh tone. Her aide's skin shimmered with a light layer of sweat on her ebony features behind black-rimmed glasses.

"Yes, Ma'am," said her aide, a recent New York University Law School graduate. "Let's sit down for a moment and cool off."

"Good idea," she replied. "They can wait."

They found two empty leather chairs into which they poured themselves sighing in the welcome coolness of the busy lobby.

"It feels heavenly," Maya gushed after a few minutes, fanning her face and drinking in the coolness. After a few more moments, she said, "We need to review our overall strategy for enforcing climate change violations."

She smiled at the thought of how enjoyable it would be to prosecute the leaders of the early twenty-first century for allowing climate change to go unchecked for decades.

"I may not be able to go after dead men, but I sure as hell can hold those in power accountable today."

Maya personified ambition, but not for herself. Her ambition was aimed at big problems. She'd first caught the public eye as a young prosecutor in Dublin, and seldom did not convict. Each conviction was strategic. Unlike her colleagues looking for advancement through high conviction rates, she chose cases to remove key players, causing entire criminal enterprises to fail under their own weight. She had a talent for identifying the right target. It was a gift.

"The water industry must be reined in. They accepted the responsibility of providing a necessity of life and have been paid handsomely for it. Corrupting that responsibility is unforgivable."

"Absolutely, ma'am," her aide agreed. "We should go, ma'am."

"Yes, I think I'm ready."

Maya stood and adjusted her light blue pantsuit. Her neck beneath her mien of dark red hair was nearly dry. She and her aide approached the bank of glass elevators framed in chrome. The traffic seemed light as several entry areas were free.

"World Police Force headquarters, please," the aide instructed the elevators' operating system, directing her voice at the intercom between the two chrome-framed doors.

A pleasant voice invited them to enter within seconds, "Please take elevator number 5 for the 121st floor."

They entered the open doors under the number 5. As the elevator rose, Maya looked out over the vast shopping center below that filled the interior of the building, reminding her of the forest-filled green valleys of home.

"Why do you think they failed to connect the lobby with the subway station?" Maya's aide asked, gazing back from where they had come.

"I wish I knew," Maya answered, still a bit uncomfortable from the walk across the plaza. "What did you think of the speech?"

"I think it went splendidly, Ma'am," her aide answered with a bright smile. "It was a good reminder of to the United Nations General Assembly of why the Global Attorney General and World Police Force were created in the first place."

"I'm glad you liked it, Maya responded. "I hope the members of the General Assembly did as well. Nobody wants another nuclear war. A small slice of sovereignty is a small price to pay for world peace and individual rights."

The elevator slowed as the floor counter in the upper right-hand corner reached 119.

"We have a few more seconds before we reach our floor," Maya said. "Is there anything more we need to discuss before this meeting?"

"No, Ma'am," her aide answered. "We are good to go."

"Excellent."

The elevator glided to a smooth stop, and the doors opened silently.

"Floor one hundred twenty-one," announced the operating system. "World Police Force Headquarters. Please watch your step exiting the elevator."

They stepped into a hallway in front of a large, brown wooden double door with a modest plaque at its center declaring this to be the headquarters of the World Police Force.

"Where's the restroom on this floor?" Maya asked.

"Just down the hall on the right, ma'am," her aide replied, pointing with a slender arm.

Maya quickly walked down the hall toward the bathroom.

"But ma'am..." her aide said worriedly, trotting alongside her boss. "We're already late for this meeting."

"They'll just have to wait a little longer," Maya said entering the bathroom.

She stifled a laugh as she saw her aide practically jumping up and down when she returned from the restroom. Maya gathered herself and opened the door of the World Police Headquarters ushering her aide in before her. The young man behind the reception desk recognized Maya instantly.

"Hello Madam Attorney, General," the receptionist greeted her. "Commander Yoshi is waiting for you in the Jersey City conference room just down the hall here to the right. I'll let him know you're here."

"Thank you," Maya answered. "We know the way."

When she and her aide arrived in front of the Jersey City conference room, Maya knocked and immediately opened the door. Maya and her aide found a nearly full conference table as they entered surrounded by men and women in World Police Force uniforms, along with a spectacular view of Jersey City's Downtown across the Hudson River. Maya appreciated the no-nonsense style and the descriptive name of the room. It reminded her of who was in charge here.

"Maya," Iygal Yoshi exclaimed, looking up from a screen emerging from the table. He gracefully rounded the large conference table, welcoming her with a peck on both cheeks. "It is so good to see you. It has been too long."

Despite the warm greeting, Maya could sense the tension in the room.

"It is nice to see you too, Iygal." She smiled up at him and made a fanning motion with her hand. "It's hot outside!" He looked good to her. But there were new lines on his dark, weathered face.

"Hot? You don't know from hot," he joked. "In Israel, this would be a nice day. And you're late."

"Maybe," Maya replied. "Sorry about being late, but a lady has to do what a lady has to do. But you look tired."

"Nothing a year or two off wouldn't fix," he retorted.

She continued to survey his features for a moment. Iygal's nomination to command the World Police Force had been controversial, to say the least. As the architect of Israel's aggressive defense strategy during the Arab Israeli Nuclear War, many had objected to his being the world's top cop. Antisemitism remained alive and well in the world, which didn't help. She could see the toll the last four years had taken.

"Wouldn't that be nice?" Maya said, her eyes sparkling.

She never ceased to be impressed by Iygal's presence, and annoyingly, slightly aroused. He was in his prime and being Commander of the World Police Force suited him. Well over six feet tall, he towered over her. He was a warrior. Lean and athletic, still in fighting condition. She liked his dark, curly hair. His brown eyes had just a hint of his Japanese father. She judged him to be handling the pressure well.

Satisfied by what she saw, Maya turned to business, "Let's get down to it. What have you got?"

"Here, sit next to me." He ushered her to an empty chair next to the one he had just vacated. Maya's aide settled into a chair at the end of the conference table and brought out her tablet.

As she sat, she wondered why he affected her when nearby. He had a physical presence, but few men did. The slightly Asian caste to his face gave him a particular appeal. But she pretended to ignore it, as did he. She knew she had a similar effect on people.

What nonsense.

She took her seat.

To get distracted when there's work to be done.

Iygal glanced at her with mischief in his eyes. He clearly enjoyed her consternation. She returned his look and asked, "Can we begin please?"

"As you wish, Madam Attorney General," he said, smiling as he bowed his head. He knew the honorific rankled her. Then, the smile vanished as his report began. "We have a new development in our ongoing investigation into the disappearance of the scientists. As you know, everyone was working on some aspect of water purification. While we've suspected several private water company executives from the start, we hadn't found a connection. Until now."

"Finally," Maya almost growled. "These bastards were involved.

"It would appear so," Iygal confirmed. "We've been monitoring the activity of chief executives of several private water companies. A select few are meeting periodically and quietly. These meetings were intended to be, and for a long time were, unnoticed and unremarkable. We've dubbed this group the 'Water Cabal.'"

"That's a sinister-sounding name. I like it," Maya said.

"And well deserved," he continued. "The most frequent attendees met this past week in Prague at the Intercontinental Hotel. We intercepted a call made shortly after the meeting by Omar Gezi, the President and CEO of the North African Water Company. The call was to one Ivan Damsky, the Managing Director of Chernaya Sobaka Okhrannaya Kompaniya, or 'Black Dog Security Company' in English."

"Damsky. Former Russian general, right?" Maya asked. "Rumors around this man abound. He's been on our radar for years. Went into private security shortly after his tour as the Commander of the Russian Forces in the Middle East following the Arab Israeli Nuclear War of 2039. Rumored to have been involved in the water riots of 2041. His clients seem to include the very rich and very corrupt."

"Yes," answered Iygal. "We met in 2039. He is an impressive man. A professional. We have no illusions about Black Dog Security. Their operatives are very well-trained, well-paid, and brutal. Many are former Russian soldiers who served under Damsky. Others are from special forces personnel from around the world. I know some of these men. They are good. Very good.

"But Omar Gezi got sloppy. The intercepted call revealed that Black Dog seems to be the enforcement arm of this Water Cabal. This relationship was carefully hidden, so it likely went on for years. We've been able to correlate these secret meetings with the disappearance of nearly every one of the missing scientists."

"Excellent work, Iygal," she said. "Naturally, I have questions and suggestions. Let's start with this Water Cabal. Who exactly are these people?"

"Omar Gezi, I mentioned. Lars Kunta, head of the South African Water Company, and Bert Gheel, the Greater Europe Water Company Managing Director, are the other two. The meeting before this one in Prague took place six days earlier at the Circle de Lorraine Club in Brussels. Just the three of them again." Iygal paused.

Dianne gasped. Maya gave her a look to remain quiet, then turned back to Iygal, whose eyebrows were ever so slightly raised. She sat up and straightened her jacket. "I know these men. I've met Kunta and Gheel several times and Gezi only once. All three were at several state functions I attended as Prime Minister. By reputation, they are aggressive businessmen. Very aggressive. But corrupt? Not according to the reports I saw at the time. Perhaps the stakes have gotten higher now that water supplies already jeopardized by climate change got worse due to radioactive contamination caused by the nuclear war."

Iygal nodded. "Between them, they control virtually all freshwater production and distribution in Europe and much of Africa. The stakes are high indeed. There are other participants, seven smaller water companies, and a few political figures are occasionally invited, but it seems these three are some sort of 'triumvirate.'"

"This is good work, Iygal," Maya said. "But I suspect there's another shoe to drop."

"As you say." He smiled in admiration and gave her a bow from his seat. "Just before the last Water Cabal meeting in Prague, an unexpected development occurred at a water symposium held in France. A previously unknown and supposedly revolutionary water purification technology from West Africa was presented. Our own water purification experts are jumping up and down. They think Ekow Aboah, the scientist responsible for the discovery, created something truly transformative. We believe the Water Cabal attempted to acquire the technology but failed and will surely try again. We believe Professor Aboah is at risk like the other scientists. They cannot afford to ignore this technology since this Waterfall Reagent, as Professor Aboah calls it, could put them out of business."

Maya appreciated the timing of his pause intended to let the gravity of the situation sink in. She sensed his well-controlled intensity. She loved seeing him this way.

Why that thought now?

Iygal continued, "Ladies and gentlemen, we have a rare opportunity here. If we do this right, we preserve a revolutionary discovery that could solve one of the world's most daunting problems and demonstrate the value of our still-new institutions to the world. We were designed to bring down corrupt, secret, worldwide organizations. We all know the world desperately needs fresh water. Let's get this done."

Iygal sat down to an enthusiastic round of applause.

"Thank you for reading us in, Iygal," Maya said as the room quieted.

"This is excellent work. All of you. But we need more. Hard evidence. We might get what we need if we catch them coming after this Professor Aboah. What is Aboah's status? Have we brought him in?"

"Agents are on their way to his home in Accra and expect to have him safe and sound later today," Iygal assured her. "The question is whether Professor Aboah will cooperate with us. His unexpected showing at the water symposium seems to have shaken the Cabal. We do not believe they are aware of our scrutiny. If Professor Aboah is willing to cooperate, we will be ready."

"I don't like using an academic as bait, Iygal," Maya said. "Are you sure there is no other way?"

"We are putting together other operational plans, but the consensus is that his cooperation gives us the greatest chance of success. I'm not happy about it either, but if he's willing, we'll use him."

Maya reluctantly agreed. "Understood. I know you will do the best you can. Do we have any news of the missing scientists?"

Iygal's face fell. "We believe it's all tied together. Unfortunately, all bad news. Every one of them is gone. At least, that's the way it looks. The Water Cabal was very thorough and brutal. Damsky's Black Dog Security is rumored to have orchestrated it, but there is no evidence yet. They are professionals.'

Maya was stunned. "In our last briefing, I was told at least half of them were likely on an extended holiday or had retired. What changed?"

"We are catching up but not fast enough. We found one of the scientists slumped over his desk in a remote part of Greece. The autopsy is underway as we speak. The others remain missing, but we're close to presuming the worst." Iygal's face hardened, and he passionately said, "That will not happen with Professor Aboah. We will bring these bastards down!"

An aide entered the conference room, coming around the table to approach Iygal.

"Report!" commanded Iygal. "You are not supposed to be here, Johnson. This meeting is need-to-knowing only."

"Yes, Sir," replied the messenger. "Apologies for the interruption, sir. I was ordered by the Intelligence Director to deliver this message for your ears only in an ultra-secure location."

"All right. Follow me." Turning to the room, he added, "The rest of you, let's take a break."

Iygal led Captain Johnson out of the conference room as several attendees stood to stretch their backs. Five minutes later, Iygal returned with a concerned look. The group returned to their seats.

Iygal stood near the closed door at the head of the conference table. "It seems Ekow Aboah was not at home when our agents arrived, having left the day before in a hurry. They are bringing his mother, Minnie Aboah, here. If she knows where he is, she has not yet said anything. She should be here by tomorrow morning."

Iygal began issuing orders to his staff in the room. Each departed shortly after receiving their instructions.

Maya was stunned but recovered quickly. She moved to where Iygal stood, discussing the timing of Mrs. Aboah's arrival.

Why would Aboah run? How would he know to run?

"Iygal," Maya said quietly, "I would like to speak with Mrs. Aboah myself. Please let me know when she arrives."

Iygal smiled, "Of course, Maya. I look forward to seeing you again." She tried to ignore his playful tone but smiled in return.

CHAPTER 6
CONFESSION

Ilse saw worry despite his barely contained excitement about the Waterfall Reagent.

He has no idea.

"Where are we going?" David asked as they rounded the fourth corner.

"Somewhere private," Ilse answered.

This will be hard for him to hear.

Her rationalizations were ready. She'd been raped. The trauma was made worse by the attacks on her reputation as a scientist as well as a botched and likely corrupt prosecution. The animal who did it had been released. A son of wealth and privilege.

They settled into two comfortable chairs she found in the corner of the conference center's lobby with a wonderful view of the well-forested slopes of the mountains surrounding Sophia Antipolis.

Turning back to face David, she looked down and said, "I guess there's no way to sugarcoat this. About six months after arriving at WIPO, I started taking money to disclose information on promising water technology in the patent applications I reviewed."

Ilse paused, took a breath, and looked at her uncle's face. She imagined his face twisting in hate, condemnation, a rebuke of their decades-long relationship. She deserved worse.

What she saw startled her.

"Tell me what happened," David said evenly. Not pity, no judgment. Not yet.

She went on hastily as if stopping would return the genie she'd just let out of the bottle.

"One of my supervisors offered me a way to make some extra money. Geneva is expensive, and WIPO patent examiners barely get by. I needed the money, but that's only part of why I did it. I was bitter. The system screwed me. Twice. My state of mind for the past five years, until virtually this moment, has been one of disdain for everything and everyone around me. Screwing the patent system, to my twisted way of thinking, was my revenge."

She did not recognize the look on David's face.

"I knew it was wrong. I just didn't care. I've been livid. I got massively abused physically. I could not get a job to do the one thing I cared most about. That monster walks free."

The simmering anger in her voice hissed like a geyser ready to explode.

David remained silent. She took a deep breath to calm herself and continued, "I'm not sure where this information goes nor what is done with it. I really didn't care. Until now."

David sat back in his chair and scanned the ceiling.

"Why are we here?" he asked quietly.

"Because I was assigned one of the Aboah patent applications. I recognized the name when we were looking for his panel discussion. The application I reviewed only covered a minor aspect of the overall technology. I didn't understand the implications. I reported it," she concluded in a detached voice.

"To whom?" David asked, worry and urgency growing in his voice.

She came to herself and looked David in the eyes. "I don't know. I never asked. It didn't matter. But Professor Aboah's presentation today shook me to my core. He's done what I always wanted to. You know this."

"Then maybe we should be celebrating." David's natural positivity kicked in. "No harm, no foul, right?"

Ilse shook her head. "You don't understand. Whoever is paying for this information must know the full scope of Professor Aboah's invention." She lowered her voice, "If what I suspect is true, Professor Aboah is in danger. I am certain he has no idea. We have to help him."

"Okay," he said slowly. "Let me get this straight. You've been paid to disclose new water technology in patent applications you've examined for the past two and a half years?"

"Right," she said, looking at her hands, embarrassed. But then she looked him straight in the eyes and said defiantly, "But none of that matters now. I'll accept whatever consequences may come. What matters now is protecting Ekow Aboah and his Waterfall Reagent."

"Even if everything you just told me is true, Ilse, I don't understand why Ekow Aboah needs protection," David answered.

"I haven't told you everything," she confessed. "I did care enough to look up three or four inventors whose inventions I reported. Three had passed away of natural causes, from what I could find. The fourth retired to Sardinia. None of it seemed suspicious. They were all elderly. Today, with our talk in the exhibit hall and then the presentation, the pieces fell into place."

David looked unconvinced.

"You said it yourself," she argued. "Where is the progress in water purification? Inventors retiring or dying unexpectedly scares me. I think Ekow Aboah is in real danger."

David sat back again. Ilse saw concern ripple across his face, but not for her this time. She could swear he was acting like he didn't believe her.

"Okay, Ilse," David sighed. "It can't hurt to talk with Professor Aboah. His session should have ended by now. Let's see what he says and then play it by ear. But I don't think you should alarm him with these stories unless we think something's really going on with him. Deal?"

Ilse shook her head and smiled. "I won't promise anything, Uncle David, if it means leaving him exposed. I have to speak with him, and I have to tell him what I believe is happening. His discovery is too important."

She was pleased David decided to go along. "All right. Let's track Professor Aboah down and have a chat."

They hurried back to the meeting room, entering as the session ended. There was a palpable buzz in the air as the audience rose and burst into conversation. People crowded the podium, peppering the professor and the other panelists with questions and exchanging contacts. Ilse and David waited patiently for the last of the audience to depart, then approached him as the professor gathered his things from a nearby chair.

"Professor Aboah?" Ilse started. "Can we speak with you for a moment, please? Perhaps somewhere less public?"

Ekow looked up and paused as if in shock. She endured this familiar reaction to her beauty. She watched him gather himself before delivering what could only be described as a one-hundred-watt smile. Both she and David smiled in return. It was infectious.

"Of course, Dr. Langstrom," he said after glancing at the name and credentials on her conference badge. "I see you are a patent examiner at WIPO. You did not happen to come across any of my applications, did you?" To David, he said, "And Dr. Jacobs, it is nice to meet you as well."

"Very impressive work, professor," David said. "I'm anxious to learn more about it. It seems you've encountered some challenges getting noticed. That's what we'd like to speak with you about. As the Chief Science Officer of Burry Water Ventures, I always seek promising new technology. Frankly, I don't understand how you've kept your Waterfall Reagent under wraps. If you have time, perhaps you could join me in my suite. We'd like to speak privately about the difficulties you've experienced."

"Of course," responded Ekow, smiling still. "How could I refuse?"

As they began walking toward the elevator, Ilse tried to make small talk. "So how was your flight in, professor?"

"Uneventful," he responded. "Thank you for asking. But what was curious was the near cancellation of our panel discussion today by the conference organizers when everyone was here and prepared. That was strange."

Ilse looked at David knowingly. "That is strange, "she agreed.

They arrived at the elevator bank, where David ordered, "Open and take us to the third floor, please."

"Yes sir," answered a voice from a speaker above the doors. "Please watch your step entering the elevator."

David led the short walk from the elevator to his room. He opened the door to his meeting suite, a well-appointed conference room with a full bar and a casual seating area with a bathroom on one side and a bedroom on the other. The floor-to-ceiling window overlooked the campus and the Mediterranean in the distance.

"I must say, Dr. Jacobs, this is a very nice suite," Ekow observed. "They must pay very well at Burry Water Ventures." They all smiled, but an awkward tension built as they took seats around the coffee table, settling into expensive leather chairs.

"Would you like a drink, professor?" asked David as he rose and went to the bar to get himself a soft drink. "Ilse?"

"I'm fine," Ilse responded. "Thank you."

"A glass of water would be wonderful. Thank you," Ekow responded. "I am always in need after a lecture or presentation. I know it is expensive. I genuinely appreciate you serving it. But the exorbitant prices should not last much longer."

"Yes, about that," David said, coming from behind the bar, placing Ekow's water on the coffee cable and sitting opposite him. "I'm afraid we didn't ask you here to license your reagent."

Ilse looked at David, suddenly frustrated. "What he means is we want to see your Waterfall Reagent distributed far and wide. We are afraid others in this world would rather that not happen. That's why we asked you up here. I believe you are in danger."

Ekow stood, all manner of friendliness gone. "Dr. Langstrom, you misled me. Is this some kind of bad joke? Good day." He headed for the door.

"Professor Aboah, wait!" She spoke quickly in clipped English, enunciating each word. "Please hear me out. I am not joking. I wish I were."

Ekow stopped and turned to face her. Her stopped him. "Dr. Langstrom, now you seek to frighten me?"

"Oh yes, professor. You should be terrified. That is why we're here. Please listen."

She could see that Ekow was not happy.

"You have my attention. Please go on, Dr. Langstrom," Ekow answered, returning to his seat.

"I suppose I should begin at the beginning," said Ilse for the second time that day. "For the past two years, I've been disclosing information from patent applications I was examining to some unknown benefactor."

Ekow looked at her, stunned. And confused.

Ilse stood and moved to the window to gather herself.

"About a year after I began passing this information, I attended a monthly meeting of the local chapter of the Chemistry Society. I rarely attended meetings like this, but the presentation was on the lack of progress in water purification technology." She and David shared a look before she continued, "That surprised me, given what I'd seen in those applications."

Ilse looked at David and then at Ekow.

"Curious about the inventors whose applications I'd flagged, I checked on their applications only to find they were abandoned or assigned. That's not unusual in and of itself, but there were no exceptions. Then I tried to find the inventors themselves. All of them had retired or died unexpectedly. Again, they were older, so nothing seemed to be out of the ordinary. I didn't think I was doing any damage. I kept on doing it."

Ilse took a breath.

"Which brings me to you, professor. Not long ago, one of your patent applications was assigned to me. The methods looked promising, but the real breakthrough must be in one of your other applications. I reported it but didn't understand the true impact until today. What some call the Water Cabal in whispers around the office undoubtedly knows all about you and your inventions. I fear they will not allow access to the Waterfall Reagent freely. Your Waterfall Reagent might put them out of business."

She paused to allow Ekow to absorb all he'd heard. He looked from Ilse to David.

"No disrespect intended, Dr. Langstrom, but Dr. Jacobs, is this true?"

"I wish I could say it wasn't, professor. I'm afraid I can corroborate at least a part of Ilse's story. I've heard mention of a group of water industry executives over late-night drinks at industry conferences rumored to be buying up new technologies. I never thought much about it since, like most industries, executives can be very aggressive. But Ilse's story is consistent with others I've heard. Hers is the first time there's been any hard evidence of anything like it really happening."

"Professor Aboah, "she began again, satisfied he was listening and understanding the magnitude of what she was telling him. "As farfetched as this may sound, I have reason to believe that you are in terrible danger. I believe there is an organization whose mission is to seek out, control, or suppress any new technology that might impact the price of water. I don't know who these people are, but I have a pretty good idea. I willfully ignored it.

"Your presentation clarified the magnitude of your discovery. It all clicked when you described your licensing challenges, and my Uncle David here had not heard of you or your invention. Your invention is more than compelling. How could it be kept off David's radar without powerful forces conspiring to make that happen?

"At this point, I need to confirm my suspicions about these other inventors' fate," she concluded. "I truly hope I'm wrong, but I don't think so."

Ekow shook his head seeming to clear his thoughts.

Ilse took it as a denial. "Please believe me, professor. I wish this was just paranoia. But it's not. It's real. Your invention is too important. *You* are too important. I want to make this right for my part in it."

Ekow raised his hand. "Dr. Langstrom, I am not shaking my head because I do not believe you, although I have difficulty doing so. I am shaking my head in wonder. You have woven quite a tale, so please give me a few moments to digest this most unpleasant dish."

Ilse returned to her seat concerned Ekow would not take her seriously.

David watched Ilse sit and then said to Ekow, "I can confirm, strange as it sounds to me as I say it, that there has been an unusual lack of progress made in water purification for over ten years. It is inexplicable, given the steady progress made in other fields. As much as I don't want to believe Ilse's story, I'm having a hard time dismissing it. Based on our long relationship, I've known her to be honest and forthright. She has nothing to gain and everything to lose by admitting what she's done. Her first-hand knowledge of the information being bought and sold is serious enough to warrant caution. You spoke of the lack of interest in your Waterfall Reagent by industry players in your presentation. Anything else you can recall over the past few months, maybe years, that seems unexplainable to you?"

Ekow stood, deep in thought, and took the place at the window just vacated by Ilse. He turned and said, "Dr. Jacobs, please call me Ekow. I know of your work and admire it. It is the only reason I am sitting here with you now. I normally do not follow people to a hotel room at a conference like this. Your presence here is and was reassuring."

"I appreciate your faith in me. Call me David. I'm sure Ilse would prefer the same."

Nodding, Ekow continued, "Back to your question then. Upon reflection, I have to admit that it seemed fate was trying to keep me from coming here and participating on the panel we just held. Flight delays. The near cancellation of the panel itself for no apparent reason. Just before the panel began today, I received a call supposedly from my mother, which nearly kept me from making it to the session. It was not my mother, so I hung up but did not have time to consider it until now. So, while you two were speaking, I have been reconsidering what otherwise seemed like random events over the past couple of years in and around the university. And there is more.

"The Waterfall Reagent should be extremely interesting to the industry. Each attempt at collaboration or licensing was quickly declined without more than a cursory review of our science. None of it makes any sense to me, but I am no expert on the commercial aspects of science. I thought it the usual large industry intransigence that resists all change not some nefarious plot to keep my Waterfall Reagent from the world. I still have a hard time believing anyone would care so much about an obscure professor from Ghana."

Ekow sat back down, looking at the two of them in turn. It was David's turn to get up and stand by the window.

"No longer obscure," quipped David while gazing at the mountains out the window. "Whether we like it or not, Ilse has identified what seems like a truly dangerous situation."

Ilse felt her face grow hot as the realization dawned on her. "That was not my intent, Uncle David. I am so sorry."

"It's okay. I'm glad you came to me. Ekow had to be warned. You've done that. Let's contact the authorities now. I know your father has connections to the World Police Force. That's where we need to go."

"Dr. Jacobs, I mean David." Ekow raised his hands. "Going to the World Police Force with this story and our only proof being the testimony of, forgive me, Ilse, a compromised patent examiner, seems like it would be a challenge. Do you really think they would believe us?"

"It's a good point," David conceded. "More evidence would be helpful."

Ilse raised her hand to get their attention. "Here's what I think we should do. Ekow, you return home to Accra as if nothing happened and no discoveries made. I'll head back to Geneva and confirm the fate of the other inventors whose patent applications I reported. If they, unlike the others, are alive and well, I'll give you a call to let you know how much I enjoyed meeting you at this conference. If I find what I expect, I'll email you saying I am not interested in collaborating with Ashesi University. In that case, I'll arrange to join you in Accra within the week. You can decide then if you want to go to the World Police Force and if you will accept my help. It's all I can do to make this right.

"Uncle David, I'll copy you on the email so you know where things stand."

Then, coming back to Ekow, she said, "I'd be surprised if you aren't being monitored at this moment, including the fact we three met here today."

Ekow looked around, uncomfortable.

"Ekow, I suggest you leave alone and return home as soon as possible. Uncle David, I'll leave a few minutes later and return to Geneva. If I go to Accra, we'll count on you to let Father know what's going on. We'll set up a secure way to communicate so you can let us know how the World Police Force responds and what we should do."

"Of course, Ilse," David said. "If you're right, your father and I will see about getting you two help. Let's pray you don't need it."

"Well, it was nice meeting the two of you." Ekow smiled again, his optimism irrepressible. "I hope we do not meet in the near future!" His gallows humor surprising them both as he walked out of the room. They watched the automatic door close behind Ekow.

David then said, "Ilse, this is crazy. You know that, right?"

"I know, but as crazy as it seems, for the first time in a very long time, I feel more like myself. Ekow is going to need help. I may not be the best person for it, but is there time to find someone else?"

"Fair enough for now," David agreed. "I don't like it, but let's run this play as you suggest. I will return to the States and do some digging. Watch your email."

* * *

It was gray and drizzling when Lincoln limousine pulled up to the entrance of the Prague Renaissance Hotel. Lars Kunta was troubled as he walked into the plush hotel lobby and was directed to the private meeting rooms in the north wing. Bert Gheel and Omar Gezi both arrived a few minutes earlier and sat expectantly on opposite sides of the conference room. Lars hardly noticed the view of the Prague Castle and Charles Bridge as he addressed them.

"Ekow Aboah spoke in Sophia Antipolis last week despite our mild discouragements and flat-footed buffoonery." He looked pointedly at Gezi. "Since when do we use crank calls from someone's mother?"

Lars knew Gezi did not appreciate being addressed this way. "I would be careful how you speak to me, Lars. None of us is above the other. All of us are in this together. Plans fail, and new ones are made. Rest assured, we will take care of this Ekow Aboah once he returns to Accra."

"It better be handled," Lars continued, ignoring the threat. "His Waterfall Reagent is powerful. Perhaps the most significant threat to our position. I hope you appreciate the gravity. Please see to it."

"Of course," Gezi responded with fake subservience. "So it shall be written, so it shall be done." He nodded to over-emphasize the point.

Bert Gheel listened to the exchange with growing annoyance. "Now, if you two are quite finished spraying at each other, perhaps you would be interested to know that this African Professor was seen speaking with David Jacobs and Ilse Langstrom. While Jacobs should be of no concern, Dr. Langstrom is one of our patent examiners at WIPO. Please do not underestimate the importance of what I'm telling you. While I'm sure she does not know for certain that we exist or are interested in Professor Aboah, in my experience, there are no coincidences. Do not leave that loose end untied, Gezi. I will monitor Dr. Jacobs' activities just in case."

CHAPTER 7

PURSUIT

"Take Route 89 toward Cape Sounion," Devang Sen instructed the self-driving rental vehicle. "Be sure to go straight south from the airport and then east on Route 89."

"Excellent choice, sir," the vehicle's operating system responded in English.

Devang enjoyed the ride to Black Dog Security's headquarters. The winding road took him through rugged hills with frequent vistas of the Aegean Sea's sapphire waters. Picturesque fishing villages punctuated the scenery south of Athens, unchanged through the centuries. Headquarters lay directly south of the city, nestled in the hills along the coast.

Devang especially liked the arid inland mountains. They reminded him of the southern Thar Desert in India.

"Not much sea there, though," he muttered absently as he gazed at the clear blue water in the small harbor. Not a pleasant thought, the Thar Desert.

"Show me our route," he ordered as the vehicle sped south down the coastal road. He liked watching his progress on this indirect way to the Black Dog headquarters.

"As you wish, sir," the vehicle responded and projected a holographic depiction of the peninsula showing the car's current location on Route 89, a red line snaking its way south, roughly bisecting the small peninsula. At the tip of the peninsula, the ancient Greek ruins of the Temple of Poseidon were depicted as a crumbling classic building. From the Temple, Route 89 turned sharply west and north, winding its way along the coast back toward Athens and his destination, the coastal town of Saronida.

Within twenty minutes, the car rounded the point of land, passing the entry to the Temple of Poseidon, and began heading north. Devang sat up to see several ships heading for the busy port of Piraeus. The ships reminded him of his childhood home in Mumbai, India's busiest port. He, his younger brother, and his elder sister would watch the ships heading out to sea from a window of the family's cube—a modular architecture India had perfected to house its massive population and manage sanitation. Housing did not mean food.

"What do you want to be when you grow up, Devang?" his brother would ask. It was a game they played often.

"I don't know. Just not here. Maybe I'll go to America. Or become a soldier of fortune. Better yet, I'll be a rich businessman," had been his flippant answer. He had not intended to become a mercenary.

Living in Turkey and running errands for Black Dog had been no plan of his. But anything was better than living in the cubes.

> *A nightmare, however well intended. There is a special place in hell for the people responsible for it.*

A pleasing tone from the vehicle interrupted his thoughts.

"Shall I answer, sir," the vehicle queried.

"Put it through," he commanded when he saw the caller's holograph on his lap.

"Devang here. How are you, Ivan?"

"How close are you?" a voice said in a heavy Russian accent with a hint of impatience.

"I should be there in about thirty minutes," Devang replied.

"Good. Make it twenty." The connection ended.

Devang sighed. "Same old Ivan."

Ivan Damsky was the Managing Director of Black Dog Security. There had been a time when Devang wouldn't have dreamed of working for a private security company, especially one like Black Dog. He remained a man of principles. It had been hard after he'd joined India's Special Forces. He had applied when he was with the rank and file.

Special Forces can change a man.

"Call Rachna Sen," he instructed his PCD.

Once he'd saved enough of his soldier's salary, he'd moved his family out of the cubes into a modest home in the Mumbai suburbs. That had been twelve years ago. Israel had nuked the militant Arab world that year. It had been too late to save his sister.

Seems like several lifetimes ago.

"Hi, Mom," Devang tried to sound cheerful when she answered his call. "How are you?"

"Devang? Is that you?" The conversation started like it always did. "I haven't heard from you in nine weeks. How can you treat your mother this way? I never know where you are or if you're all right. Have you met a girl?"

"No Mom." Devang smiled. "No one special yet. But I'm doing my best."

It was a familiar, comfortable exchange.

"So, how are you?" she asked.

"I'm fine," he assured her. "I'm in Greece on business. I called to check in with you. How is your arthritis?"

"I don't want to talk about me. I'm worried about you. You must marry Devang," she pleaded. "How else am I to be a grandmother?"

"Come on, Mom," Devang complained. "I can't promise you anything right now. One day, maybe I'll meet the right person. That's the best I can do."

"Okay, son. I understand. I don't like it, but I understand," she conceded. "Just don't make me wait too long." Then she said, "I miss her."

Devang's smile faded. "I miss her too. I think I've made my peace with it. It would be good for you to it too. We can't change the past. All we can do is honor her memory."

"I know, son," she responded. He could hear the catch in her voice. "I just miss her so much."

"I'll stop by next month, Mom," he promised, trying to lighten the mood. "I have a trip to Singapore scheduled, so I plan to swing by Mumbai the weekend after. Just don't tell anyone. I don't want a fuss. And don't you dare tell your friends who have daughters."

"I must do my part," she scolded. "I just want to see you."

"And I want to see you," he said seriously. "I have to go."

"I love you, my son," she said simply.

"I love you too," he replied and disconnected.

Why did I call her?

The dreams were always the same. The assassinations played out over and over. The Muslim in Kashmir. The Bangladeshi, the Englishman. The last, a young Chinese politician. The quiet puff of his sniper's rifle was followed by the violent explosion of the man's head.

And for what?

A nagging sense of guilt encroached on the pleasant scenery passing by. He knew why. He realized he was a dispensable pawn in the geopolitical games played by the rich and powerful. He'd caused so much pain and suffering that when it got to the point where he could no longer stand his superior officers, he quit the Special Forces.

"One day, Mom, I'll find a way help you through the pain," he said out loud, returning his gaze to the shoreline shining in the mid-day sun.

He'd felt hollow inside ever since that last mission. At least he was able to lessen the pain caused by his current employer.

Ten minutes later, the car reached Saronida. It turned inland, making its way through the small town.

"Approach destination at thirty kilometers per hour," Devang commanded.

The vehicle made a left turn up a steep hill and slowly approached a gated compound at the top.

"Stop fifty meters before the gate," he ordered.

The guards on duty were alert, surveying the streets and nearby buildings. They scanned the sky with binoculars for drones or other aircraft moving too slowly for their liking. Devang's practiced eye took it all in.

He knew his car had been spotted and was being diagnosed as a possible threat.

"Move to destination," Devang concluded.

The vehicle came to a stop at the front gate of what looked more like a medieval castle rather than the headquarters of any modern company. All of the agents simply called it the "Fortress."

A steel plaque next to the heavy gate named the residents *Chernaya Sobaka Okhrannaya Kompaniya* in Russian. *Black Dog Security Company* below in English.

Devang climbed out of the vehicle, his tall frame unfolding quickly to his full height. He approved the charge on his PCD and turned toward the big man standing before the gate. His uniform was a crisp navy blue. Two other guards flanked him two steps back.

"Hello, Igor Ivanovic," Devang greeted the man in charge as he walked up to the gate. Devang knew of Damsky's preference for Russians. He considered them predictable and reliable. "Nice to see you again. New friends?"

"Da, Sen," Ivanovic responded. "As good as seeing my piss on the sand."

Devang chuckled, hearing his heavy Russian accent. Damsky's Russians really did not like the Mediterranean heat, especially while on gate duty.

"Pleasant as always, Igor. And doing well with your English, I see." Devang smiled as he passed the sweating Russian. He approached the cameras embedded in the gate structure of reinforced concrete and heavy steel. He leaned in for a retinal scan. After a click, a metallic voice said, "Privet, Devang Sen. You are expected. Please come in." The gate silently swung open.

Devang passed through the medieval-like castle entrance which contained a guard house, served as the connection between the massive outer walls and fed into a tunnel. Inside the tunnel, he knew there were manned murder holes all around which always made him nervous.

Emerging from the tunnel, Devang came back into the sunlight to find the compound with its defenses on full display. He stopped to admire the arsenal. Tear gas launchers, large gauge automatic weaponry, and stun-level lasers invisible from the outside appeared along the wall fronting the street as well as the walls reaching toward the back of the compound. The compound was entirely enclosed by blast-proof concrete walls standing twenty feet high and five feet thick. Although the view was blocked by the large building in front of him, he pictured the walls stretched back over the top of the hill and down the gentle slope, coming together in a pointed corner topped by an onion dome. The compound was shaped like a pentagon draped across the hill. At that far point, the tower overlooked a canyon from the top of a cliff that stretched half a mile in both directions.

> *But to what end? Is Damsky expecting a full-on military assault? From whom?*

These questions always came to mind when he entered Damsky's fortified realm. He'd never cared enough to ask.

"How are you, Nikolay?" Devang asked the security guard stationed inside the walls near the tunnel exit.

The guard glared at him, saying nothing. The Russians hated small talk.

"Sorry, I asked."

Devang set off across the courtyard toward the front entrance to the three-story glass building that filled the entire front half of the compound. He watched the sliding glass doors open from halfway across the courtyard. A fit Asian man stepped through and headed in the opposite direction.

"Nice to see you, Tang," Devang said, stopping next to a massive sculpture of a snarling black dog.

"You too, Sen," Tang responded.

"Where you headed?"

"Shanghai," Tang replied.

"Right." Devang respected Tang. He was a capable operative. "Enjoy."

"Yeah, right," Tang said. "I hope things get more interesting than they've been. You?"

"That's why I'm here," Devang replied. "How is Damsky?"

"He's actually in a decent mood," Tang answered. "But that can change."

"Don't I know it. Safe travels."

Devang bounded up the long, shallow, crescent-shaped steps that fanned out from the bottom of the building like ripples in a still puddle. The front doors slid apart as he entered a large atrium two stories high, which stretched forty feet in either direction before making a sharp turn at both ends. He sauntered across the hall to a large reception desk manned by a pretty, dark-haired woman.

Devang smiled. "Hello, Doris. You look lovely as usual. How have you been?"

She returned his smile sweetly. "Fuck you, Sen," she said in an undertone, discretely making sure that her voice didn't carry. "I really have no interest to speak with you."

Devang loved her French accent. "Oh, come on, Doris." He feigned surprise. "You know it was just for fun."

"Fuck you, Sen," she repeated.

"Gladly." Devang ignored her hostility. "So...where is he?"

"Where he always is. Go on." She stuck her tongue out at him and, with a slight smile, returned to answering her calls.

Devang saw her smile as he turned.

Flowers, I think.

The bank of elevators took up the last few yards of an internal wall.

"Roses," he muttered softly to himself. Louder, to the elevator, "Third floor."

The elevator doors opened. He stepped in and caught himself reaching to press a button that was not there. The number 2 blinked in the upper right corner of the elevator. He idly wondered at the curious absurdity of a world that couldn't agree on whether the ground floor should be designated as 0 or 1.

The elevator stopped with a nearly imperceptible bounce, and the doors opened onto a large corridor, which tracked the ground-floor reception area below. He left the elevator and headed toward an ornate double door across and down the hall to the right. The left door was covered by twenty-four-karat gold Cyrillic lettering:

Владимир Дамский

Президент и

Директор компании

Below that, the translations of his name and title, first in English—

IVAN DAMSKY

MANAGING DIRECTOR

BLACK DOG SECURITY COMPANY

then beneath that in Mandarin. The non-Cyrillic characters were still in gold but only half the size.

The other door presented a two-dimensional obsidian plaque matching the statue from the courtyard. The snarling dog's eyes seemed strangely alive, glittering with malice. Devang shook his head and entered.

Another attractive woman sitting behind a large desk looked up as he entered. Without any greeting or pause in her work, she said brusquely in English, "He's vaiting for you. Go in now."

"Nice to see you too, Lyudmila," Devang joked, annoyed at the lack of welcome. He dropped his bag in an empty chair and went into Ivan Damsky inner office.

The large, well-appointed room was impressive, designed to draw one's attention to the floor-to-ceiling window framing a spectacular view. In the foreground, the town and shoreline; in the distance, large ships with several small islands behind them.

Damsky stood inside one of two large glass enclosures. Devang could have sworn he was barking at his PCD. Damsky was a large man, bald, standing well over six feet tall, middle-aged with a thick body and mottled face earned through years of drinking copious amounts of vodka.

Hard to argue with the setup.

Devang stopped about halfway across the large room in front of a giant video screen in eight large segments mounted on the inner wall. He mock-saluted the Russian General, but not with disrespect. Damsky saw Devang's salute, smiled, and ended the call with a press of a button. The smile grew wider as he exited his private office, striding toward Devang with arms outstretched.

They embraced in a traditional Russian bear hug. "It is good to see you, my friend," Damsky began. "Did you enjoy your holiday in Turkey? I hear the European tourists are particularly frisky along the Turkish coast. Especially the Nordic women. They like dark men, no?"

"Some holiday," Devang retorted. "Sitting in an out-of-the-way Turkish town with a small research center because one of their scientists just happens to stumble upon a more efficient way to pump water is not my idea of fun."

Damsky chuckled. "It's good to have less exciting assignments occasionally. I need to keep my best players rested for the biggest games."

Damsky was an avid sports fan. Devang's background as a rugby great was one of the things Damsky liked most about him.

"Sit down." He motioned Devang to the captain's chair before the large, muted screen with a sports news show playing. "One of those big games just came up."

Devang waited for Damsky to sit before taking the offered seat, showing the proper deference.

Looking vaguely toward the spectacular view outside the window, Damsky commanded in Russian, "Darken windows."

The glass faded to black as soft lights came on, turning the room into a theater.

"Merge," Damsky said in Russian.

All eight screens merged into one.

"Play Aboah," Damsky commanded.

A recording of a diminutive African man appeared on the screen, labeled "Professor Ekow Aboah." He was standing at a podium in front of a panel of other men dressed in suits and ties. It seemed a typical conference setting.

"Volume level five," Damsky instructed in Russian.

The man presented what he called his Waterfall Reagent to a surprised and excited crowd, judging by the gasps and murmurs from the invisible audience. The professor claimed this Waterfall Reagent could convert waste or seawater into drinking water. Devang was fascinated. He sat up and leaned forward in his chair.

"Where is this from?" Devang asked Damsky, still listening intently as Ekow went over the commercialization status of the Waterfall Reagent.

"Sophia Antipolis. Some sort of water symposium held each year by the International Chemical Society. This was recorded last week," Damsky explained in English. "This man should never have made it to that conference. Our client tried to keep him from going on the panel by impersonating the man's mother! Great big fuck up. Now, we must clean up the mess."

"That's where I should have been instead of Turkey," Devang said.

"*Da*," Damsky replied. "Like I said. Great big fuck up."

Devang shook his head in disbelief. The video continued, showing Ekow completing his remarks and getting peppered with questions from the audience at the apparent displeasure of the moderator, who ultimately gave up trying to move the discussion to the next panelist.

"I have an idea of what my next mission's going to be." Damsky looked at Damsky's mottled face, his red-veined nose prominently bisecting two ice-cold blue eyes. "Track down this Professor Aboah and make sure he hands over the secrets of this Waterfall Reagent."

"*Da*," Damsky said again.

Here we go again.

Devang was troubled but hid it carefully.

"Understood, sir." Devang fell into his military mode. It came easily to the former Indian Special Forces officer. "Lyudmila has the information I need?"

"*Da*," Damsky said yet again.

"Any new instructions for this one?" Devang inquired.

"*Nyet*, although our clients wish for a quick and thorough resolution. It should be no different than your previous missions," Damsky got up, poured himself an ice-cold shot of vodka, and offered Devang one, which Devang declined. Still standing, Damsky continued,

"This one should be simple, but the importance to our clients requires my direct involvement. I want reports each day until complete."

"Yes, sir," Devang responded almost automatically. Old habits die hard.

"Last thing, Sen. Like the others, the instructions require termination," Damsky finished simply. "Have a nice trip."

Turning to the middle of the room, Damsky again commanded the room's operating system in Russian, "Open windows; end video."

The view returned to the now-clear windows, and the screens turned off. Devang rose, shook Damsky's hand, and returned to the secretarial area in the anteroom. He retrieved his bag from the empty chair, gave Lyudmila a big smile, and asked, "I expect you'll send the information in the usual way?"

"It has already been sent," she answered. "*Dasvidaniya*." She returned to her work.

Devang shrugged off the curt dismissal and walked out the door. He glanced out of the large windows on the other side of the corridor, which offered a view of the interior courtyard of the building as well as the onion-shaped tower at the far point of the pentagon. His own quarters were in the north residential wing of the building. He had things to do.

CHAPTER 8
HOME

Ekow gazed at the azure water two hundred miles below as the plane rose above the basin that was the Mediterranean Sea. He enjoyed viewing the hologram in front of his seat, showing the Earth receding as the North African coast seemed to embrace Southern Europe.

> *This must have been the view of the early astronauts as they rode their ballistic missiles into space.*

The plane's altitude ticked up in the corner of the screen as it quickly obtained low earth orbit on its hyper-sonic drive before leveling off at an altitude of five hundred miles. He noticed the person sitting immediately to his right did not look comfortable.

"Are you well?" he asked solicitously. "Is this your first time on a hypersonic flight?"

"No, but thank you for asking," the diminutive older woman answered. "It's been a long time, and I never liked flying."

"What takes you to Accra, if you do not mind my asking?" Ekow asked.

"I'm visiting my daughter and her family," she replied. "She and her husband settled there ten years ago after meeting in Nice. But every time I go, I spend almost all my time with the family. I want to see more of the city and the country this time. What takes you to Accra? Going home or a visit?"

"It is my home," he answered, sitting up straighter. "Born and raised. Although I did spend many years in China for my studies."

"Really?" she said with a smile. "The special relationship between China and most African countries is well-known. Is that what brought you to China?"

Ekow put on his professorial face as he began to explain. "Just so. Ghana is an excellent example of this most momentous phenomenon. Like all modern African nations, Ghana has a checkered past. Centuries of tribal conflict were followed by European and Arab colonial periods until the middle of the twentieth century. When the British Empire crumbled following World War II, Ghana emerged as a combination of several British protectorates. Many of today's African countries formed around the same time in the same fashion, often maintaining the colonial power's language and, to an extent, their economic systems and customs."

"Fascinating," she continued smiling, enjoying the practiced delivery. "Please go on!"

"Gladly. I am pleased you are so interested." He flashed his hundred-watt smile. "Please do let me know when you have enough."

She nodded and settled in, like Ekow's grandmother on a cold night in front of the fire.

"Most African nations were on the edge of economic viability for the first fifty years of their post-colonial existence. The rise of China earlier this century unexpectedly transformed much of the African Continent. The Chinese were the first and only Great Power to tap into what has proven to be the African nations' greatest natural resource. It's people's brilliance.

"As you surmised, I am a direct beneficiary of this historical phenomenon. I received an exceptional education at Shanghai University, allowing me to do some interesting things."

"Like what?" she asked, crossing her legs and shifting in her seat to face Ekow.

"Not to sound immodest, but I obtained my bachelor's, master's, and Ph.D. from Shanghai University and have returned to Ghana, where I am a chemistry professor at Ashesi University. The Afro-Sino Alliance, as the special relationship has come to be known, has resulted in countless Africans from across the continent realizing similar benefits. Most returned home and helped foster an African Renaissance. I am proud to be part of it, as most African nations now enjoy a quality of life equal to the wealthiest nations on Earth."

"Thank you for the history lesson," she said, giving him a short bow, her hands clasped as if in prayer. "It was excellent. You must be a popular teacher."

He nodded in thanks. "You are too kind."

One of the flight attendants, a middle-aged woman, interrupted them as she worked her way down the aisles. "Would you like something to drink, sir?" she asked Ekow. "We have a nice selection of French, Italian, Egyptian, and Nigerian soft drinks." A three-dimensional image appeared above her tablet with each bottle marked. "A complete selection of fruit drinks, wine, beer, and spirits." She tapped the tablet, and a new image appeared.

"Just water, please," Ekow ordered. He was amazed by the variety of products available from places that had just begun exporting them.

Ekow glanced at the estimated arrival time and was pleased to see it had ticked down thirty-eight minutes. He and his neighbor settled into a comfortable silence.

Ekow decided to restart the conversation. "Do you travel frequently?"

"No," she replied. "While it takes far less time to get places than it used to, I still get nervous. The thought of us being in space just makes it worse. I truly appreciate the conversation. Distractions are very welcome."

"Well, at least the hyper-sonic engines do us this favor. Have you ever flown rotational? That technology has made my trips back and forth to Shanghai a fraction of the time it used to take."

Her eyes widened. "I'm not sure I could handle the pressure of that kind of plane. I've heard it's extreme. I have a hard enough time with this one."

"I completely understand." He could almost feel the takeoff's crushing pressure from the last time he'd traveled that way.

Talking about air travel innovation reminded Ekow of the lack of the same in water purification technology, as well as the strange encounter at the conference. Until that meeting, Ekow had not seen the lack of progress for what it was. Ilse Langstrom's story came straight out of a thriller vid.

> *What kind of monsters would deny the world needed technology?*
>
> *The sort of people who would have no problem thwarting an insignificant Ghanaian scientist.*

He shivered at the thought.

Moments later, Ekow felt the plane begin its descent. He and his new friend continued their conversation until the LE Hyper Orbiter landed at Kotoka International Airport. Nearly one thousand passengers quickly and efficiently disembarked. As Ekow had no bags to collect, he made it quickly through passport control and out to the airport parking area ahead of most other passengers.

After a short wait, he approached the parking garage kiosk. "Please retrieve vehicle 2A34CD."

The conveyor brought his small Fiat to the garage exit. The car door lifted straight up and out like a giant bird's wing. Ekow sat in one of the four comfortable captain's chairs and politely said, "Please take me home, Jerry."

"Yes, sir," came the soothing voice in English.

The self-driving Fiat navigated the airport exit and attached itself to the automated highway heading north toward his home in West Legon, one of several upper-middle-class suburbs just north of the Accra city center. As Fiat gathered speed, he swiveled his chair around to watch the airport retreat thinking about the Swedish patent examiner. He felt hyper-aware of everything around him. He noticed and appreciated the automated highway system's ease, efficiency, and safety. The first time in a long time, he realized. Another example of technology evolving at pace as opposed to the water industry.

"Jerry, please call home," he instructed the vehicle. A hologram of his mother, Minnie Aboah, filled the space in a few seconds.

"Hello Ekow," she said. "Welcome back."

"Hello, Mother. I am on my way home and should be there in a few minutes. There is a great deal to discuss."

"Really?" she said, her voice lilting in surprise. "Okay, then. I am here for the rest of the day. I look forward to hearing about it."

"See you soon."

The ten-minute ride home from the airport was uneventful. His car arrived at their modest, well-kept three-bedroom home in the middle of a short, quiet street that ended in a cul-de-sac. The Fiat pulled into the shallow driveway as the garage door rose, then silently docked next to his mother's identical car. The trunk opened automatically to unload the recently deposited luggage. Ekow grabbed his bag, and the trunk closed with a muffled lock.

The garage door led into the kitchen and then into an open living room, where he found his mother in the adjacent study reading a document displayed on a large wall monitor above her desk. He saw it was a Tribal Council matter.

"Hello, Mother," Ekow greeted her with a smile as he entered her office.

She got up for a hug, their embrace loving and comfortable.

"Hello, my son. An eventful trip?"

"I am not certain *eventful* would be the correct word." Ekow said, concern clearly in his voice. "More like bizarre or concerning or even frightening."

"I do not like the sound of that, Ekow. Tell me," she demanded. "Let's sit in the living room where there is more room."

Ekow put his bag on the floor as he sat. "It began when I was approached by two colleagues with a disturbing story," Ekow explained. "I am just not sure what to believe."

"I thought you went to participate on a panel at an important water symposium," Minnie replied. "Not your first time. Tell me what happened."

"Possibly everything." Ekow paused, not sure how to continue. "If what I was told at the conference is true, I could be caught up in a very dangerous stratagem. But I am getting ahead of myself. So…from the beginning."

"Good," Minnie said under her breath. "Go on, dear."

"As you know, I am excited about our progress with the Waterfall Reagent. We filed strong patent applications to prepare for commercialization. As you also know, we have been unable to find an interested partner. I believe this was due to the usual resistance newest technologies face. I learned at the conference that there may be some strange mandate among the largest and most dominant water company executives to slow or even prevent commercialization of new water technologies." Ekow shook his head. "What a tale I am telling. Crazy, is it not?" He attempted to laugh.

Minnie did not laugh. She sat straighter in her chair and made sure Ekow understood that she considered this a very serious situation.

"Please go on, son," she ordered. There was no mistaking the command.

"Of course," replied Ekow, curious about her sudden change. "As you know, I was not planning to attend this meeting but received a last-minute invitation to join a panel on water purification due to the sudden illness of a colleague."

innie watched Ekow pause and look out the picture window to the well-kept yard and the park beyond.

"Now that I am thinking on it, I used to get two to four invitations per year to speak at industry conferences. This was the first in nearly two years."

She began to feel anxious as he shook his head ruefully, then continued.

"Several odd things happened leading up to the panel session, which seemed unconnected before my encounter with Doctors Langstrom and Jacobs."

"Doctors Langstrom and Jacobs?" Minnie asked.

"Yes, but they will come into the story in a moment. Let me go over this in the order in which it occurred."

"Good," she said hiding her growing fear. "I want you to be as complete and detailed as possible."

"You know something about these water executives, don't you?" he asked, eyes widening.

"Finish your story, and I will explain."

"Of course."

She saw him shiver as if a chill ran down his spine.

"First, at the airport here in Accra. I recognized a person I saw at the university and in our neighborhood when running errands before I left for the conference. I thought perhaps he was a new neighbor and a recent hire to the administrative staff at the university. But the same person was in the boarding area for my flight to France.

"Once in France, I had this strange feeling I was being watched. I dismissed it, of course. Who would be watching me?

"Last, just as our panel session was to begin, one the conference organizers came to us with a request from their largest sponsor to cancel the panel. We refused, of course. Then another staff member came up claiming there was an emergency call from you. I took the call, but obviously, the voice was not yours."

"That last bit about the call from me, that is odd," Minnie observed.

"Odd only begins to describe these events taken as a whole," Ekow said. "While not common, on occasion, a big industry player will request a topic not be discussed due to a pending public announcement, but I have never heard of such heavy-handed tactics. The news of the near cancellation only heightened the audience's attention. It was quite a lively discussion in the end. But none of these things would result in me sharing all of this with you if it were not for what happened after the panel session ended."

Minnie put her elbows on the table and leaned forward, clasping her hands together, thumbs under her chin.

Ekow continued, "After the usual gathering at the podium immediately following a session of those whose questions remained unanswered, an unusual couple approached me."

"Doctor Langstrom and Jacobs, I presume?" Minnie asked, knowing the answer.

"Yes. Dr. Jacobs is the Chief Science Officer of the Burry Water Company. Nothing unusual there. But his companion, Dr. Langstrom, who works as a patent examiner in the Chemical Arts Division of the World Intellectual Property Office, WIPO for short. Her tale topped off a strange series of days."

"I am not surprised," Minnie offered with a concerned look.

"According to Ilse Langstrom—I do not think I will ever forget this name—she and several of her colleagues at WIPO have been accepting payments in exchange for identifying new water-related inventions disclosed in patent applications they review eighteen months before publication. She herself has reviewed one of my patent applications and reported it!"

Minnie interrupted him. "One moment, Ekow. How would she know of your inventions? Please explain more about this WIPO."

"Okay, a small step back." Ekow paused. "I sometimes forget you do not see all aspects of my work. I know you understand that patents can protect inventions so that others cannot exploit the invention without the inventor's permission. To get that protection, the World Intellectual Property Organization, or WIPO, is where you file the application for a patent. At one time, each country had its own patenting process. You can imagine the chaos that it created. Today, WIPO is the only place where patent applications are filed and reviewed. It is one of many global institutions created by the Hammurabi Code of 2046. Its purpose was to bring the world into a uniform patenting scheme to encourage innovation everywhere."

Minnie took a few heartbeats to digest this information. She had tried to understand his explanations of these things before, but she felt like an outsider when it came to the technical world, especially the patenting process.

"Go on, Ekow. I am following."

He smiled and went on. "The people who determine whether an invention is worthy of patent protection are called 'patent examiners.' Dr. Langstrom is a WIPO patent examiner. She is an accomplished chemist with a PhD in water purification. When she reviewed my patent application, she even provided guidance to me on how to strengthen the protection I might get. I confirmed it was her from the WIPO correspondence I received. We never met nor likely would have."

Minnie leaned back again, the creases in her face growing deeper. She adjusted the colorful scarf draped over her right shoulder.

"If Dr. Langstrom's story is true, she and her colleagues would be in a perfect position to carry out a scheme like this. All chemical-related patent applications from all over the world go through her department. Confidentiality of these discoveries is of the utmost importance. That she violated my rights as an inventor by disclosing my invention to unknown third parties was a criminal and moral betrayal. But it goes further, and this part is truly unbelievable. According to Dr. Langstrom, the organization to which she disclosed my invention seeks to control and suppress new technology and insists they represent a physical danger to me. While I really and truly wish to dismiss this story as impossible, I know much of it is real. I simply do not know what to make of all this."

Minnie looked at her hands clasped in her lap. She could not share much of the information she received as a tribal elder. But intelligence involving a group of water industry executives meeting secretly as a 'Water Cabal' had been received by the Tribal Elders. She was pleased that the sharing of important information like this by national intelligence agencies had become routine. The Ghanaian Intelligence Service was made aware of an ongoing investigation into this Water Cabal. They, in turn, provided such information to the Intelligence Committees of every Ghanaian Tribe large enough to have one. The requirement to circulate this kind of information had been written into the Hammurabi Code of 2046, which created the World Police Force and, apparently, this WIPO.

Minnie knew what she was about to do broke an oath she'd taken as a member of the Tribal Council, but this was her son.

"Ekow," she began, determination stiffening her back. "I am glad you shared this with me."

She tried to keep her voice steady. The shared intelligence did not just confirm the group's existence, it included reports of suspected violence against scientists who had disappeared randomly over the past few years.

She continued, "Recent intelligence shared with the Tribal Council included a report of an open investigation into an organization described as a Water Cabal. The details were few, but it mentioned a connection between missing scientists and this Water Cabal. Where did you leave things with the Swedish patent executive?"

Ekow blanched. "It's true? I cannot believe this."

Minnie remained calm on the outside, but her fear continued to grow. She knew they had to act fast. She watched Ekow try to match her calm taking a deep breath.

"Examiner, Mother. Not executive." Ekow's thoughts whirled, real fear caused his face to freeze. "She returned to her home in Geneva to investigate the fate of several inventors whose inventions she disclosed. She will contact me with a coded email if she finds anything unusual. I am beginning to feel very afraid. What should I do?"

"At this point, my son, let me see what additional information I can obtain on this Water Cabal," she said, still hiding her concern behind her best poker face. "We have contacts within the World Police Force. It is time they are tested." This she seemed to say to herself.

Minnie stood and returned to her study to access her contact database. She left Ekow sitting in the living room, stunned.

* * *

Ilse Langstrom sat on the edge of her couch, tablet on her lap, gazing out of her window at the giant lake, lost in thought. The click that accompanied the tablet's screen going blank brought her back to the moment. She pulled her knees up and leaned the tablet against her thighs, ready to type.

What choice do I have?

Determined, she began typing but then decided to dictate instead.

"Dear Professor Aboah," she began. "It was wonderful to meet you and discuss your views on European water problems. France can't seem to stop polluting its river basins, and the rest of Europe remains parched due to climate change. Your suggested solutions were insightful. We should discuss this further at future industry events. I hope to see you again soon. Sincerely, Dr. I. Langstrom, Ph.D."

She added a blind copy to David Jacobs so that he knew the game was on, and said, "Send."

Ilse took a deep breath and released it carefully. She was out of her element. She needed to figure out if doing more made sense.

What am I thinking?

She was a scientist. She approached the situation the way she would an experiment. Recording events and reviewing results gave her comfort. She dictated her internal dialogue into her PCD the way she might do a lab report. Or a journal.

"First Entry. Waterfall Journal. The name given by Ekow Aboah to his great discovery, the Waterfall Reagent, seemed a good title for this journal. It is May 17, 2051. All seventeen inventors I identified"—she faltered—"are either dead or missing. Always within a few months of my reporting."

Ilse cleared her throat and wiped at the tears in her eyes, collecting her thoughts and waiting for the roller coaster roar of the passing trolly to fade before continuing.

"I go to Accra tomorrow to offer what help I have. The Waterfall Reagent must be given to the world. As a scientist, I am both thrilled for Professor Aboah and jealous of him. He has done what I thought I was meant to do. It is time I remember that."

She put the tablet aside and hung her head. Shame transformed into rage, different from when she was publicly humiliated by the prosecutor who had set her attacker free. This rage was controlled, channeled.

"This time, there will be an accounting."

She frowned at the tablet as she saved her first journal entry. With a few swipes, she then booked a flight to Accra. She was going to do this.

* * *

David Jacobs looked at the open message from Ilse on his private email account. Only a few days had passed since the conference. He'd already gotten confirmation of the theoretical viability of the Ghanaian's discovery from his company's research and development team. The fact that this ground-breaking technology was hidden for so long was astonishing. Ilse's involvement with this

Water Cabal and its schemes seemed surreal. He reviewed his message to Bjorn Langstrom, Ilse's father and his best friend.

"Dear Bjorn, we hoped that Ilse's mental state might improve once she began working at WIPO. We hoped that relocating to Geneva would lead to new friends and relationships. It was encouraging that she accepted my invitation to accompany me to the Water Symposium last week."

"God no." He put his head in his hands. "I sound like a tour guide."

He deleted the draft and started over.

"Dear Bjorn, I hope this message finds you and Eleanor well. I'm writing you about Ilse and a situation we must discuss immediately and in person. Please let me know when we can meet in the next day or so. Sincerely, David."

He wanted to tell Bjorn about Ekow Aboah and his Waterfall Reagent, not that his daughter was likely going to prison.

A soft chime sounded indicating the arrival of another email in his account.

I guess there's no other way. Just gotta keep moving forward

David sent his message to Bjorn.

* * *

Ekow opened Ilse's message.

CHAPTER 9
RUN

Ilse sat in the Geneva International Airport, awaiting her flight to Accra. She watched the travelers passing the window of the small work cubicle she had reserved the day before. Some walked, some rode the automated walkways, and others floated on personal air scooters. Fingers poised above her open tablet, she wrote:

I depart in ninety minutes. I've taken a three-week leave from work, the first in two years. I wonder if three weeks will be enough time to see this through.

She paused and looked up again, trying to draw inspiration from the people passing by.

I find myself in a constant state of fury. It's been a full twenty-nine hours since I sent the Message.

Capitalizing *message* made sense to her. It marked the end of a long, painful time and the beginning of a new one, perhaps a short one.

I cannot shake the anger. But I am determined. Fate has given me purpose. I must succeed. Ekow must be free, his work available to everyone.

A young family of five, unusually large these days, swarmed by her window on their way to some unknown destination, frantic but smiling parents corralling the young ones who playfully leaped at the floating scooters.

I'm mad. I'm mad at the criminal justice system for being corrupt and for allowing the monster that ended my research career to go free. I'm furious at this Water Cabal for causing so many people to suffer. But most of all, I'm mad at myself. How could I help these assholes? How did I get to such a dark place?

A large crowd surged past from an arriving flight.

Journaling was cathartic. She'd forgotten how intimate and cleansing it was. Her last entry was dated more than five years earlier.

I cannot excuse what I've done. But Ekow Aboah is a second chance for me. His work was my work. He's reminded me of who I was, not what I became. I was a good person. I am back on that path. Whatever it takes.

Somehow, seeing the words on her screen made the sentiment more real. Commitment frightened her. Her anger carried her through the fear. She had to protect the Waterfall Reagent. Somehow, she would bring the Water Cabal to justice.

I'm going to Accra to help Ekow Aboah. It will be challenging to convince him that I can—he will have every reason to doubt me—but I need this. Even if Ekow refuses to allow me to accompany him, I still will find a way.

Ilse saved and closed her journal, left the privacy cube, and took the automated walkway to her gate. All that was left was to get on the plane.

A few minutes later, an announcement said, "Hyper-Sonic Flight 1542 to Accra will be ready for boarding in ten minutes."

Right on schedule.

* * *

Although Minnie was expecting Ilse Langstrom, she was startled when the house operating system announced Ilse's arrival having been deeply occupied with arrangements for Ekow's departure. Depositing the tablet on her desk, she warily approached the front door. Ekow had warned her about Ilse's beauty. When she opened the front door, she gasped.

How will he ever stay unnoticed traveling with her?

Recovering quickly, she said, "Welcome, Dr. Langstrom. We have been expecting you. Please come in."

"Thank you, Ms. Aboah," Ilse responded, unsurprised by Minnie's reaction. Minnie noticed the forced a smile as she crossed the elegant foyer and entered the living room. "It's nice to meet you."

"Please, sit down." Minnie gestured to her comfortable-looking couch, trying to keep the conversation light. "I go by Councilwoman. It is not a terribly long flight from Geneva to Accra, but traveling is always tiring. You can put your bag on the floor for now. Would you like a refreshment? Coffee, tea, perhaps water?"

Ilse carefully placed her suitcase on the floor next to the couch, then perched herself on the edge of the sofa. "No, thank you, Councilwoman. I'm fine."

Minnie sat across the coffee table on a matching loveseat. After a few seconds of awkward silence, she began, "Dr. Langstrom, I—"

"Ilse. Please call me Ilse."

Minnie frowned. She did not like being interrupted.

"Dr. Langstrom," she began again. "Please do not take this the wrong way, but I am wondering why you are here. According to my son, you are an admitted criminal. You are involved with this Water Cabal. You are a scientist. How can you help my son? All I see with you is increased risk. You stand out no matter where you go. You will have to convince me here and now that I should not have you arrested for what you have done. I have that authority as a tribal councilwoman. In fact, the police are outside waiting for my signal to do just that."

Minnie was pleased to see that Ilse was shaken. She waited as Ilse looked at the ceiling, seemingly searching for inspiration. After a moment, Ilse returned her gaze.

"I deserve your mistrust, Councilwoman. I did not expect the police, but I completely understand given the things I've done. You would be within your rights to have me arrested. I am prepared to face the consequences of my actions. I leave it for you to decide."

Ilse gained confidence as she spoke. "I am not proud of what I've done. I was acting out of pain, out of despair. But Ekow brought me back to myself. I was lost. Drifting. I had no purpose and no desire to find one. The sun would rise. I would go to work. I would come home from work. I would go to bed. I existed. Only."

Ilse seemed to be looking for some empathy by telling her story, but Minnie kept her expression neutral expecting Ilse to go on.

"To answer your first question, I am here because I know I've done some terrible things and want to make it right. I don't mean to be dramatic, but this is for me, too. Obviously, I'm not a super-secret agent or any kind of agent. But I can help. My uncle, whom Ekow met in Sophia Antipolis, and my father are well-known and respected men of science. My father has contacts at the highest level of the World Police Force. That's where Ekow must go. He needs to avoid the agents of this Water Cabal until this can happen. He cannot go directly to WPF Headquarters without being intercepted. He also cannot wait here for them to come to him. I don't think you or your tribal council can protect him. He must find a less direct way to reach the World Police Force once he puts distance between himself and his pursuers. I think I can help make this happen."

Minnie kept silent as Ilse stopped again and took a deep breath. Minnie made sure her face remained unreadable. She liked that Ilse was nervous indicated by the repeated looks around the house in an effort to settle herself. Minnie saw that Ilse's hands were already damp. Minnie was far from convinced that Isle was needed.

"I believe you are already preparing for Ekow to leave," she said. Minnie's eyes widen slightly, surprised by Ilse's guess. "I want you to know that Ekow has accomplished the very thing I was striving for as a scientist. I was well on my way to reaching my goal, or so I thought. A very difficult personal situation sent me down a path I deeply regret. Learning of Ekow's discovery rekindled my passion. His dream, my dream, now can be fulfilled. I'll do whatever it takes."

Minnie held Ilse's gaze, her own still unreadable. Minnie could see that a certain passion burned within Isle.

Maybe she can be something other than a distraction.

Finally, Minnie sighed. "I appreciate your words, Ilse. But words are not deeds."

"I am here," Ilse replied simply. "I would have resigned from WIPO already, but I didn't want to do anything that might draw attention. When Ekow's situation is sorted, I will resign. It seems clear to me, and I hope to the two of you, that Ekow must go somewhere unexpected until we can arrange for him to be taken in by the World Police Force. The way will be dangerous. I am afraid, for him and myself, but you will not find a better companion in the limited time he has. Please, Councilwoman Aboah, I must do this. I know I can help."

Minnie chose her words carefully. "Ilse, I fully expected to hand you over to the Accra Police. That remains an option. You are correct that Ekow cannot stay here. But I am deeply concerned about your involvement, not just because of what you have done but also because he must hide. Your presence will make that much more difficult."

"I understand that I attract attention. But with the proper disguise, I can blend in," Ilse responded.

Minnie studied the woman, her posture, judging her sincerity. She made her decision.

"Ekow said much the same thing when he and I discussed the merits of your involvement. Ekow was quite adamant that you should accompany him. I do not understand why, but I believe you are sincere. I do not know if you will be an asset to him or cause more problems, but I will respect my son's wishes."

Minnie watched Ilse leaned back in the couch, relief etched on her face, but Minnie was not done.

"I reached out to our contacts at the World Police Force through the Tribal Council, Minnie went on. "Ekow and I agree that he must leave as soon as possible. That would be tomorrow. I thought I would go with him, but that would be expected. Your arrival and willingness present an alternative I did not think I would choose. *You* will be going, Ilse. This will free me to pursue help from the World Police Force personally."

Minnie stood and moved toward the front door. "Please wait here." She stepped outside and waved to the two unmarked police cars at either end of the block. They silently moved off.

Out of the corner of her eye, Minnie saw Ilse wipe her hands on her thighs, pound the cushions lightly, and say under her breath, "Yes!"

Returning to the couch opposite Ilse, Minnie said, no-nonsense, "Now, since you insist on helping, let us begin."

Minnie and Ilse spent the rest of the afternoon discussing transportation, variations on disguises, and potential travel routes. Minnie was pleased to learn that Ilse had purchased several wigs and oversized clothes to hide her identity. The forethought reassured her. Despite herself, Minnie began to like the girl.

A couple of hours after Ilse's arrival, Ekow came in through the back door. Minnie had sent him to secure his laboratory notes and records. She had suggested he share copies of his work with his colleague and friend in China should he not make it to safety. She hated thinking in these terms, but what else could he do?

"You have made it to Accra." Ekow flashed his hundred-watt smile as he walked into the room. "I am glad."

Minnie and Ilse stopped sorting through the skin tones and outfits they were working with to create additional disguise options. Minnie was slightly surprised when Ilse got up and offered Ekow her hand. Ekow took it, covering her right hand with this left, showing his appreciation.

"Thank you, Ekow," Ilse said. "I had hoped for a different outcome. But I am only more determined than ever to help you. Your mother and I were busy all afternoon."

"I can see that. It is good," Ekow responded. "I want your help." Minnie did not appreciate Ekow's pointed look to which she just shrugged.

"Everything should be ready to go tomorrow morning," Minnie assured him. "We are nearly set."

"So it has come to this." Ekow sighed in resignation. "Well, if we must go, then we will go."

He perched on the couch opposite the two women, and all returned to their preparations.

* * *

The next day, Ilse and Ekow dressed and prepared for their departure. Ekow wore traditional tribal robes over a smart London suit like one of Ghana's successful businessmen. He also wore green eye contacts and a fake beard. He had elevated shoes, making him two inches taller.

Minnie did not recognize him.

Ilse wore an oversized blouse and skirt, her stomach and backside well padded. She had false teeth that were uneven at best and a mousy brown wig to complete her disguise. To Minnie's surprise, she looked twenty years older and unremarkable.

"You both look like different people," Minnie observed. "This should work, at least for a time. I will pray it is long enough."

She embraced Ekow for a long moment, not wanting to let go.

"Remember, stay away from cameras when in public," she reminded them unnecessarily. "Now, off with you before I change my mind."

She seemed about to cry.

"Thank you, Mother." Ekow smiled. "I will miss you while I am away."

"Stay safe, my son," Minnie demanded. "You have a good head. Use it!"

A tear leaked from Minnie's left eye as she watched Ekow and Ilse walk to the self-driving taxi awaiting them. He smiled and a waved goodbye. The vehicle pulled away. She stood in the doorway as the cab drove off wondering if this might be the last time she saw her son alive. Scowling, she returned inside, determined to reach the World Police Force the next day.

* * *

"We are off," Ekow said soberly to the stranger sitting in the taxi. "I am impressed that you look so different."

"You as well," Ilse replied. "Your robes make me feel like I'm traveling with royalty."

"Indeed you are," Ekow said with a smile. "Did I not mention that my father was a king? It does not mean what it used to. I never wear his royal raiment, but it is handy when you are running for your life, does it not?"

The taxi arrived at Kotoka International Airport within ten minutes.

"Going through the arrival area to a café should give us a feel for acting in our disguises in public," Ekow said. "We will get a taxi on the other side. Probably overkill to think we're being watched already, but better safe than sorry."

"Yes," Ilse responded. "I need to get used to moving around with this extra padding."

After walking to a café inside the terminal, their confidence grew. They left by the farthest exit and hailed a second taxi.

"My mother arranged for a desert vehicle to await us at one of her tribal councilman's dealerships. The owner is listed as an American limited liability company, so it cannot be traced."

"That was smart," Ilse said. "Anything to create distance between us and anything we need to touch or use. How long before we reach this dealership?"

"We should be there in just a few minutes," Ekow assured her. "Ah, here we are."

The taxi turned into the lot of a Rover dealership, which contained at least fifteen desert vehicles and many other models.

"It looks like we'll have some selection, but where are the Volvos?" Ilse asked, attempting to lighten the mood.

Ekow looked at her seriously. "I am glad you have a sense of humor, Ilse."

Ilse felt embarrassed looking at his serious face until he could no longer hold back and laughed, flashing his hundred-watt smile.

"You too, Ekow." Ilse smiled and laughed, relieved, then said, "We are well and truly on the run.

The thought sobered Ekow as the taxi came to a stop.

CHAPTER 10
ESCAPE

Ekow nodded to the manager of the car dealership. "I like this Rover."

Ekow admired the desert vehicle Minnie Aboah had organized. The Rover DMS 2050 was made for long distances across harsh landscapes and brutal weather. The brochure the manager had given Ekow explained that the shape had been borrowed from a popular camper model from the mid-20th Century. It resembled a shiny, silver pill. It was twenty feet long with three steps set seven feet down the rounded side leading into the vehicle. Above the steps, which folded seamlessly into the carriage, was a spacecraft-like door that pushed in and slid toward the rear of the car when opened. The blunt antennae on the roof connected the Rover's operating system to the satellite-based Net that provided guidance and climate control, allowing the DMS 2050 to go nearly anywhere in the world so long as there was some semblance of a road.

"Has the operating system been updated?" Ekow asked the manager as he finished circling the vehicle.

Ekow was sure the manager knew he and Ilse were important tribal council folk and he expected to be treated accordingly.

"Yes, sir," the manager responded. The Rover DMS 2050 is state-of-the-art. There is no better way to tour the desert now that the trans-desert automated highways are complete and the rest stops are built. This machine could cross without the highway, but that would be a much rougher ride."

"Excellent." Ekow smiled. "It is provisioned for our trip to Marrakesh and back, yes?"

"Absolutely," the manager assured him, glancing at Ilse. "That and a few extra items I selected myself. It should be a very nice trip. This Rover is called Nelson."

Ekow climbed the steps and pressed the opening button. The door hissed as it receded into the Rover and slid to the left to reveal the portal-like opening. Four captain's chairs occupied the front third of the vehicle. Once inside, he reached for the ceiling to get a feel for the space. Looking toward the rear of the Rover, he was pleased to see two workstations on opposite sides that could fold down into couch-like benches and two stacked sleeping births in the rear, split by a small privy between them against the rear wall.

"This is beautiful, Ekow," Ilse said, stepping into the Rover behind him. He watched her marvel at the transparent ceiling, walls, and floor and then catch herself. "I mean, Eric. I didn't realize how luxurious a trip through the desert would be."

The manager gave no indication he had heard Ilse's slip as he stepped into the Rover. She stowed her things and settled into one of the captain's chairs, surveying the interior carefully for the first time.

"It is the current standard for a Sahara Desert tour. We should enjoy this trip," Ekow said quietly, smiling as he joined her by taking another of the captain's chairs. To the manager, he said, "Thank you for your help. We will return this beautiful vehicle in ten days."

"You are welcome. Enjoy your trip," the manager said as he stepped down the stairs with a wave.

Ekow said, "Nelson, please take us to Marrakech."

The door silently slid back into place as the steps began folding into the undercarriage. There was an audible click as the door closed into its locked position.

"As you wish, sir," the Rover's operating system answered. The Rover began to move.

They watched the dealership recede as the Rover got underway. Ekow smiled as Ilse swiveled her captain's chair to face the rear of the Rover and slid to the left side workstation without getting up. The trough in the floor locked the chair in place in front of the monitor and keyboard. The Rover's walls, ceiling, and floor were opaque from the workstations to the rear.

"Ekow, is this entire car just one giant window?" she asked looking to break the silence that had settled in.

"Yes," Ekow responded. "I am told the experience with all the windows clear feels like flying only low to the ground. This feature made this Rover model very popular with tourists traveling through the desert. All sides can be darkened, as the rear panels are now. No one can see inside unless the door or one of the windows is open. The rear swings open to easily store clothes, food, drink, and other equipment. In case you were wondering, the toilet is just there." Ekow gestured to the small closet between the berths. "These Rovers are unofficially known as 'Airstreams,' a brand of mobile camping vehicle from the 1950s. They are the most common way to travel from the sub-Saharan part of Africa to Egypt, Sudan, and the Mediterranean Coast."

"I believe our departure was well timed," he added, abruptly changing the subject. "Otherwise, we would not be going anywhere, I think."

"I agree. Are you certain heading east before going north is the best route?"

Accra slid by as the Rover navigated the streets smoothly.

"Yes. There is no other way. The trans-continental highways are fast and direct, almost. These are some of the finest roads in the world. Besides, we have a stop to make along the way, do not forget."

They both fell silent, enjoying the city's sights as the DMS 2050 climbed the ramp from the surface streets and plugged into the automated highway connecting Ghana to Togo.

"Please prepare for acceleration," chimed Nelson in a friendly voice.

Ekow saw that Ilse was fascinated by the countryside, lost in thought. He tapped her knee to get her attention.

"Did you know that the trip we are taking would have been impossible a mere twenty years ago?" Ekow asked.

"I did not. I know very little about Ghana or the lands we'll be traveling through," Ilse replied honestly. "I've only been anywhere on the continent once before, with my family, as a teenager. What was different twenty years ago?"

"There were no highways. Only traditional caravan routes until the 2030s. The old route went nearly straight north from Accra to the Mediterranean coast of what used to be Libya before heading east along the coast to Cairo. Now we can go directly from Lagos to Cairo, passing close by Lake Chad and through Chad proper. We enter the Sahara from a place called Faya Largeau, cross the southeast corner of the territory once claimed by Libya, and enter southern Egypt near Abu Minqar, an ancient Sudanese trading center. We connect to another major trans-Saharan highway from Juba in South Sudan leading to Cairo there."

The Rover positioned itself to the left of the morning's commuter traffic heading for the center of Accra and accelerated to match the speed of the other vehicles in the bypass lanes. Ekow flashed a smile at Ilse as the Rover smoothly maneuvered. Ekow felt strangely optimistic.

"One-hundred and fifty miles per hour achieved," intoned Nelson. "Please provide instructions if you would like to change speed or destination."

"Thank you, Nelson," responded Ekow feeling like he was speaking with a friend. "Maintain present speed and destination."

Turning to Ilse, Ekow said," We have a long ride ahead of us. I am wondering if you would know more of African history."

"That would be a nice way to pass the time. I was so deep into the sciences that I had no time for the humanities. History was not interesting to me, so I did the minimum required in university. I barely have a working knowledge of Swedish history." Ilse shared more than she had in quite some time as her cheeks reddened slightly. She worried Ekow seemed too easy to talk with.

"Then I would be honored to tell you the African story. It will not fill the entire drive but at least the first few hours. We can discuss aspects as you wish and perhaps do some research together as we go." Ekow cringed as he realized how professorial he sounded.

Ilse tensed slightly at the lecturing tone but then joked, "That sounds genuinely educational, professor."

Ekow laughed, "Thank you for indulging me. I do not often have a captive audience of one. Lecturing in a hall can be so impersonal. Are you ready?"

"As I'll ever be," she answered.

"Okay then," Ekow began. "Other than the great North African empires created by the Egyptians, Ethiopians, and Moors, which I suspect you know even from a cursory course in world history, African history is, until the relatively recent past, a mostly mythological, oral history passed down through the generations as stories and songs. Very little was recorded before the arrival of the Arabs and Europeans. Like the rest of humanity, the people of Africa began as hunters and gatherers until civilization arose and expanded across the continent. A good way to approach African history is to divide the continent into three east-west bands: the northernmost band encompasses the Mediterranean coast from the Red Sea to the Atlantic Ocean and south to the southern edge of the Sahara Desert. The second band is Central Africa, stretching south from the southern edge of the Sahara Desert to the Gulf of Aden but north of the Great Lakes. The third band begins with the Great Lakes Region and everything south of it."

Ekow slid his captain's chair to the right-side desk terminal. "Computer, bring up a map of the African continent and present it with lines drawn across it just below the southern edge of the Sahara Desert and just north of the Great Lakes Region."

A map of Africa appeared on the monitor, and lines emerged from right to left as Ekow had instructed. Outside, the Ghanaian countryside sped past. Ekow liked that Ilse no longer noticed, engrossed already.

"The best-known parts of African history involve the ancient empires that arose along the northern coast and the Nile River. Ancient Egypt, of course. The Carthaginian Empire spread across the western half of the Mediterranean Basin from present-day Tunisia during the Ancient Greek and Roman times. The most famous Carthaginian, Hannibal, was perhaps the greatest general of that age after Alexander the Great, yet still could not overcome the rising Roman Empire. The Romans brutally destroyed Carthage after over a hundred years of war, known in Roman history as the Punic Wars. You may have heard of the Axum Empire of Ethiopia and the Cushites, a bit farther east and south of Ethiopia. The history of the rest of Africa to the south is shrouded in mythology and conjecture. It was on a different path of exploitation and poverty despite its rich history of civilization."

Ekow stopped, thinking about what he had just said. It saddened him to think that foreign exploitation and degradation had destroyed these early prosperous and stable civilizations. While no civilization had any guarantee of success, the Arab and European disregard for the African peoples' humanity took racial prejudice to an unheard-of level. But then he smiled.

"Why did you stop?" asked Ilse entranced. "And why are you smiling?"

"When I teach, my lectures are about science, particularly chemistry. Like you, science has been my focus for a very long time. I never teach about Africa or its history. I am finding it a pleasurable thing. I think I would like to do it more. Perhaps when all of this"—he spread his arms wide—"is over, I can broaden my lectures to include history. As you say, we scientists fail to make time for it. But I think it is important, yes? But where was I? Oh yes. Africa south of the Sahara.

"The Nile River did more than flood the plains of Egypt and the Nile Delta each year. Along its upper banks and at its source, the region of Nubia flourished, at first heavily influenced by Egypt but later with its own uniquely African flair. The Nile was one of the few routes from north to south with reliable water, so it was from there that civilization began to spread. Not unexpectedly, those living in villages along the river began sharing a language that was eventually classified as Nilo-Saharan. Many of the Nilo-Saharans were, and continue to be, cattle herders.

"By about 500 BCE, a West African people unrelated to the Nilo-Saharans established farms just south of the Sahara Desert. Their crops were designed for tropical climates, leading to their numbers growing and their culture expanding east and south across the continent for the next thousand years. Computer, mark where historians believe these settlements were located on our map of Africa."

Settlements appeared on the monitor far to the north of the line, marking the current southern edge of the Sahara Desert.

"As you can see, the Sahara Desert was much smaller then and only recently expanded as far south as it is today. Computer, show the expansion of the Sahara Desert slowly from 500 BCE to the present."

Ekow enjoyed this program, and it was clear Ilse was fascinated. As the monitor showed both the northern and southern edges of the Sahara Desert. The settlements previously marked were clearly south of the southern edge. A number appeared in the upper right corner of the screen, showing 500 BCE. As the number reached zero, the Sahara Desert expanded in both directions, encompassing the marked settlements, but then held steady as the number in the corner increased with an CE replacing the BCE. Around 1800 CE, the southern edge of the desert began moving quickly farther south until reaching 2051 CE, when nearly the entire northern third of the continent was clearly a desert.

"Climate change has done its part, but there are natural causes of North Africa's aridification, having to do with the Earth's natural orbital rotation. Five thousand years ago, the Sahara Desert was not a desert at all.

"But I digress. Farther north along the Nile, Nubia and Egypt ruled separate regions. There was substantial overlap between the two kingdoms over the centuries. Egypt had Egyptian and Nubian kings, the Nubians having conquered and ruled Egypt as pharaohs for about a century. Nubian and Egyptian cultures grew ever more similar, but over time, Nubian territory was absorbed into Egypt and the Sudan.

"As I mentioned earlier, my father was a King of the Ashanti Tribe in Ghana, technically making me king in my own right since he died in an accident when I was very young. I seldom speak of it as it feels so anachronistic, and I have no intention of assuming any duties as a king." His tone remained uninflected and neutral. "Genealogically, I have Bantu and Nilo-Saharan as ancestors, but most significantly, in some people's minds, I am a direct descendent of a long line of Ashanti Kings. But I am getting ahead of myself!" He chuckled, thinking about how absurd it would be if he were to exercise his rights as king.

Ilse interrupted, intrigued. "You don't want to be king? Really?"

"A king? Me?" Ekow laughed and looked at Ilse with genuine surprise. "Royalty in Africa is not like in other places. By the end of the twentieth century, most tribes had abolished the designation, and those who still have it wear it more like a name than an office. No. I am not interested in royalty."

Ekow sat quietly momentarily, reflecting on his father's life as his mother described it. He occasionally wondered what it would have been like to actually know the man. Ilse courteously gave him this moment, recognizing the reflective look on his face.

"One thousand years later," Ekow began abruptly, "the original kingdom of Ghana arose out of a cluster of fragmented trading kingdoms that developed to the north and west of Central Africa on the southern edge of the Sahara Desert. By then, the Berbers had crossed the Sahara, trading in precious metals, diamonds, and slaves. The rise of Islam followed and dominated the north of the continent. Arab traders began to reach southern and western Africa with goods and religion. The expansion of trade and Islam, which went hand in hand with the Arabs, led to trading city-states on the east coast of Africa. The Arabian colonization across the northern coast made both areas almost exclusively Arab-speaking regions.

"So, let me stop at this point and make sure you are still awake," he joked, and Ilse laughed. She was glad his mood was lightening again.

"Very much awake," she assured him, smiling.

Ekow saw that she was fascinated by this history. She seemed impressed by his deep knowledge and mesmerized by the story.

"You must be a very popular teacher at your university," Isle complimented.

The Rover crossed the border of Benin into Nigeria using the transit lanes for the north-south freeway that led from Lagos to Cairo. They were surprised to be already through the narrow country of Togo.

"This is really interesting, Ekow," Ilse enthused. "I'm not just saying that. I had no idea of how rich African history is. I think most Europeans don't. Let's make ourselves some lunch, and I hope you'll be willing to continue after."

She reached into the cupboard for two prepared lunches and popped them into the microwave oven slotted onto the wall beside the right-side workstation.

As the microwave whirred to life, Ekow sighed. "It is not surprising that Europeans know so little about us. It is our curse. The Arabs and Europeans cared little for our history or culture back then. Their primary interest was in raw materials and forced labor. Even after the emancipation from the colonialists a century ago, Africa remained largely on its own. The colonial institutions did not fit the indigenous populations. Dictators rose to step into the shoes of their former rulers. The irony of the Second Great Leap Forward caused by the

Chinese in Africa, often called the African Renaissance, is that the Chinese did not have a revelation that there was value to the African mind. It could have happened much earlier, especially after the colonists had departed. We were not ready. With the Chinese, we had good luck. Simply a happy coincidence."

Ilse laughed, but Ekow felt a deep sadness as he thought of the human capital lost over the centuries of African bondage.

"Just go on," he mused out loud softly trying not to dwell on the past.

But Ilse heard. "Please do," she said, not recognizing his pensive mood, as she handed Ekow his lunch. "By the time you finish, we'll be at Lake Chad!"

"Indeed." Ekow smiled as he dipped his spoon into the container. "But not until I have an opportunity to enjoy this gourmet meal."

Ilse was bemused by his mood swings. She had not expected him to be so open with her.

After finishing their meal, they put the biodegradable food container and utensils into the micro-incinerator, and a soft *poof* followed.

"Do continue, Ekow," Ilse encouraged. "I'm enjoying your lesson immensely."

"I am glad to hear that. But now we get to the saddest part of the story, the decline of African civilization. By the middle of the fifteenth century, when the first European ships arrived on the west coast of Africa, the continent boasted large and prosperous kingdoms. There was the Shona in the south. The proud Congo on the west coast. The Mali and other trading nations around what is today Ghana. Trade spread east as new routes were established across the Sahara to the east." Ekow's face fell as he continued. "But the slave trade began. Slavery is considered the single most significant obstacle to indigenous development in Africa. We call it the Great Bleed. The continent lost tens of thousands of souls each year. It dwarfed all other traded commodities. Human trafficking continued for nearly three hundred years. Even though the Europeans largely banned slavery by the end of the eighteenth Century, the North and South American colonies continued to fuel it."

Ilse remained silent, acknowledging his pain but unable to truly understand it.

Ekow said, "The European powers established permanent colonies in strategic locations around Africa. The pressure of the slave trade and the ivory trade that followed it created a violent cauldron that forced migrations and disintegrated traditional tribal values and structures. Perhaps the most disturbing aspect of this history is the complicity of the African kings and tribal chiefs. They were willing to trade their own people for metals, alcoholic spirits, clothes, and guns. They were willing to go to war with neighboring tribes just to capture people to sell into slavery. It was a horrible chapter."

Ekow paused to admire the prosperous Nigerian towns that whizzed by with their neat, grid design and their clean, well-kept homes as they followed the automated highway north and east toward Chad. He noted they had already passed through Togo, a very narrow country between Ghana and Nigeria.

"I never understood how these men could place such a low value on the lives of their own people. Sadly, most African political leaders following the colonial era were not much better. They ushered in decades of gross governmental mismanagement, abject poverty, homegrown terrorism, ethnic cleansing, and misery." Ekow paused again but smiled. "Happily, the story does not end there. Beginning in the early years of this century, China was the next great power to pursue the natural resources of the African continent. Their objectives were no different than previous great powers—access to minerals and other precious metals needed to fuel their domestic economy. But their method was different. Rather than simply conquer and steal, the Chinese offered what has become known as The Grand Bargain. 'Give us access to your natural resources, and we will build you dams, roads, airports, and deep-water ports,' they said. The African leaders at the time were more than happy to accept these 'gifts' from the Chinese because it only enhances their own power, wealth, and control." Ekow smiled at Ilse again. "But something unexpected occurred. To build these great infrastructure projects, the Chinese brought many of their own people to train and supervise the locals who were constructing and then maintaining these great works. They sought out the most promising students at young ages and brought them to China for education and training. Many of the Chinese working on these massive infrastructure projects brought their families for what was supposed to be a temporary assignment. Many never left. The now well-educated and trained Africans returned to work alongside their Chinese colleagues. New mixed communities formed with the Chinese immigrants joining their Ghanaians, Nigerians, or Kenyans to upgrade or build new local schools, new modern housing, and the community infrastructure rarely seen on the continent. Promising Chinese and African students were offered university opportunities in China, as had their parents before them. The universities in the African nations dramatically improved as the original generation of Africans educated in China entered public service or took professorial positions. This rising middle class no longer tolerated the corruption and inefficiencies of their truly representative governments. By the end of the 2030s, a special relationship between China and the African nations emerged as nearly a billion people in Africa rose out of poverty like the Chinese before them. Political and economic institutions are now designed to ensure this success is perpetuated. As you are seeing, the African nations we are passing through on this trip are stable and prosperous, with cooperative, multiracial, integrated communities. I am a beneficiary of the special relationship, having received an excellent education at Shanghai University."

"What about the North African countries along the Mediterranean?" Ilse asked. "When I was in Tunis in the mid-2030s, things were bleak in places. Are these countries part of the Special Relationship with China?"

"Unfortunately, they are not," Ekow answered. "It seems the combination of predominantly Arab ethnicity and Sharia Law made their leaders unwilling to embrace China. These countries remain more or less as they have been for the past several centuries."

"That is unfortunate," Ilse said. "I think things have only gotten worse since I was there. Freshwater has gotten more and more scarce."

Ekow nodded. "The North African nations were among the world's most imperiled by water shortages."

"What an incredible story," Ilse said with a small smile. "Thank you so much for sharing."

"You are quite welcome, Ilse," Ekow responded happily. "It truly was my pleasure."

Ekow and Ilse settled into a companionable silence, both lost in their thoughts as the miles passed and the day waned. They both dozed as several more hours passed, bringing them about halfway from Lagos to the small city of N'Djamena just south of Lake Chad—seven hundred miles so far.

Awaking with a start, Ilse wiped a bit of drool from the corner of her mouth and looked at Ekow, who was watching the desert pass.

"Ekow, what do you think of stopping at the next rest stop? I want to stretch my legs and have a real meal.

"That is a nice idea, but I think we should wait until after dark," Ekow replied. He rolled his captain's chair to the left side desk/workstation. "While we do have disguises, why test fate in broad daylight? Let us continue until it gets fully dark. Our disguises will be more effective. Full dark is less than two hours from now. After that, we will find the next rest stop and have a quick meal. I feel the need for a short walk myself. Our first destination is in the interior of Chad, where my mother has a friend who has promised to help us. If we keep our stops to a minimum, we should be there by morning."

"Thank you," Ilse said, moving to the bottom bunk in the left rear of the Rover and settling in with her tablet.

"Nelson," Ekow addressed the Rover's operating system. "Please stop at the first rest stop after full dark."

"Confirmed, Sir," Nelson responded. "We will stop at Rest Stop Yellow Trumpet in two hours and fourteen minutes."

* * *

Just shy of two hours later, Nelson announced, "We will be stopping in fifteen minutes at Rest Stop Yellow Trumpet. Prepare for deceleration."

Ilse set her tablet down and laid out the various pieces of her disguise. Ekow did the same on the opposite side of the Rover. Exactly fifteen minutes later, the DMS 2050 exited the automated highway and entered a large facility. The Rover seamlessly docked into a recharging station about halfway down a pier with several other unoccupied bays. The pair were fully dressed as they had been when they'd left Ekow's home in Accra the day before.

Ilse stepped out of the Rover into the darkness and chill of a late spring Sub-Saharan night. She closed her cape against the cold. She heard the whirr of the passing vehicles on the raised highway behind them.

She stood about seventy-five yards from a large dome-shaped structure.

"This rest stop is designed to resemble a Nigerian Dome." Ekow stepped down from the Rover in his West African businessman disguise. "I am glad no one else is on the platform. Shall we?"

Ekow gestured for her to precede him down the platform. She curtsied playfully but thought she really did look like a tired, middle-aged European woman. Glancing at her reflection in the windows of the vehicles they passed as they walked toward the brightly illuminated structure, she was gratified by this strange person she saw. The pageboy-style wig of light brown hair, the puffy jowls created by dental prosthetics, the hazel contact lenses she wore, and the lightweight padding that made her look twenty pounds heavier were an effective combination.

Ekow walked beside her, garbed in the robes of a Nigerian executive. She thought Ekow looked quite fine in the handsome thigh-length dashiki over a Sokoto and long drawstring trousers Minnie had chosen for him. The trousers partially hid the pair of elevator shoes she knew he'd purchased on his last run of errands the day Ilse arrived in Accra, which added two inches to his height, making them the same height. The brimless Kufi headdress completed his outfit, adding another inch to his height. Ekow had switched his trademark tortoiseshell glasses for wire-rimmed teardrop glasses.

Together, they were unremarkable.

As they neared the entrance, an intoxicated couple burst onto the platform, happily headed for one of the parked vehicles. Their private celebration passed without showing any interest in them. Startled, Ilse and Ekow hesitated until the couple passed. The look on Ekow's face made it clear he was reconsidering the idea of a stop. Then he shrugged and tilted his head toward the entrance with a smile. She sighed. They went inside.

She followed Ekow's sweeping gaze as he looked up at the ceiling of the dome once inside. "I have not been on this highway before, but I read about the Nubian rest stops. Their design is intentional and meant to remind people of where they are. The entrance from the docking piers is intended to draw visitors into the center. As you can see, three piers jut out to the east, south, and north. Every rest stop is required to have a hotel and the hotel must be to the west if the highway on north-south routes and to the north on east-west routes."

Ekow and Ilse approached the center of the domed structure. The food court tracked the contours of the round design around them.

"These rest stops are famous for their variety and quality of food. Each quarter of the circle represents cultures found on the extended imaginary line worldwide. Let us try a mix of South African and Southern European dishes."

"That sounds good," Ilse said. "Why don't you get the South African food, and I'll get the European fare? I'll meet you at the booth over toward the path to the hotel."

"Deal." Ekow smiled and strode to the southern part of the food court while Ilse went north.

Ilse made it to the comfortable booth near the escalators, which led to the enclosed overpass that crossed the highway and led to the hotel lobby. She carefully avoided eye contact with anyone as she waited for Ekow and hoped she didn't appear shifty.

Ekow arrived a few minutes later with a tray loaded with various South African dishes.

"I thought you might like to try something different," he suggested.

"That would be nice. Thank you," Ilse examined what was on Ekow's tray.

"I recommend the chakalaka and pap. It is a vegetable dish. I also have biltons and droewors, a dried meat nicely spiced," Ekow offered.

Ilse took small servings of each. The pasta dish she'd brought filled both their plates.

Ekow set to, but after a few minutes, looked up to see Ilse moving her food lazily from one side of her dish to the other, eating virtually nothing.

"Is everything all right?" he asked.

"I'm sorry, but it's just too difficult to eat with this stupid prosthetic in my mouth. I'm not really that hungry anyway," she replied softly. "I think the stress is finally catching up with me. I'm hoping a decent night's sleep will help. Why don't we get moving again? I'll take this to-go and perhaps eat it later in the Rover."

Ekow nodded and finished his food. They retrieved a biodegradable box that felt like plastic and loaded the remains of Ilse's meal into it before heading back to the Rover.

Once inside, Ekow ordered Nelson, "To Faya Largeau, Nelson."

"Right away, sir."

Once the Rover navigated them back to the highway, Ekow turned to Ilse and said, "Faya Largeau is where we will find my mother's friend, who will help us with new identity cards and passports. From there, it is another eleven hundred or so miles to Cairo. We should be there not long after sunrise. Let us get ready to retire."

"That sounds great," Ilse agreed.

Ilse folded the lower bunk on the left side of the Rover, took bedding out of the drawer below it, and made her bed. She performed her ablutions with a small sink next to the microwave between the workstation, which also served as their kitchen sink. Ekow's efforts mirrored Ilse's, and within a few minutes, they were both asleep as the Rover sped toward Faya-Largeau.

* * *

As Ilse and Ekow returned to the Rover, several surveillance cameras recorded their images. The artificial intelligence that managed the highway's rest stops matched them to the recording of their arrival. Their photos were uploaded into an algorithm that processed all such images and other data-seeking anomalies worthy of escalation to a higher degree of scrutiny. The images of Ekow and Ilse in disguise were checked against the identity of the registered owner of the Rover and correlated with any reports of stolen vehicles.

Ownership of the Rover resided in a Nigerian limited liability company, which was common enough in the region. However, neither individual recorded exiting nor entering the vehicle matched the descriptions of the individuals associated with this company. Even though there were no reports of this vehicle being stolen, a message was sent to the representative of the registered owner alerting it that its Rover was recorded at the Yellow Trumpet Rest Stop in Chad.

An incident report was logged and stored, awaiting a reply, which, if not received within two days, would result in further escalation and scrutiny. Meanwhile, the observation program followed protocol and placed the images of Ekow and Ilse in disguise in an electronic record, which was then made available to police agencies around the world. Standard operating procedure in the New World Order.

CHAPTER 11

DESCENT

The medical director, the head nurse, and the outpatient representative sat opposite Bert and Henryk Gheel at the solid oak conference table in a room designed to foster calm and reasonable discourse.

"Mr. Gheel," the medical director, who was a middle-aged, bespeckled psychiatrist in a white coat with a full head of graying hair, began, "Henryk has made much progress over the past five years, but we do not believe he is ready to be released unsupervised."

"Yes," chimed in the head nurse. She was a large, round woman with a gray bun at the nape of her neck. "Henryk still cannot control his temper. There have been many incidents over the years, at least two within the last six months, where it has been necessary to restrain and sedate him. He is a real danger should he be released."

"The last time was only because you wouldn't grant me a simple, reasonable request," Henryk interrupted with a contemptuous sneer. "You fat cow," he added quietly, under his breath, but everyone heard.

"His *simple, reasonable* request was to be left alone for an hour with one of our prettier young staff members," the nurse responded, looking at Henryk with equal disgust. "This man is sick and dangerous."

"That's not true," Henryk erupted out of his chair. "She's lying! Father, have her fired."

Bert sat quietly, observing his troubled son and the institution's staff without emotion. He could not understand how a child of his could be this deranged. Now in his late twenties, he looked like an athlete. It had to be from his mother's side. There was no history of mental illness in his family.

"Sit down, Henryk," Bert ordered. Henryk did so, still fuming. "Go on, please," Bert said reasonably to the nurse.

"As I was saying..." The nurse looked from the son to the father and back to the son. "Henryk remains a serious danger to himself and others. We do not recommend releasing him at this time."

"One moment, Nurse Muller," the medical director cut in. "While I agree Henryk needs supervision and continued treatment, it seems Mr. Gheel here would like to place Henryk in an outpatient treatment program. I see no reason why that cannot happen. Bernard?"

"But Doctor—" the head nurse began.

"That will be all, Nurse Muller. Thank you for joining us today." The medical director looked at her meaningfully.

"Yes, Doctor," the head nurse said, got up, gave the father and son a concerned look, and left the room.

Bernard, the third clinical staff member at the meeting, a small man with small hands and dark, thick glasses, spoke for the first time. "Henryk and I have had several sessions, Mr. Gheel. We think our facility outside Brussels would be a perfect fit. We are equipped specifically for people like Henryk who genuinely wish to re-enter society. How does that sound?"

"That's what I expected from you people." Henryk's expression took on an aristocratic air. "Cooperation and compliance. Bah. I had no reason to be here in the first place."

"That's enough!" Bert exploded. A rare display of emotion. "I do not know from where you came, given the excellent breeding stock of your mother and I, but you have been a spoiled brat since you were old enough to speak. It has only gotten worse as you moved into violence and debauchery. I am only considering this move because nothing has worked in the past five years. If you do not behave once on your own and comply with all requirements of this outpatient facility, I will follow Nurse Muller's recommendation to permanently commit you to a maximum-security psychotic ward for the rest of your life. Do I make myself clear?"

His eyes blazing in defiance and humiliation, Henryk said meekly, "Yes, Father."

* * *

After leaving the rest stop, Ekow shared what he knew about the man they would meet the next day.

"Agizul Amazigh is the patriarch of a Nubian family that has traded across the Sahara Desert for centuries. In this part of Africa, even today, after so much progress around the continent, we are entering an area where the laws of the modern world often clash with tradition—and tradition wins. People here were traders or hunter-gatherers unless they made their living on the black market. My uncle, and please understand this is an honorary title, is a trader who has traveled a many-colored path."

Ekow did not like Agizul Amazigh, but he was not sure why. He went on.

"My mother met him in Lagos while attending a tribal conference. He was there on business, staying in the same hotel. They first noticed one another in the bar and had one too many drinks, at least the way my mother tells it. They have a genuine love for one another, but neither would compromise. He stayed in Faya-Largeau to pursue the family business. Mother stayed in Accra as an important tribal councilwoman. Over time, their long-distance relationship turned platonic. I trust him because of my mother. Otherwise, I would not come here. In some ways, we are fortunate that he does what he does, as you will see when we get to Faya-Largeau. But that will not be until the morning, so why do we not get some sleep?"

Ilse nodded. "It's interesting how tired one can get from sitting in a car for hours. I'm ready for bed."

They readied the vehicle's beds and gratefully went to sleep.

* * *

"Hey, isn't that the guy who was ogling us in the company cafeteria?" asked Natalie as she and Ilse stood in line at a food stand in Stockholm during their lunch break. "I've seen this guy hanging around the Solna metro station several times. Listen, Ilse, I think he might be stalking us."

Ilse sighed. Natalie, her newest best friend, was suspicious of everyone and everything. Nevertheless, she dutifully glanced around, but registered nothing out of the ordinary.

"I honestly don't know what you're talking about," Ilse said with a patient smile. "I seriously doubt that someone is stalking us. Besides, why would seeing someone from work at the metro station mean we're in danger."

"I don't know," Natalie said. "I just have a terrible feeling about this guy. There's just something about him that gives me the creeps."

Ilse looked away, shaking her head.

* * *

Ilse wondered why it was so hard to open her eyes as she blinked and then forced them open. And why did she feel so tired? Had she worked late? She couldn't remember. She let her half-open eyes roam around the room. The bright fluorescent lights on the ceiling hurt. She frowned, her mind cloudy.

Where am I? What is this place?

There was an IV bag suspended from a chrome rack on her right.

A hospital? Am I in a hospital?

Confused, she murmured, "Was I in some kind of accident?" She opened her eyes wider and let her head loll to the left, then focused on Natalie.

Why is Natalie looking down at me in a hospital bed?

She blinked again to clear her eyes, then tried to speak, her voice a weak croak.

"Natalie? What...?"

"Ilse, I don't know what to say." Natalie's eyes grew and brimmed with tears. "We weren't sure you would wake up. I can't believe what that animal did to you. That lowlife will go to jail for a very long time. I swear to God he will."

What in the world is she talking about? Why is she so upset?

Suddenly, she knew. Her overwhelming terror, screaming, crying out for help, trying desperately to fight back, then the pain before darkness. Natalie leaned forward to comfort her.

They clung together, hugging and weeping. "I'm so sorry, Ilse, I'm so sorry, sweetheart."

* * *

Ilse sat in a courtroom in Stockholm, the benches overflowed with members of the press and the curious gawkers. She was, after all, the daughter of a prominent family. It was the third day of the trial. She did not want to be there, but it was essential to spare other women from what she suffered. There had been no witnesses to the rape. After her testimony, his lawyers had presented a flimsy alibi.

Ilse thought about Natalie's testimony. She'd seen the same man stalking the two of them for several days. She had warned her, but Natalie had not witnessed the attack either. Ilse's anger built.

Her own testimony had tested her sanity. Reliving the ordeal while going over the graphic details of her rape left her embarrassed and ashamed. Then, the real attacks began. Manufactured evidence designed to put into question her life's work. Every public message she'd put out reworked into a challenge to the validity of her research. She'd been terminated from her job on grounds she first heard while testifying. It felt worse than the sexual assault he'd endured. Two hours of humiliation and pain.

It had to be worth it. Justice would be done.

Today the prosecution was to enter DNA evidence that would positively identify the rapist.

I want that bastard to rot.

As they waited for the judge to return to the courtroom, a runner from the prosecutor's office arrived with a sealed envelope. He opened the envelope and drew out a single page, scanned the contents, and nodded as if it had been expected. She watched the prosecutor stand as the judge took the bench.

"Counselor, you have something to say?" the judge asked the prosecutor.

"Yes, your honor." The prosecutor hesitated. "As your Honor knows, we were scheduled to present DNA evidence today. However, it seems the rape kit and the results of the DNA tests have disappeared."

Ilse watched in confused horror as the judge grilled the prosecutor.

"Counselor, let me get this straight. We've gone through three days of testimony. You now say you no longer possess any physical evidence linking this defendant to the alleged crime?"

"Yes, your Honor," responded the prosecutor. "I'm very sorry, but with no physical evidence, the prosecution feels there is insufficient evidence to pursue this case further."

"That is your prerogative, counselor, but do consider the victim. It's not as if she did not suffer any damage. There is evidence of a crime against the defendant."

"We agree there is some evidence, your Honor, but not the evidence we need for a conviction. We are formally withdrawing the articles of prosecution."

This monster is going to go free?

Helpless to change the outcome, overcome with rage and frustration, Ilse awoke with a start, sitting up in the Rover's bed, visibly shaking and bathed in sweat. She turned toward Ekow, who looked at her worriedly from the other bunk.

"Are you okay?" he asked.

She took a deep breath and nodded.

"Sorry. Bad dream. I'll be fine."

* * *

As the horror of the nightmare receded, Ilse blinked hard before looking around the Rover in the early morning light. She took a deep breath and quickly felt herself calm. The dream faded more rapidly than ever before.

She felt good about what she was doing for the first time in years.

That must be what it is.

She was doing something truly meaningful. She hoped her new purpose would make this nightmare her last. Ilse didn't count on it. It had haunted her dreams for years. And now she put herself into a waking nightmare.

"You seem very sad," he said across the short divide. "I would like to know your story. My mother always says telling is the first step to healing."

"You have a very wise mother, but I'm not sure I'm ready to speak about these things."

Yet Ilse couldn't help but think he might be right. That she was ready to share.

Ekow stayed quiet.

Dawn broke over the desert mountains, revealing brown-colored dunes and sun-bleached rocks poking through like white islands in a brown sea. They were an hour out from Faya-Largeau. The Rover felt safe and comforting. Ilse felt an unexpected trust solidify.

Unprompted, Ilse said, "Perhaps you're right, Ekow. I've not really told anyone the whole story—not my family, not even my closest friends." She offered a sad smile. "That makes you my confessor, professor."

"I am glad to be of service, Ilse," Ekow said, with his hundred-watt smile returning, enjoying her rare jest. The atmosphere lightened.

After hesitating, Ilse began, "First of all, Ekow, I want you to know that discovering something like your Waterfall Reagent was my life's work. Unfortunately, my life got interrupted. Even though I've said it before, I will do whatever I can to keep you safe and ensure your Waterfall Reagent gets out to the world. I think you'll understand better once you hear about how I was before."

"What happened to you?" Ekow asked gently.

"Something that I wouldn't wish on anyone in this world. Violations of the most profound kind. The things that make you give up and do things you would not normally do."

Ilse winced as the pain she carried surfaced. She could sense Ekow's empathy but wondered if he could fully understand. Or whether anyone could.

Ekow gave her a warm nod and said, "No matter how many times you wash a goat, it will still smell like a goat."

Ilse burst out laughing. This ancient African proverb's nonsequitur and simple truth punctured the moment's intensity.

"Thank you for that," Ilse said, still smiling. For a moment, she felt good. "I think I'm ready for this."

Then she began.

"Like you, I was. No, I am passionate about chemistry. Part of that comes from my parents, both accomplished scientists. But the real drive came from what I saw as a child on a family holiday. I was ten years old when we visited a seaside resort in Tunisia. On an otherwise regular excursion from the resort to see the Sahara Desert, our bus stopped for a break in a village near the desert's northern edge, which sat on the banks of a large saltwater lake. Curious about the town, I wandered through an arch from the square where the bus stopped to get a better look at the lake. I saw what seemed like an endless stream of women and girls, some heading around the far side of the lake, the others returning, but all carrying pots, plastic water jugs, and any number of other items designed for carrying water. Fascinated, I followed one of the women into another part of the village to see what she would do with the jug. I watched her enter her adobe hut with the water and place it carefully in a shady spot, taking a tiny amount for her young son to drink before drinking herself. It dawned on me that these people had no water in the village. It just wasn't right."

A look of childish outrage flitted across her face.

"I started walking without thinking about where I was going. The next thing I knew, I was lost. Frightened, I ran the wrong way. The longer I searched, the more frightened I became. It was brutally hot, probably forty-five degrees. I thought I was going to die of thirst. Then I found him."

The memory was fresh even after fifteen years. The anger and frustration ignited.

"In a ruined shell of a building, I came across a boy about my age on his side, clutching his stomach and whimpering in pain. Next to him was a bucket of water and a cup. He glanced at me with hope, but I could only think about how thirsty I was. So, I grabbed the cup, dipped it into the bucket of water, and drank.

"The next thing I knew, I was on the ground near the boy, stomach cramps making me double over. I tried to vomit, but nothing came out. I felt so sick I could not move. I don't know how long I sat there, but I was hysterical, crying when my father found me still sitting near the boy, who had died. The water in that water bottle he gave me tasted better than anything I'd ever had before."

"Oh my," exclaimed Ekow. "How terrible."

"Yes. It was. I was miserable for the rest of the trip. I couldn't get that boy's face out of my head. On the bus ride back to the resort, my father tried to comfort me by explaining that the boy likely died of dehydration from drinking the water from the nearby Salt Lake. I kept asking him, 'But there is all that water in the Salt Lake. Why can't they just change it so they can drink it?' He kept answering the same way. 'Ilse, I'm so sorry, but no one knows how to change salt water into drinking water in quantities that would solve the problem at a price that these people could afford.'

"That made no sense to me, so I swore I would find a way to turn salt water into drinking water. That large salt-lake held so much water, so there had to be a way."

Ekow nodded in agreement. "I understand your feelings exactly. But please continue."

Ilse gazed out the Rover's window, taking a few deep breaths to calm herself. The quiet, still beauty of the passing desert mesmerized her for a moment. It had been years since she shared so much with anyone. Looking back at Ekow, she found him sitting patiently, watching her with an encouraging smile. She met his gaze and went on.

"From then on, all I wanted to do was learn everything I could about water and how to purify it. At university, I focused my studies on chemistry and water purification. I became an expert in water purification technology. I discovered the cost of the research I wanted to pursue could only be funded by the private water industry."

The irony was not lost on either of them.

"It was not easy finding a company willing to fund the research I wanted, but I was determined. After a year of searching, Uncle David, whom you met at the conference, introduced me to the managing director of the Stockholm office of the Greater European Water Company. It was a perfect fit. They had just started an initiative on water purification. My university research provided a jump start for their program. It was probably the happiest time of my life. I was pursuing my lifetime goal and getting paid for it. I made friends at work and around Stockholm. I was even promoted to head of research in my lab after six months. Right after the promotion is when it happened."

Ilse flushed, her breath coming in small gasps. The thought of reliving that horrific experience always terrified her.

Best not to think about it. That will make it stop.

The pain and humiliation from the memory of that nightmare welled, nevertheless. Her eyes glistened with tears, giving her a haunted, ephemeral look.

"It is going to be hard, Ilse," Ekow said. "You know that. We just met, but I am more than willing to listen. One thing overrides all others when one feels as intensely as you do. Leaving it unsaid only causes it to fester. You need to leach it. I hope you will continue."

She took several deep, rhythmic breaths to calm herself. The panic, as well as the remembered physical pain, receded.

"This is very difficult for me, Ekow. I appreciate your willingness to listen but please don't tell me it's going to be hard. That does not help. What helps me the most is knowing that your Waterfall Reagent actually exists. I've resented everyone since that wonderful life was ripped from me so brutally. But your discovery has given me a new purpose. That's why I'm here now. I feel confident again. I think I can speak of what happened for the first time."

Ekow smiled reassuringly, trying not to show his apprehension. He remained silent, waiting for her to continue.

"One night, I was working late at the lab. Something I did often. I was excited about my work. We were making real progress. I was so focused I paid little attention to what was happening around me. A good friend, maybe my best friend, saw it coming and tried to warn me. Earlier that day, she pointed out an ordinary-looking man who she thought was following us. But she wasn't completely sure. Besides, this was the Center of Stockholm, one of the safest places in Europe. That I was in danger simply did not make sense to me. I ignored her concerns when I returned to the lab."

Her face reddened again, but her lips compressed, a look of determination flashing across her face.

"Whatever happened, Ilse, it was not your fault. You must see that," Ekow soothed.

"I know that intellectually." Her voice broke as she took a swig of water to hold back a sob. "But emotionally, I am so angry at myself for feeling, no being, so powerless in the moment. I wasn't able to fight him off. I was naïve. I was alone at night in the lab, trying to finish an important experiment. Somehow, he got into the building.

"There were warning signs that night. Still, I ignored them. I heard noises that sounded enough like a tree branch tapping on the window outside in the wind, even though I knew in the back of my mind that there were no trees nearby. The next thing I knew, I was down on the floor, and he was ripping my clothes off."

She stopped and stood in the Rover. After a moment, without room to pace, she sat back down, her back straight and her voice a monotone.

"I screamed and tried to scratch his face. He twisted my arm up my back and broke it. There was no one there to hear, no one there to help."

Ekow shook his head.

"He gagged me and tied me to a stool so that the seat was in my belly and my arms lashed behind even though he knew he'd broken my arm. He tied my ankles to the stool, legs spread apart. My arm throbbed with excruciating pain. It happened so quickly that I was in shock. I prayed for it to be a nightmare from which I would awake.

"He took me from behind. That's when the real pain started."

"I am so sorry, Ilse," Ekow began.

"Just let me finish. Please. He left me lying on the floor of the lab bleeding until the cleaning crew came in and found me an hour or so later, I am told. I was unconscious."

She sat expressionless and numb, focused on the field of cacti unfolding next to the highway, which had giant red sand dunes behind it. Isle felt like it was somebody else's life.

"Amazingly, they caught the bastard." Tears began to fall silently down her face. "But he got away with it. There was no question it was him. A friend lied in court to give him an alibi. But the worst thing was their destruction of my professional reputation with false accusations of plagiarism, reporting non-existent experimental results and other lies about my work so that my testimony wouldn't be believed. Then physical evidence went missing, and the case was dropped."

She sat up straighter and focused on Ekow, her eyes hardening. No longer numb, she balled her fists in her lap. "As far as I know, that animal is still out there, ready to hurt someone else. They just… They just let him go." A few seconds later, she concluded, "I couldn't find an industry job anywhere. My life was over."

She finished her story like a puff of wind that slides off a sail. She stared out the window at the passing shoreline of Lake Chad, feeling the same astonishment and disbelief as the day it happened.

"How is that possible?" asked Ekow, appalled.

"I've never been able to verify all of the facts around the missing evidence, but I know who my attacker is. He is the son of the managing director of the company I was working for. Henryk Gheel is his name. A privileged, disturbed monster. Out there. Doing God knows what to someone else. For all I know, his father is a member of this Water Cabal. He fits the profile. Successful but ambitious still. Controls the Greater European Water Company completely."

A disturbing thought caused her eyes to turn from granite to ice.

> *What horrific irony it would be if I was helping the father of the man who ravaged me?*

Ilse looked at Ekow in dismay, praying it was not true.

Ekow took her hands, looked deep into her eyes, and said with conviction, "It is a travesty that this monster did not receive the punishment he deserved. I am thinking, however, that this world will have consequences for him one day. I am truly sorry you experienced such cruelty, Ilse. No one should have to go through such a thing. I am hoping the telling will begin to help the teller."

Ilse took another deep breath, released it. "Is that another of your mother's sayings?"

"No. This one is my own." He smiled. "I have many more, as you will see the more time you are forced to spend with me."

She smiled again sadly, but his positivity was infectious. She began to feel a bit better, able to speak comfortably again.

"After the attack, I was in the hospital for three weeks. Each day, I was forced to relive the assault. Day after day. The humiliation. The anger. First, the questions from the police. Then, my family and the prosecutors. The worst were his defense lawyers. Horrible." She shuddered. "During the trial, I learned who my attacker's father was. I am pretty sure I know what happened to the DNA evidence. Gheel's father paid to make it disappear. He also had to have funded the character attacks that killed my career. But nothing could be proven.

It should not have mattered. I identified the bastard. I relived the trauma over and over for everyone's entertainment. He should be rotting in jail," she said as her anger returned.

Then she went on matter-of-factly.

"Once the trial ended, I could not get my life back together. The anger, frustration, and unfairness of it all caused me to fall into a deep depression. The damage to my professional reputation serious. I considered ending my life just to stop the pain. I could not get it out of my head. At some point, maybe six months later, I realized that killing myself was the dumbest thing I could do. Henryk Gheel had taken enough from me. I was not willing to give up my life. It wasn't much, but it got me through those very dark days. I couldn't even think about the Greater Europe Water Company without shaking with rage. Saying it even now is hard for me. Uncle David was the one who suggested applying for the position with WIPO."

Ekow thought it best just to let Ilse's story settle. They sat in a comfortable silence as the sun rose over the desert passing by outside, the morning shadows almost visibly retreating.

After what seemed like a long time, Ilse said simply, "I don't know if this strange confessional will help, Ekow, but I want to thank you for listening. Finding people, I can talk to about this has been hard."

"I am more than glad to be of some help," Ekow answered, and the silence resumed.

About an hour later, the Rover's operating system announced, "We are approaching Faya-Largeau. Please prepare for deceleration."

"Thank you, Nelson," Ekow responded. "Please take us to 459 Airport Road."

"Very good, sir," Nelson confirmed. "We will arrive in approximately twenty-nine minutes and thirty-six seconds."

"Your accuracy is appreciated," Ekow joked, smiling at Ilse. "Please message Agizul Amazigh informing him of our approximate arrival time."

"Very good, sir," Nelson repeated.

More seriously, he told Ilse, "I hope he is there when we arrive. I do not want to linger anywhere too long. It would be best if we were moving again before sunset."

"Should we don our disguises?" Ilse asked as she sat at one of the workstations, feeling better than she had in a long time. The confession had worked.

Ekow pondered the question, then shook his head. "I do not think we will need them at this time."

"That's a relief," Ilse said. She pulled up a summary of Faya-Largeau's history and current situation. "Would you like to hear a bit about the city?"

"Please," Ekow said. "It would be good to know more."

"Okay then." Ilse sat up straighter, reading with a bit of a flare. "Faya-Largeau is an ancient oasis just inside the southern fringes of the Sahara Desert and the largest city in northern Chad. It lies at the crossroads of several ancient trade routes. With considerable underground water, it evolved into a regional capital, but being already within the Sahara, the population remains small. Climate change has caused the average temperature during the warmer months to exceed one hundred twenty degrees. Yet, its location has permitted it to become a prosperous regional transit point for trade, scientific research into the great desert, climate change, and a tourist center. Its fundamental challenge, as in much of Sub-Saharan Africa, is the availability of fresh water. The famous underground water reserves are nearly depleted."

"Interesting," Ekow said. "Is there mention of the thriving black market in that summary?"

"Nothing about that," Ilse answered. "Why do you ask?"

"Because this is what I know of this place. I am certain that my mother's friend, Agizul, is a legitimate businessman. But he has a less legitimate business on the side. That is why we are going there."

Roughly thirty minutes later, the Rover turned into a large warehouse facility and came to a stop. It was deserted that early in the morning, but Ekow knew security teams manned this place and Agizul's home compound ceaselessly.

* * *

Agizul Amazigh stood in the small security office that housed the network operating center for his modern office complex that included warehouses. A security camera showed a desert vehicle enter the grounds on one of the many screens displaying images from all around his property. He still could not quite believe that Minnie's egghead son was actually in serious trouble. He had known the boy since he was a toddler and trouble was never part of his story. He smiled as he thought of the Lagos hotel where he had met Ekow's mother, a random connection in a random restaurant. Minnie had been at the next table, and he'd had a tough time concentrating on the conversation at his own. By the time they had finished their dinners, they managed to signal one another to meet in the hotel lounge for an after-dinner drink. It was the beginning of a love affair that spanned decades.

Ekow needing my help. I never would have believed it possible.

* * *

Ekow was amazed at how large the warehouse and grounds were.

"My mother comes here on occasion to visit Agizul. They met when I was very young, and Agizul has been like an uncle to me. My mother shared her impressions of this place with me, and this seems far more significant than what she described. Clearly, Agizul is doing quite well."

Ilse nodded. "It does seem a large, well-kept place. Can you tell me again who this person is and why we should trust him?"

"He is more than my mother's lover. He is her friend, and I know he cares deeply for her. And so he cares for those things she cares for, including me, even though I am certain he does not like me. The feeling is mutual, but we tolerate one another out of respect for my mother.

"Another certainty is that he knows the desert like few others. He is a direct descendant of the Tuareg people, the Nubian branch of the Berbers. They were once nomadic shepherds of various livestock and traded goods in and around the Sahara Desert. Today, Agizul's family business specializes in transportation and shipping across harsh environments. A natural inheritance, if you will. He is very, very good at it."

"So he knows the desert and cares for your family. What is the problem here?"

"Well, there are the things he does that fall outside his day-to-day transportation business," Ekow continued. "That part we do not discuss but have always known is there. As a Tribal Council Member, the relationship with Agizul always posed a potential problem for my mother. There is irony in both our lives as I seek help from this man. Are you ready? Even this early, the asphalt will be scorching and soft."

"I'm ready," Ilse responded, checking her shoes.

The vehicle stopped, the car door opened, and they made what seemed like a mad dash across the burning asphalt. Ilse felt the tar begin to stick to her shoe, but she made it across. A tall, handsome, middle-aged African man stood in the doorway, motioning them in. Agizul welcomed Ekow with a familial embrace.

"It is good to see you, Ekow. It has been a long time. I wish your first visit here had been under different circumstances. Welcome to Faya-Largeau." Agizul's eyes widened as he turned to Ilse. "Please introduce me to your companion, young man."

"This is Dr. Ilse Langstrom, Agizul," Ekow began. "She is helping me for reasons I cannot fathom. Yet here she is. We truly appreciate your willingness to help as well. As much as I want to stay and see everything, we must depart before dusk. I fear we are being pursued."

Agizul ushered them into a conference room off the reception area. No one else appeared to be there.

"Where are your employees?" Ekow asked. "It is the middle of the day in the middle of the week."

"I thought it best to greet you without prying eyes," he replied. "I am fully aware of your predicament. Given the nature of what you are up against, I suspected you might be followed. We will not stay here long. I have arranged a safe place for you to spend the rest of the day and the night and a different vehicle to depart once your identification papers and pay cards are ready. Unfortunately, that will not happen until first thing tomorrow. So, let's get the Rover into a garage, get your things, and turn over control of it to me. We will leave this facility by a lesser-known exit. You now are truly on the run."

CHAPTER 12
RELENTLESS

Omar Gezi always enjoyed the helicopter view of the Greek Ilses on the approach to the Black Dog Headquarters. The aircraft rounded a hillside to reveal a pentagon-shaped complex spread out below, quickly rising to meet him. Gezi climbed out as the propellers slowed to a stop. A dangerous-looking man and a stunning woman were there to greet him.

"Ivan Damsky. It is good to see you."

"And you, Omar." Damsky took his hand firmly. "It has been too long." He eyed the gleaming Bell 75000 that had just landed in a soft rush of wind over Gezi's shoulder. "These Bells are so different than the screeching monsters we used to fly. They are sleek, beautiful, quiet, and deadly."

"Yes, they are Ivan Ivanovic," Gezi responded. "That's why I fly them."

Gezi's scanned the 'copter pad, the entrance to the building, and settled on the woman standing beside Damsky.

Releasing Damsky's hand, Gezi smiled and said, "I see you have a beautiful bird of your own."

"I do what I can," Damsky demurred.

"What do I call you?" he asked.

"Hanka, Sir. At your service," she said with a slight bow and a neutral look.

Gezi nodded his approval. "We'll see about that." To Damsky, he said, "Let's go inside. We have things to discuss."

"Of course. My office then."

"Lead on!" Gezi ordered abruptly jerking his head toward the rooftop elevator bank at the corner, indicating that Damsky and Hanka should precede him.

Gezi followed Damsky and Hanka to the rooftop lists trailed by his two security guards, who had exited the helicopter behind him in silence when they landed. Gezi could tell this visit was bothering Damsky.

"Ivan, relax," Gezi said. "This won't take long."

The doors slid silently open, and the impromptu entourage quickly filled the lift. Gezi noticed the cameras in opposite corners of the lift reminding him that Damsky was no fool. He expected every word and movement to be monitored.

When the elevator doors opened on the second floor, Gezi's security guards quickly filed out first and then made way for Hanka. Once the group was out of the lift, she turned to Gezi. "Sir, with your permission, I will happily show your associates to a waiting area while you speak with General Damsky."

The two men looked to Gezi for instructions. He smiled at her and nodded to his men.

"This way, gentlemen," she said as she led them down the hall. Her voice faded as she asked, "May I offer you coffee?"

Damsky and Gezi turned to the right to reach Damsky's office suite. Damsky pulled open the door, allowing Gezi to precede him into the suite. For a moment, Gezi's eyes lingered on the Chernaya Sobaka Okhrannaya Kompaniya sign on the door and the vicious-looking black dog opposite.

"I do like your mascot," Gezi said with an amused smile.

I truly loved that animal," Damsky replied thoughtfully.

Damsky led Gezi through his outer office past a luxurious seating area and into a glass-enclosed inner room. A large desk dominated the far side, with a small sitting area just to the right of the entry. Behind the desk was the panoramic view of the Greek coast. Once inside, Gezi paused to enjoy the view then sat down in the chair opposite the door and pulled it up to the small conference table as Damsky silently closed the door behind them.

"Would you like a drink?" Damsky offered.

"That would be nice," Gezi said. "I've always liked your scotch."

"My pleasure," Damsky said, walking up to the small bar in the corner opposite the small conference table. "Glenn Fiddich Black, neat, as usual?"

"Perfect."

Damsky prepared two tumblers a quarter full, brought them to the table, and sat opposite Gezi.

"Ivan, do you recall when we first met?" Gezi mused as Damsky settled into the comfortable conference chair.

"Of course. How could I forget? Tripoli. 2041. A few short years after the Arab Israeli Nuclear War." He took a sip of his whiskey. "A horrible time. I even keep a few reminders here in this office." He gestured toward the framed photograph showing an aerial view of Damascus just after the Israeli attack.

"Yes. Damascus. 2039." Gezi shook his head. "Those clever Jews. They destroyed that city and so many others. The Israelis called it the Iron Cap, right?"

" 'Iron Dome,' actually," Damsky answered. "Brilliant technology. You're thinking of the key feature to it, the containment dome, or 'Cap,' as the Israelis called it. We called it the 'Shapka.' The Arabs thought their out-of-date nukes would finally destroy the Jews. The Iron Dome Cap brought their own nukes down on their heads obliterating them swiftly, completely, and with no retaliation. As I said. Brilliant."

"I always wondered why you were chosen to lead the Russian humanitarian forces into Damascus after it was destroyed," Gezi continued. "Not exactly the skill set of a war-tested general."

"On the contrary, my friend." Damsky realized Gezi was playing an odd game he'd thought they were well past. He sat up straighter and stopped drinking the whiskey wondering what Gezi was after.

"A wartime leader is exactly what was needed. Instead of search and destroy, it was search and rescue. Very similar processes." Damsky paused, considering his words. "First, finding people healthy enough to function. Then using them to deal with the aftermath of radiation sickness and a host of other maladies caused by the blast. Avoiding the inevitable starvation and creating reasonable living conditions all the while protecting my own soldiers from harm."

"Lessons well learned, my friend."

"That's for certain, Omar," Damsky continued. "We got so good at this that we were deployed to Baghdad, then Tripoli, then Riyadh. After Riyadh, I'd had enough. That's when I resigned my commission. I wasn't serving Mother Russia, and there was money to be made privately."

"Do you remember our first meeting in Tripoli in 2041?" Gezi asked.

Damsky hesitated. Gezi was a dangerous man. At the time, he was one of the up-and-coming young executives making a name for himself in the Middle East. He was then in charge of the North African Water Company's Security Division, also known as NAW.

"I do. The Israeli attack was fortuitous for your company." Damsky decided that sharing his take on the situation from that time was no gamble. He still spoke carefully, "NAW had just completed a roll-up of smaller regional water companies unable to recover from the Israeli attack. The war opened the door for NAW to take complete control of water distribution throughout the Middle East. To this day, NAW controls all the water from Morocco to Turkey, across the Sahara and the Saudi peninsula, and down the Persian Gulf, including Iran. The only exception is Israel. The Israelis maintain their water independence as one would expect."

Gezi was impressed but not surprised by Damsky's understanding of his company. "That insane war was my ticket as well. I worked hard to gain control of my company. There aren't many heads of security who reach the top executive of any company, let alone one the size and wealth of NAW."

"Of course, Omar. I always admired your abilities. Our meeting in Tripoli was auspicious for us both. I had no idea you would be so successful. Your business has always been appreciated."

Damsky hoped Gezi would get to the point. He was tired of the dance.

"This goes both ways, my friend. That is why I retained your firm on an exclusive basis. I couldn't have made a better business decision. I need you to validate my trust in your abilities again."

Finally, they were at the heart of it. Dansky asked, "What is so different about this Ghanaian? I presume that's why you are here. We've done this dance quite a few times before."

"Yes. It is the Ghanaian. Not that he is special. But I suppose, in a way, he is. It is his invention that is special. He has discovered how to turn lead into gold. In this case, the lead is water. Any water. The gold is fresh drinking water. At scale. Anywhere on the planet. We need this technology. If fully disseminated out of our control, it could end my business. The end of the water industry as we know it. I need you, Damsky, to personally see to this."

Damsky whistled softly. "Okay, Omar, I already have one of my best men tracking the African, but I will take direct control. Expect nothing less."

"I *do* expect nothing less." Gezi's look was uncompromising. "This assignment cannot fail."

Gezi finished his drink and stood.

"I must return to Tripoli. I expect daily reports beginning tomorrow morning and continuing until this matter is resolved."

Damsky stiffened slightly. His eyes glittered dangerously at the curt tone of Gezi's voice. He detested anyone, even Gezi, issuing orders to him. But he kept his tone even as he gestured toward his office door.

"Let me walk you back to the 'copter."

* * *

Lars Kunta led the large delegation of water company executives into a long conference room in the United Nations building in New York for a meeting with the board of UN-Water, the umbrella agency coordinating efforts to address the worldwide water crisis. The group of sixteen men and eleven women from around the world settled around the thirty-foot-long dark mahogany conference table, their aids finding chairs against the wall behind them. The industry executives were at one end of the table, the politicians at the other. The Senior Program Managers flanked the Chair and Vice Chair of UN-Water, a handsome, gray-haired man next to a woman of middle age to whom the years had not been kind.

The Chair opened the meeting. "Welcome, ladies and gentlemen. We at UN-Water truly value your participation in these meetings. The water crisis grows ever more precarious each year. Weather patterns continue to change, and drought-stricken areas grow. We understand you have shareholders to look after, but we appreciate your critical role in helping those in need gain access to fresh water at a fair value. Only through public-private cooperation can we make it through these dangerous times."

"Thank you for the warm welcome, Mr. Chairman," Lars stood as he began to speak on behalf of the industry delegation. "We appreciate your getting right down to business. How do we deliver fresh water to everyone at a fair price? The price is as low as it can be given our costs to source and distribute it. As this agency knows, we build into prices the cost of regulatory compliance in every jurisdiction we operate. We have a simple request which we believe can reduce the price of water. If we lower the regulatory burden in a few key areas together, we believe this will allow us to pass the savings through to our customers without compromising water quality."

"But Mr. Kunta," one of the senior program managers said, whose name tag identified her as Angolan. "How can you guarantee that quality standards will be maintained? The failure to keep water quality acceptable across the board is what led to the regulations in the first place."

"You are correct, and your concerns are well-founded," Lars acknowledged. "But please recall these regulations were put in place early in the privatization process and the early days of the water crisis. We are confident the free market will police itself now that the market is more mature. No one will pay for poor-quality water. Any company selling it will quickly lose its business to competitors who can deliver. The regulations are no longer needed as they are currently written."

"How would you address the situation where there is only one supplier, Mr. Kunta?" asked another senior program manager from Jordan.

"As you will see in our presentation, in addition to eliminating certain costly regulations, we suggest easing the qualifications to enter the water industry so that every community always has at least two water suppliers."

"So let us move on to your proposals, Mr. Kunta." The chairman looked left and then to the right at his fellow board members, keeping his expression neutral even though he suspected several of his senior managers were being paid by the industry people at the other end of the table.

"Thank you, Mr. Chairman," Lars said, gesturing to his aids to pass out the binders they brought with them. "The binders you are receiving now contain our detailed proposal. Here, we will cover only the highlights. You will need time to digest the information, but we are confident you will find it fair and reasonable."

Lars knew they would. He also knew their profits were going to rise substantially. He smiled at the UN-Water board reassuringly.

* * *

Devang arrived in Accra the day after he met with Damsky and was not happy to learn that Aboah had not been seen for two days. Eight days had passed since his presentation at the water symposium, Ekow Aboah's profile and known schedule had not indicated any travel in the near term. Yet the scientist was gone.

Devang was suspicious.

"He must have been tipped off," he told his Ghanaian colleague with whom he was watching the Aboah home. "But by whom?"

"I do not know, sir," the Ghanaian said. "We followed standard operating procedures. Twenty-four-hour surveillance of the Aboah home began two days ago and is ongoing. Minnie Aboah continues her normal day-to-day activity, giving no indication of where her son may be. We know Ekow Aboah told his university he was going on holiday in a remote part of Africa, which is difficult to confirm, but we have assets pursuing that angle. But it seems clear it is a ruse. The Aboah home is bugged, but we must tread carefully around Minnie Aboah. She is a powerful member of her Tribal Council."

Devang needed something to break soon. He was getting impatient. He continued to review Aboah's dossier.

"Child prodigy in chemistry. Recruited by the Chinese at the age of fourteen for education at Shanghai University. Superior performance and high regard from his years there. Excellent prospects while working on a reagent to purify water," Devang read from the text on the car's monitor next to a photo of Aboah's face while parked across the street and around the block from the Aboah home. "How did you disappear so completely and so quickly, my friend?" he spoke a bit louder to the image before him.

"What was that, sir?" asked his companion.

"Ekow Aboah was warned somehow. Of what? By whom and why? Too many questions already."

The vehicle signaled an incoming call from Black Dog headquarters. Damsky wanted his update.

* * *

Immediately after Gezi's copter sped off into the afternoon sky, Damsky returned to his office. He was in a foul mood and determined to delve into the project personally. Devang's reports so far had been disappointing, and he knew the lack of progress prompted Gezi's visit.

"Connect me with Sen," he ordered his PCD,

Devang's face appeared on his PCD screen. "Yes, general."

"Sen, I want an update. Omar Gezi just left, and neither of us is happy about this project's progress."

"General, I think Aboah was warned. I have no idea how that might be, but there must be a mole somewhere in our client's organization."

"That would explain his unscheduled departure," Damsky responded. "Is there anything new at the Aboah house?"

"No, General," Devang answered. "I think this is a dead end. We'll continue to monitor his mother's activity, but I don't expect anything to come of it. We need better intel."

"Yes, we do," Damsky agreed. "I'll contact you again in twelve hours unless I hear from you."

"Roger that, Sir. Sen out."

"What are we missing?" he asked his assistant now sitting where Gezi had sat just a few minutes before. "Hanka, get me a list of every person Ekow Aboah spoke with at that chemistry conference. My guess is that this Ghanaian was approached there. I bet it's one of Gheel's sources. That spiderweb of his is too large and unwieldy," he continued, switching to Russian. "We have to find out who.""

"Of course, Ivan Ivanovic," Hanka responded also in Russian. "I will begin immediately."

Damsky never liked the fastidious Belgian, and he knew Gezi detested him as well. But what Damsky really did not like was the sheer number of informants Gheel employed. It was impossible to manage such a large group of people well, and leaks were inevitable. Leaks made his job harder—much harder.

"Good." He switched to English. "We'll need Gezi to get us a list of all the people in the Belgian's network. Once the list comes through, cross-reference all the names against all known contacts of Ekow Aboah over the past two months. Bring any match to me immediately."

"As you say, General," she replied and got up to return to her desk in the outer office.

He smiled, admiring the sway of Hanka's hips as she walked, tilting back in his chair to appreciate the show.

* * *

The following day, Damsky had the two lists he needed. Sure enough, twelve of the International Chemistry Society conference attendees were also part of Gheel's network.

"Hanka," Damsky yelled to her through the open door. He enjoyed being a bit boorish. It felt more traditional somehow. "Please come here."

"Yes, sir," Hanka responded through the PCD on her desk.

Damsky watched her cross the large outer office to sit in one of the guest chairs opposite his desk. She flashed a smile as she sat.

"How can I help you, sir?" she asked with just a touch of flirtiness.

Switching to Russian, Damsky was all business, "We need to track the activities of each of the twelve people you identified since the end of the conference through today. And I need it today."

"Yes, sir," Hanka answered, also in Russian. "Right away, sir."

Damsky reported the progress to Gezi through a secure channel. Gezi's reply was curt, "Keep me posted."

By noon, Hanka entered Damsky's inner office and placed a dossier on his desk for each person on the list. Damsky looked at her and smiled, "This will earn you a nice bonus, my dear. Thank you."

"It should, sir," Hanka responded. Her walk back across the office seemed to have an extra sway.

Damsky began reviewing each folder. Ilse Langstrom quickly stood out. After returning from the conference, Ilse Langstrom had taken a leave of absence from her job at WIPO less than a week ago. Her first destination from Geneva had been Accra. How she could have known about the African Project was a mystery. He pulled up her WIPO identification page on his screen and stared in amazement at the face gazing back at him.

"Hanka, come here for a moment," he called.

She appeared at his door with an expectant look. Damsky looked between his secretary and the face on the screen. He was having a hard time taking his eyes off the screen.

"As gorgeous as you are, my dear, this woman could be even more so." Damsky held up his tablet for Hanka to see.

Hanka stared into his eyes for an extra moment, saying nothing.

* * *

Devang ordered the vehicle to connect with Damsky. It was time for another report of nothing new, but before he could begin, Damsky called.

"Devang, I know who tipped him off. She is probably traveling with him. I'm sending you the dossier on Ilse Langstrom now."

"Roger, General. Received. We'll review and make recommendations within the hour," Devang responded.

"One more thing. Included in the dossier is an explanation of what is at stake. Far more than either of us understood. I expect results," Damsky ordered.

"Yes, sir," replied Devang. "Sen out."

Devang opened the electronic folder and began examining the three-dimensional images that appeared in the air in front of them.

"Let's see who we're dealing with and what this is all about," Devang muttered almost to himself but included the agent sitting in the car with him.

The image that appeared on the car's screen surprised the two men. They looked at each other and smiled.

"Wow," Devang breathed. He felt a warm glow rising from his middle, a strange feeling he couldn't explain. Ilse Langstrom's eyes held a fractured aspect that cooled and hardened the warmth. The longer he gazed at her, the more certain he became. He was seeing his sister's eyes, only more mature. If she'd lived. Ilse Langstrom was a survivor. But then his discipline kicked in. He crushed his strange reaction. She was a target. He took a deep breath and gathered himself. He gave his body and head a quick shake.

"You okay, boss?" asked his companion.

Slightly embarrassed that he'd shown a vulnerability in front of another agent, Devang responded more aggressively than needed. "I'm fine. You don't need to worry about me." And then said more mildly, "Extraordinary beauty, though. Let's widen the net immediately. How hard can it be to find a tall, beautiful European woman traveling with a short African man?"

* * *

Approximately eleven hours following Ekow and Ilse's departure from the Yellow Flower Rest Stop in Chad, the Black Dog search algorithms discovered they had been there. Although their disguises hid their identities well, the rest of the evidence fit. It was straightforward to trace the vehicle held in the name of a Nigerian limited company tied to the brother of one of Minnie Aboah's fellow council members. That connection made the likelihood of a positive identification ninety-nine percent. The resulting report was uploaded for review at the Black Dog headquarters in Greece.

Devang Sen was not surprised as he calmly watched the video from the rest stop. Their disguises were impressive but useless now—only they didn't know it.

"They always make mistakes," he said quietly from the back seat.

Arthur Mensah, another Ghanaian agent sitting in the front seat of the stake-out vehicle, turned and asked, "Sorry, boss. I did not catch that. Can you say again?"

"No worries, Art," Devang replied. "Just talking to myself. We're done here. Please take me to the office. Just to be sure, we'll continue surveillance of Councilwoman Aboah."

He shook his head as he watched the video again, which showed the Ghanaian man and the European woman getting into a desert Rover. Devang smiled like a predator who knew a kill was coming. Using his PCD, he began issuing orders to the Black Dog operatives in the Accra facility as he prepared to depart for Faya-Largeau.

CHAPTER 13
HOPE

When David arrived, Bjorn Langstrom was waiting at the baggage claim at Gothenburg Airport.

"Welcome to Sweden, David," Bjorn said, arms wide, inviting a hug.

"It is good to be here again," David said, embracing his old friend. "I wish it were under different circumstances."

"I understand," Bjorn replied. "No one's happy about this, least of all me."

David plucked his bag from the cubby hole above which his name blinked. He only had one small suitcase.

"I love the luggage claim system you have here. I'm so tired of the old conveyor belt and the competition to get one's bag, not to mention the bags all look the same. I hope other airports adopt this system soon." David said.

"I'm glad," Bjorn answered, unable to keep the pleased tone out of his voice. "We're very proud of it."

The two men headed for the lift to the airport garage.

"Sector 5, Level 2, please," Bjorn instructed the lift in Swedish.

David felt the lift rise gently, watching the location indicator above the sliding doors turn from Level 0 to 2. The lift slowed to a stop for a moment before moving horizontally to the left. When the location indicator read Section 5, it stopped, opened, and announced in English, "Section 5, Level 2. Watch your step when exiting. Have a nice day."

David sighed at the ease and efficiency of the Gotenborg Airport systems. Bjorn just kept smiling.

David sighed again as they neared Bjorn's 2020 vintage Tesla 1, one of the first mass-produced fully electric cars. David loved antique cars, especially those from the early electric vehicle era.

"It's a fun car, I know," Bjorn said. "But not for me right now. It will be fun to drive again when we get through this thing with Ilse."

David nodded, his whimsical look turning somber.

Once in the Tesla, Bjorn drove them manually out of the parking lot to the airport exit opposite the automated highway entrance and maneuvered the car next to a white, oval-shaped connection pod. The Tesla's modified receptors opened on its front and back bumpers while what looked like the mandibles of a giant insect extended from the pod, first along the length of the car and then out to both ends of the vehicle. Once locked in, Bjorn relinquished control as the pod and car moved onto the on-ramp to the automated highway.

David marveled at the seemingly flawless process and watched another pod replace the one connected to the Tesla and fill the slot behind for the next car already linked to it. The pod carefully merged them into ongoing traffic, each lane to the left moving at increasingly staggered rates of speed, allowing vehicles to accelerate smoothly between lanes.

The pod settled them in the lane second from the right and asked, through the Tesla's operating system, "What is your destination? Do you have a preferred exit? At what speed do you wish to travel?"

"Gothenburg University, exit 9, 150 miles per hour, please," Bjorn responded.

"Thank you," the pod acknowledged. "Please hold on as we accelerate."

The pod took the Tesla to the faster lanes, accelerating to the requested speed. It settled in the second lane from the left, a mere ten feet from the vehicles in front, back, and on both sides. Larger, slower vehicles traveled in the right lanes, as did vehicles exiting to surface streets. They were about thirty miles from the exit to Bjorn's home near the University. More than a few fellow travelers gawked at the vintage car as it passed.

"I so enjoy coming to Sweden just to see the latest truly useful technology," David mused as the pods around them smoothly transitioned their cargo back and forth across the highway like an intricate, mechanized dance. "This automated highway system works so much better than the patchwork quilt of self-driving electric vehicles, legacy freeways, and the few automated highways we have in the States."

"Yes." Bjorn chuckled. "My hat's off to our engineers. They do make things more efficient."

"I'm sorry I've been so vague about Ilse's situation," David began, abruptly changing the subject. "I just thought this discussion needed to happen in person."

"I understand and appreciate your discretion," Bjorn answered. "From what little you've shared, I am grateful you are involved and willing to come all this way. Let's wait until we get home before getting into it."

A few minutes later, their pod danced the Tesla back across the lanes as it announced, in a smooth, inhuman tone, "University of Gothenburg exit. Warning. Vehicle slowing. Prepare to exit the highway."

The highway disgorged the Tesla onto a ramp with a large slot on the left side into which the pod slid seamlessly. At the bottom of the ramp, the pod disconnected from the Tesla, saying, "Thank you for using the Gothenburg Automated Highway System. Have a nice day."

Bjorn took back control of the car to drive the short two miles of surface streets to his home. The design of local roads had changed little over the last century except for the busy bicycle lanes paralleling each surface street and the slate gray color of the road surface.

"Even your surface streets set an example of what is possible," David said, shaking his head.

"Swedish science," Bjorn responded proudly. "Combining all sorts of recycled materials, including rubber from used tires, one-time-use plastics, and organic materials from our landfills wasn't easy but completely sensible when considering how much of this garbage we all have. A reagent developed at our university breaks the petroleum-based waste down. We mix the sludge with organic waste and add a catalyzer, also invented here, to get the road's base material. It's become one of Sweden's most successful exports.

"But that's enough bragging for one day," Bjorn said, smiling at David as he turned the Tesla into the driveway at the front of his home. "Here we are."

David grabbed his bag from the trunk and followed Bjorn into the small but neat house through the front door, then deposited the bag on the floor in the entry.

Bjorn turned and asked, "Would you like some coffee?"

"Oh, yes, please," David replied.

Bjorn nodded toward the first door on the left as he continued down the corridor to the kitchen. "Go on into the study and make yourself at home. I'll be right back."

David opened the door and entered the familiar study where they'd had many excellent discussions. As he settled into one of the two comfortable armchairs in front of the fireplace, he overheard Bjorn instruct the coffeemaker to prepare two cups of cappuccino. David glanced around the room, not surprised to find the desk as neatly organized as ever and the paintings hung on the wall intermixed with framed certificates for the awards Bjorn had received over the years. He noticed the collection of photos on his friend's desk had changed.

Bjorn entered the study and handed him one of the wonderfully fragrant mugs of steaming hot cappuccino, then sat in the other armchair in front of the fireplace.

"Thank you, sir," David intoned as he sipped the hot, fragrant liquid. "How is Louise?"

"My wife is a story that can wait, my friend. Let's take one thing at a time," Bjorn responded.

"Of course," David said, still curious, and now concerned, but he let it pass. "Ilse first. Let's cut to the chase. No need to sugarcoat this. Ilse could be in grave danger. That's why I'm here. She's managed to get herself caught up in a situation involving a mysterious group some have called a Water Cabal. At this very moment, some terrible people could be pursuing both Ilse and a Ghanaian scientist she is with named Ekow Aboah. Professor Aboah has made a remarkable discovery. He's developed a reagent that turns salt water and wastewater into fresh water. At scale. He calls it the Waterfall Reagent."

Bjorn's eyes widened. "What? What do you mean Ilse could be in danger? From some water cabal? Who is this Aboah person? I don't understand."

David had expected Bjorn to be upset and confused. "Let me just tell you the whole story. We both know Ilse hasn't been herself for several years, so we don't have to get into the why. Still, I was encouraged that she was willing to join me at the Chemistry Society's Annual Water Symposium in Sophia Antipolis."

Bjorn interrupted, "Louise and I truly appreciate all you've done for her, David. More than you know."

David nervously ran a hand through his hair. "I've been more than happy to do it. I love Ilse as if she were my own daughter. Anyway, everything was going more or less as I hoped until we attended a session where this Ghanaian scientist presented the most amazing water purification technology I've ever seen. His discovery is truly monumental. It can purify nearly any quantity or quality of water, fresh or salt, polluted or waste, in minutes. Chemically speaking, the reagent he invented is a work of art. The resulting fresh water is easily filtered from a benign biodegradable byproduct with several interesting uses. Needless to say, I was flabbergasted. But Ilse looked troubled. After the presentation, she sat me down and told me things I did not, at first, believe. But I'm afraid those things are true, which is why I'm here."

David paused, trying to think of a tactful way to tell his friend about his daughter's transgressions. Still, nothing clever surfaced, so he just continued.

"Ilse confessed to me that she and several of her colleagues at WIPO have been accepting payments in exchange for confidential information about new water purification inventions appearing in pending patent applications. Apparently, Ilse recognized Aboah and the Waterfall Reagent from a related case she reviewed some months earlier. She said she didn't realize the significance of his Waterfall Reagent because what she saw was tangential to the main invention. When she saw Professor Aboah's presentation, what she'd reviewed had a new meaning."

David expected Bjorn to react more strongly to the corruption at WIPO, especially Ilse's involvement. Instead, he just sat there listening carefully, so David continued.

"Aboah complained about being unable to get any traction in the industry for his discovery. Ilse was certain his failures were due to what she and her colleagues had been doing. She believes Aboah is in trouble. She told me she'd heard rumors from the other examiners about a 'Water Cabal,' a group of powerful water company executives bent on controlling all new water purification technology. Ilse thinks this cabal is willing to employ any means necessary to make certain competing technology never sees the light of day. She tried to find the inventors whose technologies she'd reported and found all had passed away or just disappeared."

Bjorn still said nothing.

"How can you just sit there, Bjorn?" David asked, exasperated. "Doesn't any of this bother you? It's mortified me."

"Because getting upset, or otherwise emotionally charged, isn't going to change anything," Bjorn replied calmly. "What you're telling me troubles me deeply, and obviously, I'm very concerned for Ilse, but until you finish, I can't know how to feel or what I might do to help. Please conclude your story as quickly as you can."

"Okay," David said relieved. "It was weird to see you just sit there with no reaction. So, back to the story and its end."

"We met with Professor Aboah after the session, Ilse shared her concerns for his safety and we all agreed that Ilse would look into the fate of other inventors whose patent applications she'd examined and disclosed. She was to send a coded email to me and Professor Aboah if all had died or disappeared. That email came two days ago. We have a real problem on our hands."

David's last words hung in the air, feeling terrible. The silence dragged on seemingly forever.

Bjorn leaned forward in his chair and studied his shoes, oddly noticing they needed a shine.

Ilse has been through so much. And now this.

"David, thank you for coming here straight away. This is disturbing on so many levels. I'm still processing the fact that Ilse is involved in this mess. I cannot believe Ekow Aboah's work has gone unnoticed by the scientific community. Frankly, I cannot believe a lot of things right now."

"I know. It's all just nuts." David shook his head in disbelief. "Well, part of the plan we cooked up was my coming to you due to your connections at the World Police Force should I receive the email I did. Ilse has gone to Ghana to offer what help she can to Professor Aboah. At this point, she and Ekow Aboah could be anywhere. Somewhere in the Sahara Desert, South America, or even Asia, for all I know. Ilse is bent on ensuring access to the Waterfall Reagent equitably reaches the public. It was the first time she's shown real emotion and determination in years. About the only silver lining around this dark cloud. We have to find a way to help them."

Bjorn put the heel of his hands on both temples for a moment. Regaining his composure, he brought them down, and looking at David, he said, "This just gets worse and worse. What I'm about to share with you is highly confidential police information. Normally, I would just thank you and send you home. But you're directly involved now, so we'll have to go in together."

"What? Go in where?" David asked nervously.

"To the World Police Force, of course. It's why you came to me. It was the right thing to do. There is an ongoing investigation into a group called the 'Water Cabal.' The World Police Force contacted me some time ago when they were alerted that some lesser-known chemists had been reported missing. They eventually learned that in each case, the date the person was reported missing was shortly after a small group of water company executives met quietly in various places around the world. These scientists vanished without a trace. The World Police Force came to me to verify the chemistry."

David was stunned by Bjorn's revelation. "You knew about this?" He was amazed. "And you're involved?"

Bjorn shook his head. "Only to the extent I just shared. Obviously, I never expected Ilse to have anything to do with it. But I have a colleague, a great friend actually, from Japan. His name is Katsumi Yoshi. You may have heard of him."

David shook his head a second time. "Of course, I know who he is. You're friends with Dr. Yoshi? What else have you been up to I don't know about?"

Bjorn looked sheepish but said, "I'm sure there are things you're doing I can't or shouldn't know about."

"Other than this mess, I'm not sure what that might be." David scoffed. "But regarding Dr. Yoshi, I've heard rumors he's working on a new propulsion system based entirely on folding time and space. If it were anyone else, I'd call it science fiction. But what does he have to do with Ilse's situation? And how do you know him?"

"I've known Katsumi since my graduate school days," Bjorn said, his face growing long as he remembered. "We were closer then, but we stay in touch. He ended up marrying a fiery Israeli general with whom he had two children. Although the family frequently traveled to Japan, the children were raised mostly in Israel. One of those two children grew up to be the architect of the Israeli nuclear offensive, which was so devastatingly successful. His name is Iygal Yoshi."

David's eyes grew wider. "I never made that connection. The Commander of the World Police Force and Katsumi Yoshi—amazing. How did Katsumi weather the confirmation process? That had to have been absolutely brutal."

"It was tough, but they are quite a family. Iygal's experience and abilities were obvious to many. His mix of cultures and nationalities made him a top choice. His family's notoriety was a double-edged sword. Still, ultimately, at least to my mind, that's what got him across the finish line. He was by far the best choice. This was a rare moment of the powers that be doing the right thing."

David searched his memory for what he could remember of the Commander. He recalled that he was best known for his role in the Israeli nuclear first strike in 2039. His appointment as the Commander of the World Police Force had been highly controversial, but since taking up the position, the reports in the international press had been glowing.

As if hearing David's thoughts, Bjorn said, "The fact that he was so intimately involved with the Israeli nuclear attack made his confirmation difficult, to say the least. Nevertheless, a consensus was reached, and he was chosen. It wasn't easy, but Katsumi is a public figure, so he understood the challenges his son's confirmation involved. Katsumi recommended me to the WPF for the investigation into the missing chemists. I've met Iygal several times over the years. He is every bit as impressive as his father. He'll want to know about all of this, assuming he doesn't already know. I'll let Katsumi know we're coming."

"Where are we going?" David asked. He was impressed yet again by his friend's familiarity with such well-known and powerful people.

"To New York," Bjorn responded. "This can't wait and cannot be done in any other way but face-to-face. The stakes are simply too high."

Bjorn spoke to the house operating system in Swedish, "Isaac, please request a meeting or call with Iygal Yoshi and send a message to Katsumi Yoshi that I am coming to New York tomorrow. Please make a reservation for two of us, David Jacobs and me, on the first transport to New York tomorrow morning. Thank you."

David sat silently, wondering how well he really knew his friend. But then he remembered the missing photos on Bjorn's desk.

"Bjorn, please tell me what's going on with Louise," he asked. "Why are her pictures gone?"

* * *

Katsumi Yoshi welcomed them into his well-appointed office at Columbia University. David was surprised to find that Katsumi was nearly six feet tall and very fit. For some reason, he'd expected a small, elderly man.

"Gentlemen, welcome." Katsumi greeted each with a brief bow and handshake. "We have much to discuss and very little time for niceties, I'm afraid. Iygal is on his way. Hopefully, this meeting will end your active role in this, and we can let the professionals take over. It is good to see you, Bjorn."

"It is good to see you as well, Katsumi," Bjorn responded.

David just sat staring at Katsumi as if in a daze.

"David, are you okay?" Bjorn asked.

"Yes, of course. My apologies." He couldn't stop thinking that this must have been like meeting Albert Einstein. "Dr. Yoshi, just let me say how pleased I am to have the opportunity to meet you. I admire your work immensely, although it is far outside my own area of expertise."

"Thank you, David. Given what Bjorn has told me of you, I have a hard time believing it is over your head." Katsumi smiled graciously. He spoke softly and without a glimpse of ego. "And please," he added, "Call me Katsumi."

David smiled in return, clearly enjoying the compliment. Bjorn looked at his friend, slightly bemused, but his thoughts immediately returned to his worry for his daughter.

"I suppose the fact that she is motivated again is something," he said aloud without realizing it.

"Excuse me?" both David and Katsumi said simultaneously.

"I'm desperately worried about Ilse," he sighed. "The idea that these bastards are willing to *disappear* innocent scientists speaks volumes about what they might do should they find her before the World Police Force do."

The three men regarded each other in silence. A moment later, there was a discrete knock on the door.

"Yes, Hiroshi?" inquired Katsumi.

"Pardon the interruption, Master Yoshi, but your son is here," Katsumi's assistant announced in a deferential tone with a bow.

David stood in a daze as Iygal Yoshi entered his father's office with two other officers from the World Police Force. David had never seen any members of the World Police Force in person. Like billions of others, he saw them on the video feeds, but up close and personal, they were very different—more vibrant, almost like cartoon superheroes wearing uniforms and protective gear projecting the 'WPF' symbol to the world. David shook his head to clear away the vision.

"Gentlemen, my son, Iygal." Katsumi introduced them.

Iygal had a firm handshake that projected confidence.

"Professor Langstrom, it is good to see you again," Iygal said. "I am very sorry for your daughter's predicament, but I assure you we'll do everything possible to keep her from harm."

"Thank you, Iygal, it is nice to see you again too. I'd like you to meet a very old and dear friend of mine, David Jacobs. He was with my daughter when they met Ekow Aboah and knows more than anyone about where Ekow Aboah and Ilse might be. I hope you can help."

Iygal turned to David, briefly looking him in the eye as he shook his hand. Through that simple exchange, David knew Iygal was someone exceptional. What he'd heard and read about the first and only Commander of the World Police Force became much easier to believe.

"It is a pleasure to meet you, Dr. Jacobs," Iygal said smoothly.

"And I you, Commander," David responded recovering his composure quickly.

David stepped back so that Iygal could address the small group. Iygal nodded while seeming to continually assess the room. David realized Bjorn Langstrom had met Iygal many times and undoubtedly heard more about him from his father. Iygal began.

"First, allow me to introduce two of my intelligence officers, Major Busco from Detroit and Lieutenant Schwarz from Munich."

Each of the men nodded as they were introduced.

"They and their teams have already begun searching for your daughter and Professor Aboah. We are certain the Water Cabal is as well. As far as we can tell, the pair are still ahead of their pursuers, but probably not by much." He turned to David with an expectant look and asked politely, "Dr. Jacobs, what more can you tell us?"

David frowned at Bjorn meaningfully and, with concern on his face, turned to Iygal and his officers.

"I would think that by now you'll have been apprised of Ilse Langstrom's history?" he asked.

"Of course, Doctor," replied Captain Busco. "Rest assured, we have studied all of the players in this game carefully."

"Then you know that she was not only badly injured but seriously traumatized several years ago and has yet to fully recover," he continued. "She was just twenty-three when she was attacked. She's twenty-eight now. It's been four years since she took the job at the World Intellectual Property Office, but she has had no interests outside work. So, I invited her to accompany me to the International Chemistry Society's Annual Water Symposium, hoping she would discover that she enjoyed interacting with her peers again. The last thing I expected was what happened."

David then related what happened during their attendance at the panel discussion, where Ekow Aboah had presented his technology. He told of Ilse's strange reaction, her confession to him, and their meeting with Ekow shortly thereafter. He explained their plan to contact each other by coded email. "And then I came to Bjorn, who brought me to you."

CHAPTER 14
HELP

The next day, Bjorn and David accompanied Iygal to the World Police Force Headquarters in the Freedom Tower in downtown New York City. David noticed that Bjorn seemed familiar with the room they were brought to—a very large, octagon-shaped room with fifteen-foot ceilings. David counted two professionals for every wall of the octagon. Floor-to-ceiling video feeds filled five of the eight walls, showing various places and people worldwide. News feeds marched down three walls dedicated to the list of white, blue, and red headlines. The two western-facing sides of the octagon were windows with a view across the Hudson River to New Jersey. A quiet hum of competence pervaded everything he could see.

"Welcome to the World Police Force network operating center," Iygal said. "Right this way."

Iygal ushered them into a conference room adjacent to the western-facing wall of the room without a screen. David enjoyed the view of the Jersey City skyline across the Hudson River before he entered the windowless conference room. A half dozen people, besides Iygal, were there, some seated, others standing. A striking woman with a mass of bright red-orange hair piled on her head nodded to him. David's jaw dropped. It was the Global Attorney General, Maya Yardfeather. She stood to one side, conversing with an attractive middle-aged African woman.

Maya Yardfeather stepped forward to welcome Bjorn and David. With a wave of her arm, she invited the African woman to join them.

"Gentlemen," she said, turning to all three as she introduced herself, "I am Maya Yardfeather, Global Attorney General, and before I leave for my next meeting, I wanted to properly introduce you to Ekow Aboah's mother, Councilwoman Minnie Aboah. Councilwoman Aboah, please meet Doctors Bjorn Langstrom and David Jacobs. As I think you may already know, Professor Langstrom is Ilse's father, and Dr. Jacobs, their family friend, is Ilse's godfather. He met your son at the International Chemistry Society's Annual Water Symposium in Sophia Antipolis."

Minnie nodded and shook their hands. "It is nice to meet you, gentlemen. I wish it were under different circumstances. Ekow was quite disturbed when he returned from Sophia Antipolis, as was I when he related the nature of your meeting, Dr. Jacobs."

"Please call me David, Councilwoman," David told her. "I can assure you that the revelations of that day were as new to me as they were to your son."

"I realize that," she replied. "I am grateful that you and Dr. Langstrom acted decisively. It may have saved my son's life. I also wish to thank you and Professor Langstrom for helping raise the profile of the situation. I have done what I can from my side. I just hope it is enough." Concern was etched on her face.

"As do we, Councilwoman," interjected Bjorn. "Both of them are at great risk. I'm afraid all we can do now is pray these people can succeed in their mission."

Maya Yardfeather said, "Councilwoman Aboah, Professor Langstrom, and Dr. Jacobs, I want to assure you that this investigation has been elevated to our highest priority status. I'd also welcome you to the World Police Force Network Operating Center. Our NOC. Few civilians ever see this room. We are pooling considerable resources into formulating plans for finding and extracting your daughter and"—she turned to Minnie—"your son, Councilwoman. At the same time, we plan on dealing with those who pursue them.

"Unfortunately, another urgent matter demands my immediate attention, so if you'll forgive me for rushing off..." She turned and signaled to Iygal, who politely rose from a chair where he was speaking with another individual. "Commander Yoshi, I leave the rest in your capable hands."

"Thank you, Maya. Won't you all please be seated?"

The three made themselves comfortable as Maya Yardfeather returned to her own seat and began to gather her things. Iygal turned to address the assembled group.

"As you all know, Professor Langstrom's daughter, Dr. Ilse Langstrom, and Councilwoman Minnie Aboah's son, Professor Ekow Aboah, are being pursued by agents of a rogue collection of water industry moguls who some call the Water Cabal. It's a ghost we've been chasing for some years. Councilwoman Aboah, Professor Langstrom, and Dr. Jacobs are here to provide background information, so feel free to ask them whatever questions you deem necessary. I want suggestions by the end of the day, and I expect the final plans to be formulated by 15:00 tomorrow."

Maya rose to depart as the agents prepared themselves for questioning. This was followed by a short, terse, semi-private pause with Iygal, who briefly rose from his chair again. He nodded, and as she took her leave, returned to his seat.

"We are ready to begin," Iygal said crisply, all business now.

The two agents David and Bjorn had met the previous night were there. The three civilians sat opposite them, with Iygal at the head of a sleek-looking white marble conference table. The other two lower-ranking officers were aiding Iygal and the other officers.

"We will start with Dr. Jacobs and his arrangements with Ilse and Ekow," said Iygal. "Then I would have Councilwoman Aboah share the plan she, Ekow, and Ilse agreed upon and executed following Ilse's arrival in Accra. After that, perhaps Professor Langstrom can share his thoughts on what we might expect of Ilse under these circumstances."

The World Police Force agents looked to David to begin.

"That's fine, Commander," David began. "My part is short. As you all know, there is no need to retell it here in detail. You all know what was happening with the patent examiners at WIPO and how she reacted to Professor Aboah's presentation."

"Excuse me, Dr. Jacobs," Iygal interrupted his narrative. "Captain Busco, make a note to investigate who the other patent examiners are who have been cooperating with the Water Cabal."

"Yes, Sir." Captain Busco turned to one of the two aids, whispering instructions.

"Dr. Jacobs, please continue," offered Iygal.

"Certainly, Commander. Again, you all know we met with Professor Aboah, and he agreed to Ilse's plan, which was simple and potentially lifesaving."

"And what was that plan, Dr. Jacobs?" Major Shwarz asked.

"Simply put, if she found that the other inventors reported to the Water Cabal came to nefarious ends, she would send an email signal to Professor Aboah, with a blind copy to me, ostensibly turning down an opportunity to work at Ashesi University. If the whole thing was a false alarm, call him or send a message thanking the Professor for meeting with us. Ilse sent the email turning down the university job four days ago. She's likely in Accra to do whatever she can to help Professor Aboah find his way to you. For my part, I went to her father because we knew of his work with the World Police Force."

"Thank you, Dr. Jacobs," Iygal said. "That is helpful. Hearing the narrative again, even in summary form, may trigger new ideas and questions. Did Ilse mention what she intended to do once she reached Accra?"

"No. We intentionally didn't discuss that. She wasn't even sure Professor Aboah would accept her help or what help she could offer. But she was determined. I knew there was no stopping her, so I did what I could to support the plan," David answered.

"Thank you, again, Dr. Jacobs. Is there anything else you would like to share at this time?" Iygal asked.

"No, Commander," David replied.

Turning to his officers and aids, he said, "Ladies and gentlemen, is there anything more for Dr. Jacobs?"

The senior officers shook their heads, so Iygal returned to David and said, "Again, thank you for your cooperation. Please remain available for any further questions should they arise."

"Of course," replied David.

Turning to Minnie, Iygal asked, "Staying with the topic of their plans, Councilwoman, what can you tell us?"

Minnie Aboah surveyed the room. She liked what she saw, so she began, "To the extent I know their plans, much as Dr. Jacobs shared, the less I knew, the better. I can tell you that Ilse Langstrom came to our Accra home. She and my son left together for Faya-Largeau to meet up with a friend who was to provide them with new identities. The last I heard from my friend was three days ago when they arrived at his complex. He has not communicated with me since. They were to leave in disguise for Cairo two days ago. I expected to hear from my friend once they departed. I have not. I am very concerned about all of them."

"Councilwoman, we have to know who your friend is in Faya-Largeau," Iygal said, more gently than she expected.

"Yes. Of course," she said reluctantly. "His name is Agizul Amazigh. He has a successful trading company based in Faya-Largeau. He and I have been friends for many years." There were unshed tears in Minnie's eyes.

"We'll also look into Mr. Amazigh's situation. Lieutenant Schwartz, please be sure to find out his whereabouts," he ordered.

"Right away, Sir," Lieutenant Schwartz replied, turning to the same aid Captain Busco had used for another whispered conversation.

"Next question. This one is for all three of you," Iygal prompted. "We need to know about their friends and family wherever they may be around the world to figure out where they might go."

Minnie answered quickly, "Ekow's closest friends outside of Ghana would be in Shanghai. They are Jekyll and Leon Dong. Jekyll was one of his colleagues at Shanghai University. Leon is Jekyll's sister and Ekow's very serious girlfriend. All his other friends are from Ghana. As for family, our closest relatives live in Ghana, Nigeria, and Togo."

"Thank you, Councilwoman," said Iygal. "Please provide us with their names and contact information."

"Of course, sir," Minnie responded.

Iygal turned to Bjorn Langstrom. Bjorn sat up straighter as if he looked forward to the prospect of making a meaningful contribution.

"Ilse did not have many friends, especially after the incident, but I believe there are two women with whom she has stayed in touch. Natalie Roche and Anika Mortensen. Natalie Roche is a professional chemist. She worked with Ilse at the Greater Europe Water Company before Ilse joined WIPO. Natalie lives and works in Stockholm. Anika Mortenson is someone she met at university. Anika is a chemical engineer who works in the oil and gas industry, at least what's left of it. I don't know where she's working now, but it's remote, given what I understand she does.

"What does she do, Professor?" Iygal asked.

"Ilse used to joke that Anika got to blow things up for a living. She's a refinery safety expert."

"Any idea where she may be currently?" Iygal asked.

"I'm afraid I don't. But there are only so many places where such facilities are permitted. She should not be too hard to find."

"Major Busco, please get started on the possible locations for Anika Mortensen. It could be our best lead yet," he ordered. Turning back to Bjorn, "Tell me about your family, please."

"We do not have many relatives," Bjorn seemed to sadden. "Ilse is an only child, as are my wife and I. Our parents have passed, and their siblings and cousins all live in Sweden. I would guess a mere handful are still alive. I'll gather their contact information and get you what I can tomorrow."

"Dr. Jacobs?" Iygal asked. "Any thoughts here?"

"No, Commander."

"Okay," Iygal said. "Let us move on. We have been discussing several important topics but are getting no context. Now would be a good time to review Ilse and Ekow's personal histories. Reviewing them may jog a forgotten memory associated with a person, place, or experience. Professor, let's start with Ilse."

"Oh dear." Bjorn was caught a bit off guard. "I'm afraid I'm unsure how to respond to that."

"I'll explain, Professor," Iygal responded understanding Bjorn's anxiety.

"Let's discuss things relevant to her situation now. For example, why was she suddenly so willing to go from a government official taking bribes to wanting to be a hero?"

"I wish I had a good answer. The idea that Ilse was willing to go down that dark path contradicts her nature. She is a good person—a very good person." Bjorn's eyes began to tear. He turned away for a moment, embarrassed. "My Ilse is a sweet, sweet person. When she was younger, she sometimes attracted bad people through no fault of her own. She was too trusting in our institutions to keep her safe. Before her assault, she was a gifted young scientist committed to the challenge of solving the water crisis. Her spirit was broken by pain, embarrassment, and humiliation caused by the assault she endured and buried when the man responsible was allowed to escape justice. She is still clinically depressed, as far as I know. Depressed people do things they normally would not. Ilse is not a vengeful person, but her depression twisted her to the point where she had an opportunity to get back at the system, and she took it."

Bjorn looked out the conference room window at the buildings across the river in New Jersey. He took a deep breath and continued in a drained, monotone voice.

"The patent examiner position was the first thing she seriously considered doing after the trial. It took two years for her to even think about returning to the workforce. We were all thrilled she got the job. Ilse acted like she was, but it was painfully obvious she was not. Nevertheless, we all thought that for her to return to the world, she moved to Geneva and began work. We looked in on her occasionally as we've shared and enlisted David's help to do the same."

Iygal felt Bjorn's pain as Bjorn sat back, scowling slightly, clearly thinking about what he might have done to change things for his daughter.

"Thank you, Bjorn. That was very helpful," Iygal said, searching Bjorn's face. "Ladies and gentlemen, Ilse's passion for science never left her. Perhaps it was buried in her shame, humiliation, and despair. Discovering Aboah's work rekindled it. Ilse could be on a crusade and willing to take dangerous risks, which concerns me most about her.

"I agree, Commander," added David. "Ilse said as much to me in Sophia Antipolis."

"One last point," Bjorn said. "I want to re-emphasize that Ilse remains in a fragile mental state even though it's been years since the attack. She may think sacrificing her life for this cause would be a fair trade. I am counting on all of you to stop that from happening."

Bjorn finished talking and looked around at the group. While all were sympathetic, there was nothing anyone could say. David started and stopped himself several times before lapsing back to silence with a faraway look on his face.

Minnie's eyes misted. Although she read the dossier on Ilse Langstrom, hearing it from her father helped her to better understand the haunted look in Ilse's eyes when they met.

"I am sorry to hear this story," Minnie said, reassuring Bjorn. "Your daughter is stronger than you may know. She is a survivor. I saw this. She is a good companion for my son."

Bjorn looked at her with a sad, thankful smile.

"Thank you, Professor," Iygal said. "Your theory of motive makes sense. We'll work with this until someone can show me a more compelling one."

Both the World Police Force senior officers nodded their agreement.

Iygal continued, "Professor, please tell us more about these friends of Ilse's. When and where did they meet? When was the last time they met, if you know?"

"I don't know too many details about either woman I mentioned. As I said, Natalie Roche worked with Ilse at the Greater Europe Water Company. She was already there when Ilse started, so that would have been about two years before the attack. Natalie was the only person outside the police and prosecutors Ilse would talk to about her ordeal. I am in touch with her periodically. I'm not certain where she works or where she lives, but I have her PCD ID. I am certain she would be willing to answer any questions once she knows the danger Ilse is in."

"Again, thank you, Professor," Iygal said, looking at Captain Bucsco. "Captain Busco, please get Natalie Roche's contacts from the Professor's PCD."

"Yes, sir," Captain Busco responded. "Professor, if you please?"

Bjorn pointed his PCD in Captain Busco's general direction. He said, "Find Natalie Roche's contact information and transfer it to Captain Busco's PCD."

"Commander?" Another aide at the table looked up from her screen. "Please forgive the interruption, sir. We have located Anika Mortenson. She works in Venezuela for the Shell/Exxon Companies out of Guyana City."

Turning to Bjorn, Iygal said, "I know you said you don't know much about Anika Mortensen, but anything you can tell us could help."

"I'm afraid I know very little," replied Bjorn. "We met several times, but that was years ago when she and Ilse were at University. I haven't seen her since they graduated. There was an occasional short call when she tried to reach Ilse, but otherwise, nothing."

"Thank you, Professor. You don't know what you don't know."

Turning to Captain Busco again, Iygal ordered, "Make Guyana City a likely destination for our scientists. It's time to execute our plan. Dispatch teams to Accra, Faya-Largeau, Cairo, Shanghai, Guyana City, and Stockholm immediately. They could emerge in one of these places—or none. Let's keep looking for signals on the 'net, including tracking Black Dog operatives. Damsky could lead us to them as easily as anything else."

Iygal now turned to Minnie. "Councilwoman, please tell us about Ekow's friends in Shanghai and any other friends or family that could be a destination for them."

"Of course, Commander," replied Minnie, eager to do something. "Jekyll Dong was one of the first people Ekow met at Shanghai University. Ekow was only fifteen years old then, and Jekyll was just a few years older, a child prodigy in his own right. They had much in common and became fast friends and roommates for many years while Ekow was in Shanghai.

"While Ekow focused on water purification, Jekyll wanted to join the Chinese Space Agency, hoping to participate in the first human exploration of the outer planets. As far as I know, Jekyll still lives in Shanghai and remains one of Ekow's best friends."

Minnie paused and took a breath before continuing. "Leon, Jekyll's sister, also lives in Shanghai. She and Ekow met through Jekyll. I don't recall the specifics, but they developed a very loving relationship. I believe Ekow intends to marry this woman. I am not particularly thrilled with this choice. I have nothing against Leon, but the mainland Chinese remain very intolerant of interracial marriages, especially with Africans. It is particularly frustrating for we Africans given the nearly total integration of the Chinese who immigrated to various countries around Africa and despite the close political relationship that evolved between China and many African nations over the past several decades. My understanding is that Leon is a successful investment banker. That is really all I know about any Shanghai friends."

Iygal turned to his senior officers once again and said, "Gentlemen, let's see if we can't get more information about other places Professor Aboah might seek safer harbor in Shanghai. Look for former instructors, mentors, and classmates in China and Ghana. We have a lot of work to do. Dismissed."

"Thank you, Councilwoman. Please give Captain Busco as much information as possible about your son's friends and acquaintances in Ghana. To be thorough, also include Togo and Nigeria. While these are less likely places for him to go, we cannot afford to leave any stone unturned."

Iygal watched his officers move off at a professional clip. Finding the Langstrom girl and bringing Ekow Aboah in was important, but so was the prospect of a massive win against a sophisticated worldwide criminal organization like the Water Cabal.

> *The World Police Force needs to prove its worth. I'm bringing these motherfucking water assholes to justice.*

Iygal tamped his rising anger back down in an instant. He returned his attention to his three guests. "We still have much to do here. I should have asked this sooner. Can any of you contact Ilse or Ekow?"

David piped up, his face turning red, "I can."

All the heads in the room turned toward him.

"You can?" Iygal asked, frowning at David. "You might have shared that bit of information sooner, Doctor."

"Sorry about that. I suppose I should have. I think my nerves got the best of me."

"David, please," implored Bjorn.

"Yes, yes, of course. Before Ilse left the conference in France, we discussed how to reach each other if they had to run. For the first three weeks, they are supposed to check a series of chat rooms for coded messages from me every two days. If things went longer, we would use a different method based on their circumstances. I can leave a message for her to find tomorrow. Should I? What should the message be?"

"Yes, Doctor. Please do," Iygal said, shaking his head in disbelief. "Tell them that help is on the way."

* * *

Ilse watched the people coming and going from the Cairo coffee shop from an alley across the street. Public computer terminals were available, so it seemed a good place to check for messages. Her dark brown hair, typically worn loose, was now a nondescript gray brown worn in a tight bun at the nape of her neck, aging her by fifteen years. Her gray-blue contact lenses and dental prosthetic completed her disguise. She looked up and down the street one last time for anyone who might be watching. Seeing nothing unusual, she crossed the street and entered the café.

"Three international credits per minute," said the disheveled, sweaty clerk at the counter. "In advance."

She stiffened at the sour sweat smell wafting from the man but brought out her new PCD and paid. Ilse quickly moved away, releasing the breath she'd been holding. She sat down at one of the small cubicles that lined the back wall of the cafe, addressed the consol, and logged on. Ilse worked through the agreed series of chat rooms, spending at most thirty seconds in any one. Her heart skipped when she saw the coded message from David waiting in the eleventh chat room. It read:

"The night is dark, but the light is coming. 2."

She exhaled, not realizing how long she'd been holding her breath. She carefully scanned the shop to make sure no one was watching before typing a response:

"Echoes of the Old Kingdom once divided. 4. Friends are always a help."

She logged off and left the café, forgetting to move at the pace of an older person. She tried not to smile, but the news was good. They now had a chance.

CHAPTER 15

SHANGHAI

Leon Dong enjoyed riding the high-speed air trains around Shanghai. The ultra-sensitive solar panels on the top of the lightweight, wheel-less chain of carriages riding the air compressors offered a steady low hum as they zipped otherwise silently between the high-rise buildings of the Chinese financial center. The severely squared streets below reminded her of a giant microchip.

> *Ekow was so excited the first time we went on the air train together.*

His eyes wide and face bright, she smiled fondly at the memory. Then the scene faded.

> *He won't change—not my Ekow. I don't care what trouble he's gotten himself into.*

She knew little of his predicament, but she was determined to help. She glanced at her older brother, Jekyll, as the airport came into view through the narrow passage created by a cluster of impossibly tall high-rise apartment buildings.

"Jekyll, we have to do something," Leon said. She saw that her brother was truly frightened.

"What am I supposed to do?" Jekyll asked in return. "Am I to jump out of my skin? Frankly, I am not happy about this, but I will not behave like a frightened child."

"This is all your fault, you know. You were the one who set us up at that dump of an Irish Pub," she answered. "You could not stop talking about him. Ekow this. Ekow that. It's a wonder *you* didn't fall in love with him."

She remembered their first meeting as if it were yesterday. His smile had glowed when they were introduced. She'd caught the knowing gleam in his eye—and the appreciation. Her cheeks reddened.

"Oh, I did, sister," he said, shaking his head. "Everyone does. That's why I'm here as well. I just didn't expect the two of you to get so involved so quickly."

"What was I supposed to do?" she asked, turning to look him in the eye. "He is the love of my life. I am his." She sat back against the seat and looked at the carriage's ceiling. "I just wish Mother and Father were more accepting."

"Given how busy you were and that you stopped seeing them when you had time because you were with him, what did you expect?" Jekyll pointed out reasonably. "And then you two moved in together again without telling them. If Mom hadn't stopped by unexpectedly, they might never have known. Did you really expect it to go well when you finally came clean?"

Before she could answer, the train settled onto the airport station grooved dock with a light bump. She had no good answer anyway.

The doors opened, and they stepped out onto the platform together. As they turned to the stairs and escalators leading down to the monorail train between the airport terminals, the air train rose and sped off to the next stop with a hum that quickly faded.

Once on the long escalator, moving quickly down the long drop to the monorail station, she asked, "Where are we to meet them? I know this is all cloak and dagger, but at least tell me that much now that we're here."

"I wish I could. I've never seen Ekow like this. Something serious is happening, and as much as I love him, I'm not sure we should be involved."

Jekyll twisted his hands in the annoying way he did when he was nervous and trying to hide it. It was weirdly contagious and made Leon more nervous. As close siblings, they easily triggered each other.

"All right then," Leon said with a sigh. "Have it your way. But let's at least get a coffee while we're waiting."

They rode the monorail to Terminal 4 and then moved into the airport arrival area, where they found the usual, overpriced café with mediocre coffee and ordered. They sat at a retractable table that opened from a nearby wall. After a few minutes, Leon could not sit silently. "Can you tell me again what Ekow's message said?"

It was Jekyll's turn to be exasperated. "How many times do I have to tell you? He made a point that we speak rather than message each other. He then called from a location I didn't recognize and said, 'Check your messages and don't tell Leon.' So, I'm already in trouble for letting you know."

"Okay. I get it. But I just need to hear it again," she said.

Jekyll sighed. "There was a game we would play when we first met where we would play at being secret agents."

Leon shook her head. Grown men?

"Don't judge, Leon. We were young and working hard at school. Anyway, in the game, if we included 'Message' in any communication, it was a code word for going to a particular chat room on the 'net. I wasn't sure what I was seeing, it had been so long, but I checked the chat room, and sure enough, there was a message. 'Coming tomorrow with a friend. Meet airport Terminal 4 between 10:00 and 15:00. Will find you.' That's it. Now stop asking."

"Don't get angry with me," Leon demanded. "I'm just as worried as you. This is entirely out of Ekow's character to be so secretive and cautious. You said he sounded frightened when he called. Are you sure this isn't one of your elaborate pranks?

Jekyll tried to refrain from wringing his hands. He just couldn't. "Not this time, Leon," Jekyll replied. "I wish it were."

Leon eyed him, annoyed, as they resigned themselves to the wait.

* * *

They arrived at the Shanghai Airport two hours before Jekyll and Leon.

"We will not be sitting together on the plane, you understand, Ilse?" Ekow had explained on their way to Cairo International Airport. "When we arrive, if we are on time, we should have about two hours before my friend gets to the airport. Pass by the entrance to Terminal 4, through which you come every hour on the hour. I will follow you at a distance to know which entrance to Terminal 4 you use. Once I see my friend, I will signal you on the next pass by wiping my forehead. Continue for another minute, and then slowly turn around and follow me to the ladies' room near the end of the Terminal. Wait in there while I meet with my friend. It will not be more than two or three minutes. Once the plan for leaving the airport is settled, I will knock on the lady's room door loudly. When you come out, I will be waiting. Follow me to the next Terminal, where we will leave together."

"I get it, Ekow. It's simple and easy to execute," Ilse had agreed. "But I must say doing this stuff is beyond strange for me."

"For me, too, but what choice do we have?" Ekow had agreed.

The last few days had been a whirlwind of driving, hiding, and flying. They collected their new identification and untraceable unlimited pay cards from Agizul Amazigh, completed the eleven-hundred-mile desert crossing, and hid for a day in Cairo before departing for Shanghai. They left the Rover with Agizul in exchange for a slightly nicer Jeep Model. So far, the journey had passed without incident. Nevertheless, the stress exhausted them both.

Upon arrival in Shanghai, Ekow had watched Ilse get off the plane just in front of a tall, distinguished-looking German man. He'd trailed her at a reasonable distance and watched as she walked beside the random German, almost like a husband and wife traveling together. Once they both passed through passport control, she left the German's proximity after pretending to grab luggage from the far side of the conveyor belt. She went through customs without any questions and left Terminal 3 as if to leave the airport. She turned right, walked to Terminal 4, and entered as if she were picking up a family member or friend, noting the large capital 'A' above the entrance.

Ekow pretended to have a connecting flight and followed Ilse to Terminal 4, but he did not stay close enough to see which entry she used. He'd continued to Terminal 5 to bide his time for their first pass and wait for Jekyll to arrive. He'd imagined Ilse doing the same in Terminal 4.

He and Ilse made two passes before Jekyll and Leon arrived and sat in the café. Ekow was coming around for a third pass when he spotted Jekyll and Leon at the Terminal 4 Café.

What is Leon doing here?

The entrance they used for their passes was beyond the café, so as Ekow passed Ilse, he stopped, took off his headdress, and wiped his forehead. He continued in the same direction for another minute before glancing behind him to see Ilse casually walking toward him. He passed Leon and Jekyll without acknowledging their presence and continued around the Terminal with Ilse in tow. He was elated and upset at the sight of Leon but not surprised.

He approached the area where Leon and Jekyll were sitting. It was less than an hour since Leon and Jekyll had arrived.

"Thank you for being here, my friends," Ekow said without moving his jaw and just loudly enough for Jekyll and Leon to hear. "Follow me in three minutes if you would."

The apparent stranger continued strolling down the concourse. Leon and Jekyll looked at each other, suspecting the obvious. After the allotted time passed, they got up and walked off, following their disguised friend.

Ekow continued until he came to a less crowded area between two terminals with restrooms across from a bookstore. He loitered in the bookstore until his friends came around the corner. As they passed, he went behind them and whispered just loud enough to hear, "Come to the men's toilet."

Jekyll followed while Leon took a seat in the concourse. When Jekyll entered, the bathroom was empty except for his strange-looking friend, who came up and gave him a big hug.

"Thank you for coming, Jekyll," Ekow gushed. "It is wonderful to see a friendly face, but I am putting you in danger just by meeting like this. I do not know if we are being followed or whether our communication devices are compromised, which is why I wanted to see you in person. Let us meet at that restaurant on Yunnan South Road in three hours, and I will explain. I will be in the back room with my companion, who I will introduce to you both. I truly wish you had not brought Leon. I did not want anyone else to be at risk."

"Don't bring Leon?" Jekyll chuckled. "You, of all people, should know that wasn't going to happen. I know the place. There have been so many good times there. And one more thing. Don't forget everything that happened in the concourse was recorded, will be processed, and will likely wind up in the wrong hands."

"We did try to take that into account, Jekyll," Ekow responded with a worried look at Leon. "But thank you for the reminder."

* * *

The Black Dog agent at Control reviewed the processed security recordings showing an African man approaching a Chinese man and woman in the Terminal 4 café of a Shanghai airport. The couple clearly did not recognize the man who approached them. The man continued without any apparent contact, after which the two had a short discussion before getting up and walking in the same direction as the African man. Shortly after, the cameras at the end of Terminal 4 showed the African man and the Chinese man sitting at the café a few minutes earlier, leaving the men's toilet a few minutes apart. The Chinese man collected the Chinese woman and left the airport by air-train. The African man banged on the woman's restroom door and walked slowly toward Terminal 5. The recording from Terminal 5 showed the African man being joined by a European woman, and together they left the airport by taxi.

"Sir, I've got them," the Black Dog agent called to his supervisor.

"Let me see," the supervisor said.

"Of course, sir. The African man appeared in both Terminal 4 and Terminal 5 in ways inconsistent with regular travel," the agent offered.

The supervisor knew these recordings were restricted to the airport authorities and Shanghai Police. Still, copies are always provided to the Security Agency of the People's Republic of China. Black Dog received its copy of the footage from its Chinese agents placed in the airport authority.

"Good work," said the supervisor. "Let's find that taxi. Hack the taxi service's server and find out where those two went."

"Yes, sir," confirmed the agent.

Later, the two agents viewed a video showing the disguised Ekow Aboah and Ilse Langstrom exiting the taxi and entering the central station of the Automated Public Walkways three hours earlier, which they used to disappear into the sea of humanity.

* * *

At the appointed time, Jekyll and Leon casually approached the Irish pub on Qilianshan Road, located around the corner from Shanghai University.

"I hope this was a good idea, Jekyll," Leon complained. "The people chasing Ekow probably know this was your favorite watering hole while attending university. I could always find you two here, playing darts and drinking that horrible dark Irish beer."

"I don't disagree," Jekyll glanced down at her with a frown. "I was surprised he chose this place. It's also where you two first met."

They entered through the dark, heavy wooden doors. The smell of stale beer immediately assaulted their noses.

"Phew," Jekyll pinched his nose. "I can't believe we spent so much time here. I forgot how bad it smelled."

"I couldn't understand it either," Leon responded, taking a handkerchief from her sleeve and holding it over her nose. "Because of that, I almost didn't come the night I met Ekow."

The siblings went through the sparsely populated front bar area to the empty back room, which doubled as a game room with a billiards table and darts that quickly converted into a dance hall. Ekow sat in the far corner at a small table with his back to the wall. Next to him was a middle-aged, non-descript Caucasian woman.

Leon rushed around the billiards table to jump into Ekow's arms just as he stood.

"Ekow, I have been so worried about you," Leon said, looking into his eyes before kissing him soundly.

"I can imagine," Ekow gave Jekyll a sidelong look as Jekyll shrugged his shoulders. "I didn't mean for you to know until this was over."

"Well, that's just ridiculous, Ekow." Leon's face colored as she began to get angry. "I don't need protection. You do." She then looked at Ilse. "And who is this?"

Leon studied the large black glasses. The hair was pinned up behind her head, partially covered by a scarf. Dangly earrings, which drew one's attention away from her face. But her eyes were arresting even behind the glasses. Perfectly spaced on either side of a lovely, not too small, sculpted nose. Her brown eye color didn't look quite right on that face.

She must have been beautiful once.

"A friend," he answered. "A very good friend."

"Hello, Leon. I've heard so much about you," Ilse said, standing and offering her hand.

Leon looked up at the tall European woman and cautiously took Ilse's hand.

"I have no idea what this is about, who you are or why you're here," Leon said. "I'd like to understand what's happening."

"Leon," Ekow jumped in. "More than a reasonable question. Dr. Ilse Langstrom is a patent agent in the Chemical Arts Unit of the World Intellectual Property Organization. She has graciously offered to help me at great risk to herself. I accepted her offer and we have been traveling together since."

"That's quite all right, Ekow," Ilse interrupted. "She has every right to be suspicious of me." To Leon, she continued, "I am here because I wish to see Ekow live through the next week and because his Waterfall Reagent must not be kept from the world."

"I don't mean to be rude, Dr. Langstrom, but I still don't understand why he would choose a middle-aged woman as a companion," Leon answered.

"Let me explain," Ekow asked. "I am sure you will be understanding." He looked around as if counting the few people in the pub. "It should be safe to speak here, I think. Come, let us sit down."

Leon followed Ekow to a carefully selected table out of the view of anyone who might pass by the game room/dance hall doorway. Ekow sat close to her, tightly clasping her hand under the table. Leon watched him closely more curious than angry.

"Do start from the beginning," Leon said wanting to hear the story. "It's been many months since I last saw you, and this was not what I was expecting."

"I do apologize, my lotus blossom," Ekow cooed. "I will tell you everything. You must know that I..." He paused. "That *we* have nothing to hide." He looked meaningfully at Ilse.

"Where to begin?" Ekow asked no one in particular. Then he looked at his friends with no hint of his usual good humor. "You both know of my work on the Waterfall Reagent. That has gone well. In fact, it is better than any of us expected. That is why I have not been to Shanghai in so long."

He smiled at Leon and said, "For being missing from here for too long, I do apologize, my love." He then went on serious once again.

"You both know how hard it is to commercialize any new technology. Apparently, there is a mysterious organization determined to control all water purification technology like mine. It's made up of viciously ruthless executives representing half a dozen or more of the largest water companies in the world."

"You must be joking, Ekow," Jekyll interjected.

"I wish I were, my friend," Ekow responded. Looking now to Ilse, he said. "Ilse, please share what you know."

"Of course, Ekow." Looking at Jekyll and Leon, she said, "As Ekow said, I am, or at least was, a patent examiner working at the World Intellectual Property Office. As a chemist, I worked in the chemical arts department that examines patent applications based on chemical discoveries to see whether they present inventions that qualify for patent protection."

"Nine months ago, I examined one of Ekow's patent applications, which presented an aspect of his Waterfall Reagent that was an invention in and of itself but did not disclose the details of the reagent itself. Due to my narrow view of the overall process, I did not fully grasp the revolutionary chemistry Ekow had discovered." She paused. "Jekyll, I suspect you know a bit about the patenting process but let me briefly explain it for Leon's benefit. Once an inventor wishes to get protection for an invention, he or she must file a patent application at WIPO. There used to be national and regional patent offices. The Code of Hammurabi of 2045 did more than create a World Police Force and a Global Attorney General. It also consolidated all national and regional patent offices into WIPO. Eighteen months after filing, every application is published, thus ending the window for working under stealth mode. Before the eighteen-month deadline, secrecy is paramount."

Jekyll nodded. "That it is. And hard to maintain around a bunch of academics where collaboration is in their DNA."

"Just so, Jekyll. Thank you," Ilse agreed. "I tell you this so that you understand the rest of my story. It is not good, and I am not proud of it. I and several other patent examiners were part of a group that took money in exchange for alerting one of our supervisors when an interesting invention in the water purification field crossed our desks. The money was good, and I had reasons to feel justified. But what matters is that after Ekow's patent crossed my desk, I thought the invention interesting enough to report and collect my pay."

Jekyll's intent interest turned to horror. He stood angrily. "I'm not sure I care to hear the rest of this. Ekow, this woman should be in jail."

Ilse sighed. "I agree with you. I intend to turn myself in once Ekow is safe and his discovery made available to the world. But there is more."

"Jekyll, please sit. We should not draw any undue attention," Ekow pleaded.

Jekyll sat reluctantly, stubborn judgment on his face. "Go on then."

Ilse nodded. "As terrible as what I've done is, it may get worse. As you just heard, Ekow intended to broadly license his invention to get it into as many hands as possible. He wants the Waterfall Reagent for the entire world. The few offers he received required exclusivity. That was the trigger. His desire to broadly disseminate the Waterfall Reagent made him a threat to this Water Cabal. If he could not be bought, he would have to be removed. Just like several other inventors-scientists whose patent applications I reviewed and reported."

Ilse paused to allow the last to sink in. Leon and Jekyll both sat back, fear etched on their faces. After a moment, she concluded, "We believe that whoever is now pursuing us"—she paused again—"is capable of anything."

A leaden silence followed her words.

Leon was the first to speak. She asked Ilse in an even but troubled tone, "Just so I understand what you're telling us, do you mean to say that you accepted payments for giving confidential information about patent applications containing water technology before they became public?"

"Yes, that's exactly what I mean," Ilse looked at her feet, embarrassed.

Jekyll's anger had not faded. "Leon, she is a corrupt patent examiner who sold out Ekow's and many other inventors' years of hard work— their blood, sweat, and tears."

Ekow appreciated his control. "Obviously, what Ilse did was reprehensible on many levels. But that is why she is here now. She is risking her own life to help me and willingly accepts this as part of her penance. Considering what pursues us, in my view, it fully pays the debt."

Ilse continued, "Until I saw Ekow's presentation in Sophia Antipolis a couple of weeks ago, I had no remorse. It was no more than a way to pick up some extra spending money. It never even occurred to me to consider the amount of damage I might do. Nor did I care. However, misguided that may have been, I felt justified. But upon seeing the complete picture of Ekow's brilliant solution, all the pieces of what was going on behind the scenes began to fall into place. Ekow's life was at risk. So I am here to do what I can to help make the dissemination of the Reagent happen, including protecting the creative genius behind it," she finished, fervently, determined.

Jekyll remained doubtful and angry. "Dr. Langstrom, you are saying the right things. But turtles do not shed their shells so easily. I am sorry, but you have no credibility with me." Turning to Ekow, he said, "Ekow, you are trusting a corrupt bureaucrat with your life? Why haven't you gone to the police? Why are you hiding on your own?"

"These are fair questions, my friend," Ekow answered. "It is not something I chose willingly. But it seems the depth of this group's power and influence make the local authorities anywhere suspect. My mother, through her contacts, knew of this Water Cabal. Ilse's godfather, David Jacobs, who was with her in Sophia Antipolis, is a close friend of Ilse's father, Professor Bjorn Langstrom. Professor Langstrom has direct ties to the World Police Force. We are trying to organize our rescue through our three elders."

Incredulous, Jekyll interrupted, "Bjorn Langstrom of Gothenburg University? This is his daughter? He is a famous, well-respected scientist. What happened to you, Dr. Langstrom?" He looked again at Ilse in wonder.

"I completely understand your doubts, Professor Dong," Ilse replied, returning to her normally even-keeled demeanor. "What happened to me is not important now. What is important is staying ahead of those who are pursuing us."

"Yes," agreed Ekow. "Our plan is to stay on the move until the World Police Force can figure out how to take us in. It is truly our only hope."

Leon and Jekyll looked at each other with fear in their eyes. Jekyll broke the connection and said, "So where to next, Ekow? You cannot stay in Shanghai for long. Your relationship with Leon and me is known. It would not take long for people with the kind of resources you are describing to find you here."

"I agree," Ekow said, sadness and exhaustion entering his voice.

"But surely a few days would be possible," Leon pleaded. "Ekow, you cannot leave immediately. There are places in Shanghai that would be difficult for anyone to discover. Even with all the cameras, this is a giant city. Everyone knows where the blind spots are. People hide here for years. Let's put our heads together and figure out where we can stash you and Ilse. But I am not sure you should remain together."

"Leon, please," Ekow pleaded, mistaking her strategy for jealousy. "She is with us, and I trust her. For my sake, please."

"I am not jealous, Ekow." Leon looked at him flatly. "This is not emotional. I think the two of you should separate. It would make it harder for anyone to find one person as opposed to the two of you.

If you've been traveling as a pair, this might help throw them off your trail."

"I think she may be right, Ekow." Ilse supported Leon's point. "Racially mixed relationships still get attention, if not the scorn of earlier decades. Together, we draw more attention than when separated." She turned to Leon and Jekyll. "I know and understand why you would not want me involved, but please take care of Ekow. He is the important one. I am not. I will contact my uncle again to see if there are any new messages. I will also look into where we will go next, which I think should be a place they do not expect. I would share it with you, Leon, and Jekyll, but the less you know about our plans, the better. Ekow, as we discussed, if separated, I will leave word for you tomorrow. If it turns out to be urgent, I'll call. Good luck and enjoy the time you have with your friends." Before anyone could object, Ilse rose to her feet, turned, and walked out of the pub.

"That did not end well," Ekow groused. "Leon, I am surprised you were so aggressive. You know how I feel about you."

"I know, Ekow," Leon replied. "But I am afraid for you. I know it's serious. Who you partner with in these circumstances is critical. I wanted to know who your partner was."

Jekyll chimed in, "Not to mention that she screwed over so many inventors."

"I think you should consider moving on from her." She said finally.

"I am afraid I must continue on with Ilse," Ekow told her, intrigued by Leon's behavior. "I trust her implicitly. While I initially felt the same way you do, I have learned much about her these past few days. She is not a bad person. I believe she deeply regrets what she did and genuinely is trying to help. Finally, she is our conduit to the outside world while we are on the run with a direct line to her uncle. We are in this together, she and I. Now, where should we go?"

"I know just the place," Jekyll smiled. "I think you will agree once we get there."

* * *

Ilse left the Irish pub, relieved. She knew exactly where she was heading. The Longmont Shanghai Hotel had been in the old French Concession for over fifty years and provided easy access to Hongqiao and Pu Dong International airports. It was only minutes away from the central business and shopping districts and had excellent access to the Shanghai public moving walkways and commuter lines, while still being far enough out of the way to be private. It was also nicely appointed, so she'd enjoyed staying there the multiple times she'd attended scientific conferences in Shanghai and collaborated with Shanghai University researchers.

The commuter lines got her to the hotel within an hour of leaving Ekow and his friends. She needed to get to a net café and make sure she could leave a message for David Jacobs. But first, she wanted to check in, shower, and eat something.

"Good evening, miss," the hotel's front desk clerk said, trying not to be too obvious while he eyed her up and down. "Can I help you?"

"Yes, please," Ilse responded, trying not to look at the large gap between his two front teeth. There had been periods in Asia when crooked teeth had become popular. She was dismayed that the strange fad was again fashionable in China. "I'd like a single room for two nights, please. In the left tower on the 155th floor."

"Aha. Then you have stayed with us before." The clerk smiled again. Ilse tried not to cringe as she presented her fake pay card with its corresponding identification. He checked his screen and confirmed her request. "We do have such a room available," he announced. He processed her card and ID and then handed them back to her. "You may go right up. Would you like help with your bags, Ms. Borg?" He glanced around but saw no baggage, and his face registered momentary confusion.

"Thank you, no," Ilse responded with a friendly smile. She realized her mistake. She wanted to remain as unnoticeable as possible. "That will not be necessary. I'm traveling lightly on this short trip." When checking in, she should have made it clear that her only bag was her backpack.

"Of course, Ms. Borg," the clerk understood. Or at least pretended to.

With that, Ilse walked briskly but not hurriedly away from the front desk. She felt his eyes on her backside and all the other parts of her as she headed for the bank of elevators. This clerk seemed interested despite her disguise.

Once in her suite, Ilse used the room's operating system access codes. "Access code LSH15527. Please have a Chinese chicken salad delivered as soon as possible. Also, please request a wake-up call tomorrow morning at 06:30 with classical music and a European continental breakfast."

After her meal was delivered, she removed much of her disguise to eat. The thought of following dinner with a steaming hot shower felt divine. She barely made it to bed before her exhausted body gave out. She was asleep shortly after her head hit the pillow.

Ilse awoke the following day to the sounds of Mozart's Requiem and the sun streaming through her hotel room window like a million bright ambassadors of morning. For a moment, she wasn't sure where she was. Then the fog cleared, and the truth of her situation came rushing back like the tide in a fast-forwarded video. Her breakfast would be arriving within half an hour.

She got out of bed, got her disguise on, and was ready for the day. After a leisurely breakfast, possible since she'd figured out how to eat in her disguise, she went to the nearby net café she'd spotted on her way into the hotel the previous afternoon. Once logged in, she searched the designated chat rooms for messages from David.

She found a message in the fifth chat room. "Chariots of Fire," posted three days ago. That was good news. David and her father made contact with the World Police Force, and they were on board with bringing them in. Now, she and Ekow just needed to figure out how to remain free until that could happen.

As agreed, she searched the chat rooms to make sure she didn't miss any messages. Maybe the World Police Force had a plan. She found "Shadows in the Middles" in the eleventh chat room, left just the day before. She froze. The good feeling evaporated like mist in an intense sun. They were here in Shanghai. She had to find Ekow. They had to leave. With shaky hands, she posted in the fifth chat room, "Mother," and logged off.

Ilse quickly returned to her hotel room, pulled out one of the limited-use communication devices she and Ekow purchased when they arrived, and punched the connect button to Ekow's contact.

"Yes, Ilse. How are you today?" Ekow sounded quite happy and cheerful. She hated to ruin it for him.

"I'm fine, Ekow. But we cannot stay in Shanghai. The Water Cabal knows we're here. I just picked up a message from David Jacobs.

There is some good news, too. The World Police Force is on board with coming to get us, but that will not help us today. We must go."

Ekow sounded crestfallen. "If we must, then we must. Please meet me at the Western Transit Center at the Ningbo exit."

"Got it. I will see you there as soon as I can," she replied.

After finishing her call, Ilse pulled up her account on the video screen and checked out.

* * *

Ekow disconnected from the call, fell back on the pillow, and looked at Leon sadly. "I must leave today. The sooner, the better. This Water Cabal seems extremely resourceful. Their agents are in Shanghai searching for us. I am sorry, my love."

"Where will you go?" Leon asked. "You cannot run forever."

"You are right about that, my love. We cannot run forever. But we can stay ahead of these monsters long enough to reach help. Ilse also told me the World Police Force has been informed and mobilized. All we need to do is walk into their open arms. We just do not yet know where this embrace awaits."

"This is crazy." Leon began crying quietly. "We can protect you here. We have friends. We can move you and that woman as needed."

"I cannot continue to put you, your brother, or any of our other friends at risk," Ekow replied simply. "We will go where they do not expect and contact the World Police Force from there. They will come in time."

"Where is that?" Leon asked. "I must know."

"The less you know, the better," Ekow responded. "Let us not part arguing. I will return to you. If there is any lesson to be learned from all of this, it is that I love you with all my heart, and I can no longer wait to be with you always."

He got on his knees in the bed, and the covers fell away, revealing his ebony body. Leon sat up.

"When this is over, will you marry me?" Ekow earnestly looked into her eyes.

"Of course, you knucklehead," cried Leon. "You took long enough to ask." Leon smiled through her tears. He stood up and pulled her into his arms.

"I love you," Ekow breathed, tenderly kissing her.

"And I you," Leon replied after the kiss. She pushed him back slightly. "But we can't tell anyone until this ends. What can I do to help? There must be something."

They sat on the edge of the bed together as Ekow took her question seriously.

"Leon, I am in real danger. Just by coming here, I have jeopardized you and your brother. We planned to rent a car, drive from Shanghai to Ningbo, and fly from there to the next destination. You and Jekyll must leave Shanghai until this is over. You should drive us to Ningbo and then go on a holiday for a week, maybe more. Our connection is known. They will come for you unless you cannot be found. This situation will resolve itself one way or the other in less than a week."

Leon reluctantly agreed amongst tears, some for the joy of being engaged and some for the worry she had for her beloved's fate. They dressed and, within twenty minutes, departed to pick up Jekyll and meet Ilse.

* * *

The World Police Force mobilized considerable resources. Within five hours of Iygal's order to deploy, strike teams of ten men and women were on their way or had arrived at the destinations flagged by Minnie Aboah, Bjorn Langstrom, and David Jacobs.

"Team Accra, report," Major Schwarz ordered, watching the moving of the men on the ground.

"This is Team Accra Leader. We have contacted our local agents and confirmed that professionals are pursuing Aboah and Langstrom."

"Move on to Faya-Largeau in support. Repeat. Move on to Faya-Largeau," ordered Major Schwarz.

"Roger that, Major," acknowledged Team Accra Leader. "We'll report upon arrival. Out."

"Team Faya, report," ordered Captain Busco at another moving image on a different wall. "Where is Agizul Amazigh?"

"This is Team Faya Leader. The subject is missing. His armed vehicle is still on its side on the Western Road. Appears the subject was abducted. Local authorities and the subject's employees already searching. Joining search."

"Ten Four, Team Faya Leader," Busco announced. "Team Accra coming your way. ETA 18:00. This search is mission priority one. Acknowledge."

"Acknowledged. Team Faya Leader out."

Team Stockholm located Natalie Roche at home the evening they arrived. Natalie was surprised by the loud knock on her door. She said in a loud, confident voice, "Who is it?"

"We are with the World Police Force. We are looking for Natalie Roche. Is she home?" a voice said from the other side of the door. "Is it important that we speak with her."

Natalie peeked through the peephole in the door and saw two well-dressed men in professional-looking suits. "I'm Natalie Roche. Now, what is this about?" she asked reasonably.

"It's about Ilse Langstrom. May we come in?" Agent Dominguez asked, even keeled.

Natalie decided to open the door. "Can I see identification, please?" she asked.

The two agents pulled out their shields and held them up for Natalie to inspect.

"Okay. Come in," Natalie said.

She led them to her modest living room in a small, one-bedroom flat. Outside the picture window, the agents admired the view of the archipelago's many waterways.

"Please sit and explain what is going on," Natalie demanded.

"I am Agent Dominguez, and my colleague is Agent Charles. We are trying to find Ilse Langstrom. We wondered if you had heard from her recently?"

"It's been months since Ilse and I last spoke," Natalie explained. "Please, can you just tell me what this is all about?"

"I cannot give you details now, ma'am," Agent Dominguez answered. "I am sorry. But I must inform you that you are at risk. With your permission, we would like to extend a protective perimeter around your flat."

Natalie's face paled. "For what? I don't understand. Is that really necessary?"

"Better safe than sorry, I'm afraid. May we proceed?" asked the agent.

"Of course," she replied and sat heavily on her living room couch, stunned.

What could Ilse have gotten herself into?

One agent unpacked her gear while the other agent took his bag into the hall, calling the agents at the entrance to the building and around the block. "Execute Safe Haven. I repeat. Safe Haven."

"Team Stockholm to HQ. Do you read?" Agent Dominguez asked.

"Loud and clear, Team Stockholm," was the answer. "Status report."

"Team Stockholm executing Safe Haven. Reviewing security footage. Remain ready to relocate if needed."

Team Cairo made contact with their local counterparts. There was no sign of Ekow Aboah, Ilse Langstrom, or any Water Cabal agents. However, Team Cairo did report that two Black Dog Cairo agents were missing. They had no other information.

Team Venezuela found Anika Mortensen at her office in the Shell/Exxon oil fields outside Ciudad Guyana, supervising an active drilling site. They gathered no new intelligence there so Team Venezuela executed Safe Haven for Anika.

"Team Shanghai, report," ordered Iygal.

"This is Team Shanghai Leader. Neither subject was at home nor at work. We reviewed recordings of the past twenty-four to forty-eight hours from all major transit centers, including bus stations, train stations, and airports. We located recordings of the Dongs in the Shanghai Pu Dong Airport. We believe Ekow Aboah arrived from Cairo at 10:15 hours today and met with the Dongs in disguise. Aboah left the airport with a middle-aged Caucasian woman, who we believe was Ilse Langstrom, also in disguise. We continue to review recordings and will maintain surveillance of the Shanghai transit centers."

"Thank you, Team Shanghai Leader," Iygal responded. "I'm going to have Team Cairo join you in China to aid in the search. Keep me apprised of any new developments."

"Yes, sir," was the response.

"Computer, raise Team Cairo," ordered Iygal.

"Cairo Team Leader here, Sir," came a voice in roughly thirty seconds.

"The subjects appear to be in Shanghai. Eight of your team should be sent there immediately. Two of your best should remain in Cairo to monitor the search for the missing Black Dog agents. Something is off there, and we need more intel."

"Yes, sir," responded the Cairo Team Leader. "Anything else, sir?"

"No. New York out," Iygal ended the communication. Turning to Major Schwartz, he ordered, "Ready the transport to Shanghai. We depart in ten."

CHAPTER 16
BETRAYAL

Devang stepped down from the Black Dog chopper into Faya-Largeau, the largest town in northern Chad, compact briefcase in hand. The sudden rush of heat felt like a blast from a furnace. Batu, a Black Dog Security agent, awaited him on the tarmac and walked just behind and to the left as they entered the private terminal. Devang barely registered the giant hut-shaped structure he strode through the airport. He turned to Batu.

"Do we have information on the man they met?" Devang asked.

"Yes, sir," responded Batu Panton, the Chad Sector Chief. "His name Is Azigul Amazigh. He is a local businessman of some import. We must move carefully with this one. He has strong connections to the desert smugglers. A powerful and dangerous man locally. We should not underestimate him."

"Understood, Batu. Where do we find this smuggler?"

"His compound is at the north end of town near the entrance to the Trans-Sahara Highway. His home is less formidable. I propose we visit him there."

Devang admired the discrete, nicely appointed black Peugeot Electric SUV waiting there. Thankfully, the Peugeot was air-conditioned, and they sat in the middle two captains' chairs.

"Take us to the residence," he instructed.

"Botha," Batu said in French, "take us to the Amazigh residence. Please obey commands from Devang Sen as well." Then, in English, "Sir, please speak at the signal so that Botha can capture your voice print."

"Botha, is it?" Devang smiled. He found the African custom of naming their vehicle operating systems after both famous and infamous former African leaders amusing.

"Yes, sir. Thank you, sir. Your voice is registered," answered Botha.

The Peugeot departed from the terminal and merged into the right-hand lane of the well-maintained road. Faya-Largeau was a small town on the outskirts of the desert. They did not have far to go, nor was there much traffic. They arrived in the designated district and made their approach to the residence.

"Botha, slow down as we near our destination and make sure the windows are partially opaque as we drive by," Devang ordered.

"Acknowledged, sir," Botha responded, winding through the light traffic until they came to a corner and slowed.

"Travel the speed limit," ordered Devang.

The Peugeot sped up slightly and turned left at the next corner.

Devang spotted the residential compound, which took up a good third of the block. The well-fortified stone residence had a deep setback and was surrounded by a six-foot-high brick wall.

"The building lies a third of the way forward from the rear property line. The front gate is a graphite-steel alloy typically used in bank vaults. At least two well-armed guards, possibly with lasers, man the guardhouse. Other security measures are unknown. Amazigh is prepared for a significant assault," Batu concluded.

"Damn," Devang agreed. "It *would* take a small army to overcome these defenses. We're not doing it that way."

The Peugeot passed the compound unremarked, but Devang noted the security cameras recording all vehicles on this part of the road. They turned right at the next corner.

"Did you record our passing?" Devang asked, knowing the answer. "Do we have drone footage? Any satellite imagery? I want to know what we're dealing with."

"Yes, sir," responded Batu. "All of it. Botha, take us to the company offices in the town center."

Botha took them back the way they'd come and, within twenty minutes, pulled up in front of a well-maintained, albeit drab, concrete building. Painted in shades of brownish-gray, Devang thought building's paint resembled two-tone mud, but if the aim was for the structure to avoid undue attention, it succeeded.

The two men exited the vehicle and entered the building to find a large, clean, air-conditioned, open room well-equipped as a remote temporary control center. Batu led him to a conference room that was the heart of the operation.

"Would you like a coffee or biscuits?" Batu offered.

"A coffee sounds excellent, Batu. We'll worry about food later," Devang responded. "Please get me the information on the Amazigh compound. We must move quickly and quietly."

Batu stepped back into the open area and called the agents to join them. They gathered their notepads and laptops, filed into the conference room, and sat.

"Impressive," Devang complimented Batu, surveying the bright-eyed people in the conference room as he placed his briefcase on the table and opened it.

Batu glanced at the PCD in his left hand. "Sir, the information you requested is being uploaded now. It will be accessible in moments from any of your communication devices," Batu announced with satisfaction. The other agents sat quietly, awaiting their orders.

"Thank you, Batu," Devang said. He took his tablet from the case, located the files Batu's people had provided, and quickly scrolled through a selection of folders, which he floated in the air in front of him so that the group could follow along. He selected a virtual folder, which immediately opened in full color. They had a birds-eye view of the Amazigh compound.

"We can clearly see the street side of the compound," Devang observed. "The layout reminds me of a small castle. Have someone count the guards every hour to see whether the numbers change at night or any other time. My bet is they don't."

Batu glanced at his handheld unit again quickly and told Devang, "The drone footage is available now, sir." Another folder appeared in the corner of the holographic display. Devang ordered the folder to open and the video to play.

The image began high above the earth, then zoomed in and finally stopped at thirty-five feet, high enough to get clear pictures of the area. Fortifications were at each of the compound's back corners.

"There are no mounted weapons that I can see, but the help is well-armed," Devang observed. "It seems storming the castle is still a bad idea. A clandestine operation would be equally bad since getting in and out would be hard enough. Carrying a body? Never."

"I am following, sir. By now, you should have satellite images of the local area," Batu said.

Devang smiled as the next file appeared. He was beginning to like Batu and his team. "Thank you. Do you know any nearby areas where the road is narrow and perhaps vehicles might be vulnerable? It seems our best option is to lure him into an ambush."

"Let me do a quick search of the roadways and surrounding terrain. Yes, here we are," Batu said, pressing a key that added yet another file to Devang's folder, which opened. "From near the Amazigh compound into the center of the town, there are two possible choke points for an ambush," Batu concluded.

"Agreed," Devang said as he studied the image. "Neither is ideal, but it's all we have. When is his next expected departure from the compound?"

"Based on the historical satellite imagery and our limited surveillance over the past few days, we expect him to leave the compound late tomorrow morning for a meeting in town. His vehicle must pass through one of the two potential ambush points," Batu responded.

"Excellent," Devang said, satisfied. "Marshal our people. We need teams at each location. Choose an appropriate meeting point at 0600 hours' tomorrow."

"Yes sir," Batu looked around the conference room at his agents. "You all heard Agent Sen's orders."

Within seconds, they dispersed to assemble strike teams. Devang was beginning to feel good about this operation.

* * *

"Okay, my friend," Agizul smiled at Muhammed, his confidant and bodyguard for many years. "I will humor you and take the fortified Rover. I will see you when I return after midday."

"Open," Muhammad commanded. The door to the armored vehicle's rear seating area slid open to the right, revealing thick walls and fortified glass. Muhammed nodded. "Right, boss. Be careful."

"You need to stop worrying," Agizul joked. "The feud with the Hutus has been resolved. I am more worried about this business with Minnie's boy. That scares me."

"Do not make light of this, boss." Muhammad remained severe. "The organization that pursues him is not to be taken lightly. My contacts tell me they are merciless. We do not want to face them if it can be avoided."

"Agreed," Agizul said, stepping into the cabin of the large Rover, a modified desert transport vehicle. The doors closed and locked, and the Rover headed toward the exit gate. Agizul contemplated Muhammed, the stoic figure who stood at the entrance, watching his employer's vehicle drive away. He smiled to himself. "Take me to the Irish Pub in town, Habré," Agizul instructed the car. "Moderate speed. No rush today."

"Yes, sir," responded Habré. "We should arrive at our destination in thirteen minutes."

"Open the BBC news feed," Agizul ordered. The screen in front of his seat glowed into a scene Agizul had seen too often: water lines in Eastern Europe. The journalist droned on about the shortages.

A deafening *WHOMP!* rocked the Rover hard to one side, throwing Agizul into the reinforced door, a stabbing pain shooting through his head. He remained in his harness. Like a child's untippable toy, the Rover came back to its center without stopping.

"We have been attacked, sir," Habré's electronic voice intoned, placidly announcing the attack as it would have had they arrived at the restaurant.

"What was that?" a rattled Agizul shouted toward the empty left front seat where drivers used to sit. Force of habit. Electric self-driving vehicles were new in Faya-Largeau.

"An anti-tank shell, shot from forty-five degrees to our right front, but now is one hundred eighty degrees behind us," continued Amin's unperturbed electronic voice.

"Get us out of here!" Agizul shouted, but then realized the Rover was already accelerating. He paused to check himself for injuries. Happy to find himself intact, he ordered, "Habré, contact Muhammad now."

"Yes, boss," Muhammed's voice came through.

"Code red. Not sure if there is pursuit but attacked with military-grade munitions. Serious. Returning now to compound. Out!"

"Return to the compound now," he ordered Habré just as another loud *WHOMP!* slammed into the left side of the vehicle, knocking it off the road and onto its side. Agizul drifted into unconsciousness to the sound of Habré's disembodied voice repeating, "Emergency! Emergency! Emergency!"

* * *

Agizul awoke in a fog. As his eyes cleared, he took in his surroundings. He tried to raise his hand to rub away some of the grit in his eyes, only to find his arms tightly tied to a straight-back chair. He was naked, and his legs were bound by zip ties to the chair legs. Two lengths of thick, black rope pulled tight across his chest and around his upper thighs made it impossible for him to do anything but squirm. Cool air blowing down from above made him shiver. When he moved his right shoulder, a sharp pain shot down his arm. He noticed a heavy feeling on the right side of his face and felt his swollen cheek with his tongue.

I must have been taken when the Rover turned over, he thought more calmly than he would have expected. *I am in deep shit.*

He winced as a bright light snapped on and shone directly into his eyes, painfully blinding him.

"Good. You're awake," came a voice from behind the light. "I suspect you're trying to figure out who we are or why you've been taken. Let me help with that. We are Hutu and will require a king's ransom for your safe return. At least, that is what the demand will be. My interest is in where a Ghanaian man and a Swedish woman went after meeting with you."

"I do not know what you are talking about," Agizul snarled. "Hiding behind a bright light, binding me like a pig. I am Agizul Amazigh. Head Chief of the Tuergo Tribe. How dare you treat me like this. If I am not released unharmed at once, there will be hell to pay."

"I expected that kind of bravado, Mr. Amazigh. Let me introduce myself. My name is Dev Rao," Devang lied as he lowered the light. Batu rolled into view a cart with an ancient car battery and a few wicked-looking instruments. "We can do this the hard way, or you can cooperate. We'll get what we want one way or the other."

Agizul's eyes widened at the sight of the instruments of torture and the large Indian man. Obviously, these Hutu Tribesman were professionals. This would be made to look like a random kidnapping for money. Unless he cooperated. Even then, his chances of survival were slim. His mind focused as he considered his limited options.

242

"Okay. Let me understand my choices," Agizul replied evenly. "I tell you to go to hell, after which I will last for some time under the barbaric playfulness of your friend. Then I will either die from the torture, or you will keep me alive to suffer more and then kill me. If I cooperate, I tell you all I know, you torture me anyway to make sure I did not leave anything out. Then you kill me. I am trying to figure out what is in my best interest here. I am dead if I do, I am dead if I do not. It will just take longer to happen." Agizul smiled, impressing himself with how calm he sounded.

"I see your point," Devang said thoughtfully. "I have a third option for you." His eyes narrowed. "You can cooperate, and we will let you go. You tell your friends and your organization that we were Hutu radicals and that you escaped. That makes it a heroic story. If I later discover you've left anything out, then I, or someone like me, will return to kill you. How do you like my third option?"

"How do I know you are not lying?" Agizul asked, knowing the answer. He tried adjusting his position on the chair, but was met with another searing flash of pain from his shoulder. He felt his calm dissolve as the pain caused him to moan. The damage done by the car crash was taking its toll.

"You don't," Devang answered. "We don't have much time, and yours has run out. What will it be? I'll give you ten seconds to make up your mind. Computer, set a countdown at ten seconds. On my mark. Begin." Devang held his wrist device up for Agizul to see.

The wrist piece counted down to five, four, three...

"Okay! Okay!" cried Agizul, making his choice. "I will cooperate!"

I am sorry, Minnie.

"Wise choice, but just to make sure you are sincere..." Devang looked at Batu. "Please ensure Mr. Amazigh cooperates thoroughly."

* * *

"We have their new identities and where they were headed from Faya-Largeau," Devang reported to the Black Dog Control Center. "I'm headed to Cairo within the hour. I will check in upon arrival."

"Roger, Mr. Sen. Safe travels," dispatch from Control responded.

Devang sat in the Faya-Largeau airport, waiting for the plane to finish refueling. It was the only one on the tarmac.

"Your cooperation is very much appreciated, Mr. Carter," Devang said as he transferred the funds for the plane's use to its befuddled owner thirty minutes earlier.

"You're welcome, sir," he answered. "You'll contact me about where to pick it up, yes?"

"Yes. Besides, what I've transferred would cover replacing this plane."

"Indeed," the man answered. "It is a pleasure doing business with you."

Devang preferred a transaction rather than taking the plane by force, which he would have done if the owner had proved less amendable. Within thirty minutes, the self-flying Cessna lifted off on its way to Cairo. Devang sat in a plush reclining seat in the middle of the plane, nine identical empty seats around him. He sorted through the now complete files on the two people he was chasing. There was nothing significantly new about Aboah. A few older acquaintances had been added to the list, and a few new possible sources of assistance were added. He turned to the Langstrom file. The trial transcript and police report from the attack on the girl mentioned in the earlier summary had been added.

"Now, what do we have here?" Devang murmured softly as he opened the police report on Ilse Langstrom's assault. After thirty seconds of reading, he looked away, up, and out the window. He couldn't help but think of his sister. A beautiful, sweet, innocent girl of sixteen, only two years older than he. The authorities refused to believe her at first. They never found the man who did it. She'd never been the same. She killed herself just over a year later. He'd found her body at the bottom of a ravine not far from their Cube.

He read on—the trial transcript, the press coverage, the character assassination. He could not seem to close the file. He found himself reading it over and over, unable to stop. He brought up Ilse's image from her registration badge at the Sofia Antipolis conference. Her photo and his long-dead sister seemed to converge. This hazy combination filled his head as he leaned back and dozed off for a needed rest for the remainder of the flight.

Devang landed in Cairo two hours after leaving Faya-Largeau, rested and clear-headed. As he stepped off the plane, he was met by two local Black Dog agents—*Damsky is a perfectionist*—thought Devang. Devang greeted his Cairo colleagues.

"Kassab and Bahar, it is good to meet you. What news?" Devang asked as they approached the terminal shaped like a small pyramid.

"Based on the intel you provided us from Faya-Largeau, we traced where they stayed and when they left. They departed Cairo yesterday, Mr. Sen," Bahar said. "They were only here for one day. They stayed in a cheap hotel near the airport and took the first flight to Shanghai. They are most likely heading to meet the Dongs."

"Yes. So it would seem. How many others are in your local detail, Kassab?" Devang asked.

"Just we two," Kassab replied. "We reported to Control, advising them of your arrival along with the last known contact and presumed destination of Ekow Aboah and Ilse Langstrom. Sir, if you wish, we can accompany you on your plane, assuming you will go directly to Shanghai. Control will likely instruct us to head there to provide backup for those agents. I think traveling with you would probably be more expedient."

"Thank you, Kassab. Let's discuss our next steps at the local office," Devang said as the three got into a nearly identical Peugeot to the one used in Faya-Largeau. The agents sat in the two forward seats, leaving one of the back seats for Devang, making his next move that much easier. As soon as they were settled, Devang drew his sidearm and killed Kassab and Bahar.

He couldn't save his sister. He'd managed to protect several of the scientists he'd been sent after. He'd do the same for Ekow but Ilse Langstrom was different. This felt like a second chance.

A faint burning smell hung in the air. Devang leaned back and admired his laser pistol, a marvelous example of Chinese-Ethiopian weapon design. It was compact and produced a silent, invisible energy beam that instantly cauterized whatever wound it made. A single shot to the back of the head resulted in no blood or noise. The distance selector was on the short-range setting, although the weapon had a range of up to half a mile. Neither agent knew what hit him.

"To the New Zaballah dump," Devang ordered the Peugeot. "And please darken the window shading."

The operating system responded in English, "Yes, sir. If you like, I am called Hosni. It appears that New Zaballah Dump is closed."

Devang just shook his head. "Thank you, Hosni. I am aware. Please proceed as instructed." A moment later, he shouted, "Hosni, Alpha, Zero, Nine."

"Received, sir," Hosni responded.

"Erase any recordings you have of today in our system, including complete or partial copies. Disconnect from the 'net immediately. Cease all automatic communications except those necessary for navigation."

"Acknowledged and completed, sir," Hosni said in a flat metallic voice a moment later.

"That will be all for now," Devang concluded. "Alert me when we are one mile from our destination."

On the drive to the abandoned Cairo Dump, Devang considered his situation. He had just killed two Black Dog agents, taking pieces off the board. He needed to do the same in Shanghai.

The dump was deserted without monitoring devices. Devang disposed of the bodies and headed back to the airport. When he arrived, he reported to Control.

"I met Kassab and Bahar. They informed me that our targets are en route to Shanghai. Heading to the airport now. Over."

"Roger that, Mr. Sen," replied Control in the same voice as before. "Let us know when you've contacted our Shanghai group."

"Will do. Over and out."

The adrenaline rush from the kill had subsided to a low level of intensity. Every step brought increasing clarity. He'd been waiting for an opportunity like this. Black Dog was vulnerable and didn't know it. Helping the fleeing scientists could bring Black Dog into direct conflict with the World Police Force. It would be a fitting end.

The vehicle pulled up to the airport's main entrance. Devang issued his final command to the Peugeot operating system, "Hosni, please park in the structure across the street and display your *do not disturb* message. Await orders there."

"Yes, sir," Hosni responded and eased away from the curb after Devang closed the door.

Devang re-boarded the plane he'd borrowed in Faya-Largeau, which taxied out onto the runway. As the plane took off, he began formulating plans.

The autopilot announced, "Shanghai in three hours, sir."

* * *

"This is Team Faya Leader reporting in. Over."

"Report, Team Leader," Captain Busco answered from World Police headquarters.

"The Subject has been located. He is a little worse for wear but alive," the team leader shared. "We're debriefing now to determine the identities and disguises of the ultimate quarry. He is cooperating."

"Roger that, Team Leader," Busco confirmed. "Nice work. I look forward to your full report. But what of Waterfall?"

"Black Dog is very close to them, sir," answered the team leader. "We're uploading their aliases and disguises now. They were heading for Cairo from here, but beyond that, the subject wasn't sure."

"Roger, team leader," acknowledged Busco. "Wrap up in Faya and take your team to Cairo. We have to find them!"

* * *

"No response, sir," said the Black Dog Control Center's communications officer. "It's been four hours since Kassab and Bahar last checked in."

Damsky frowned. "Something is not right," he said in his thick Russian accent. "Get me Sen."

he communications officer turned back to his console and connected Damsky to Devang Sen.

"Sen here," came the familiar voice over the com.

Damsky wasted no time on pleasantries. "When was the last time you had contact with our Cairo agents?"

"Three hours ago, sir," responded Devang. "Why do you ask?"

"We cannot reach them," Damsky snapped, unable to pronounce the w correctly in English. "I want them in Shanghai."

"Neither of them said a word to me about that. Why wasn't I advised?" Devang asked testily enough to sound believable. "We already had a plane in Cairo. It would have made more sense for them to accompany me. Surely, our Shanghai agents could use their help."

249

"I assumed they would have accompanied you without being told. I also assumed you would have ordered them to, Devang," an annoyed Damsky retorted, the only time he let his Russian slip when he pronounced his name. "What was their last location?"

"Cairo airport," Devang responded calmly.

"We will investigate. Damsky out!"

Devang almost laughed at Damsky's accent, but he knew it was only nerves.

> *He knows something is up but isn't sure what. I have some time.*

Damsky cut off the connection with Devang. Damsky replayed the earlier conversation with Sen in his head.

> *Something in Sen's voice was off. He said all the right things and did all the right things, but something was not right.*

Damsky's preternatural instincts were formidable. He was rarely wrong when it came to reading other's intentions and loyalties.

> *I hope I'm wrong, but I cannot take a chance with this assignment.*

To his aid, he said, "Track Devang's route and activity from when he left for Ghana."

> *Everything was routine until this communication from Shanghai. This could be a big problem.*

"And get me Tang," he ordered. "Now!"

"Yes, sir," responded the communications officer. "He is on the line now."

"Tang, what is your status?" asked Damsky.

"I've got eyes on one of the targets, sir. The Swede. She has been in and out of her hotel," Tang responded.

"Did Devang contact you when he arrived?"

"He let me know he was in Shanghai, yes. He said he was searching for the Ghanaian."

"Be careful, Tang. Devang Sen may have turned. If you see him, take him into custody. If he resists, you are ordered to kill him."

The Control Center staff gasped. Damsky's face turned very red. Livid, he said in measured tones, "If he has betrayed me, I want his death to be very slow and very painful."

To his aide, Damsky ordered, "Get my transport ready. Tell the pilot we go to Shanghai."

CHAPTER 17
NINGBO

Devang stalked Li Tang, the lone Black Dog agent tailing Ilse Langstrom. He watched as Tang finished a conversation on his communicator and immediately looked up and around. Devang ducked behind the corner of the building just in time.

Damsky knows.

He mirrored Tang's gaze as they watched Ilse emerge from the hotel with her backpack and hurriedly walk toward the public transport. She was in a different disguise from the one she had on at the Mali rest stop, but he and Tang had no trouble recognizing her. She looked worried.

Maybe she knows Black Dog is closing in.

Tang peeled away from the small shop where he'd been standing pretending to read the news on his tablet and followed at an appropriate distance. Devang followed.

From a safe distance behind Tang, Devang watched Ilse get onto the public transport crowded with people moving at various speeds on five separate tracks in each direction. The tracks increased in speed as she moved left from one to the next until she was on the fourth, which moved at twenty miles per hour. She looked behind her, trying to see if there was any pursuit, but Devang could tell she didn't spot Tang. She began to walk forward along the fourth track with others who wished to continue moving while on the walkways.

She stayed off the fastest track. Good.

Tang followed, blending in well. Devang mirrored him.

Teenagers laughed as they jumped back and forth from track to track, not caring that they were jostling others. Ilse navigated around the scowling adults and avoided the teenagers. She knew how to use the Chinese moving sidewalks.

Tang expertly moved along the walkways in front of him. Devang kept them both in his line of sight and matched their pace.

Ilse's chosen transport headed toward the west side of the city. All Devang could do was follow and stay out of sight. He considered what he knew of the Black Dog agent ahead of him.

> *Li Tang. A good agent by all accounts. Skilled in all forms of martial arts and weapons, but so were all the Black Dog agents. The question is: How good are you?*

He vaguely recalled meeting Tang a few years before and very recently when he'd arrived at Black Dog headquarters to meet with Damsky for this assignment.

> *No element of surprise this time. Tang has to know I'm coming.*

After about thirty minutes, Ilse began moving back to the right of the transport, to the slower tracks, and stepped off at the westernmost Transit Center in Shanghai.

> *This Transit Center is going to be my only chance at Tang. They must be heading west, mostly likely Ningbo, in a private vehicle. Sizable airport. Makes sense. This transport center must be where they're going to rendezvous.*

He saw Tang reporting in on his PCD.

> *Damsky will figure this out as easily as I have. But first things first. If I can take care of Tang, Damsky won't know exactly where they are in Ningbo.*

Devang stepped off the transport and into the station, closing on Tang.

> *I need to do this before Ilse stops moving to wait for her friends, letting Tang find a defensible observation point.*

Devang glided diagonally to his right to flank Tang.

> *He tends to look left and behind more thoroughly than to the right. Good. A bad habit.*

Devang hid behind others moving through the Transit Center as he planned his move on Tang. Devang exploded from behind a blind spot created by two people with large bags, taking Tang into a hallway to their left in one smooth athletic burst but not taking him to the ground. Devang flowed from Tang's side to behind him as Tang began a countermove, his training kicking in a fraction of a second too late. From behind, Devang snapped his neck and continued to keep the now-dead agent on his feet, supporting him as if he were helping a drunk friend.

A short way down the hall was a public bathroom with twelve private stalls, eight occupied. Devang wrestled the body into one of the open rooms, sat him on the toilet, and shut the door. A couple of mildly curious people watched the two of them go in. One elbowed the other, pointing, and the other snickered before moving on. Once inside, Devang positioned Tang's body so that Tang's head would jam against the bathroom door as he stepped out. It would take time for any maintenance crew to realize it was more than just a bad lock. He left quickly.

Devang headed to the Transit Station exit nearest the onramp to the Ningbo automated highway.

There you are.

He watched the disguised Ilse get into a Kia sedan, where he could see two black-haired heads in the rear seats. As the Kia passed, heading to the nearby onramp, Ekow Aboah, his appearance unmistakable in the heart of Asia, looked out the window at something above Devang's head.

"Get me a ride to Ningbo," Devang said into his PCD. After a few seconds, a vehicle detached from the taxi line across the street.

* * *

Damsky was fit to be tied.

"Try Li Tang again, damn it!" he yelled at the communications officer on the company plane. "I have no eyes on the targets." In the next breath, "Devang Sen will pay."

They'd lost touch with Tang when he was in the westernmost Shanghai transit center, still five hours from landing in Shanghai.

"Too many things point to Ningbo. Change course immediately. We are going to Ningbo," Damsky ordered.

As the transport descended toward the Ningbo Airport, Damsky announced, "We are about to land. Devang Sen is now a confirmed hostile. You all know his skill. Be sharp or be dead."

Damsky landed with a large contingent of Black Dog agents at Ningbo Airport. The agents deplaned and melted into the terminal, assuming pre-arranged positions throughout the facility.

Why would Devang turn?

Damsky followed his agents off the plane, shaking his head.

* * *

Devang followed the Dongs' Kia almost all the way from Shanghai to Ningbo, then sped ahead of them to arrive about thirty minutes earlier. He chose a defensible location within sight of the aunt's residence and quickly exited his vehicle. He looked at the time on his PCD.

> *Twenty-five minutes before they get here.* Devang rolled his eyes. *These amateurs will come straight here. They've gotta know their every move is being watched.*

After five minutes of waiting, Devang left his hiding place to find the Black Dog agents surveilling the aunt's house. He quickly but carefully circled the residence, navigating the surrounding neighborhood.

> *It should be easy to find these guys.*

A minute later, Devang spotted an agent on the roof of a commercial building with a clear line of sight to the Dong residence.

> *The sniper.*

"Where is your partner?" he said softly, patiently waiting for movement.

Black Dog agents always survey in pairs.

Devang found the other agent across the street from the Dong residence inside an empty flat. He noticed the blinds being pulled slightly back as the agent peeked through the window.

"Okay, I've got you now," he said to no one. "The sniper first."

Devang carefully made his way to the commercial building, deftly picked the lock to get inside and found the stairwell to the roof. He quietly climbed the stairs, opened the roof door, and stepped out in a crouch. He listened for a moment. Hearing nothing, he rose slightly and, still in a crouch, slowly edged his way around the rectangular structure that housed the stairwell access door. He quickly looked around the corner, then ducked back to stay hidden. The agent had his gear set up near the roof's edge, his full attention on the Dong home. Rather than approach the agent across the open roof, Devang flicked his hand-held laser to the on position, stepped out quickly from behind the stair cover, aimed, and fired at the Black Dog sniper's head. Devang approached the sniper carefully and then sighed at the look of surprise on the agent's face as the laser burned a tiny but deadly hole through his skull.

Halfway there.

He left the body where it lay and returned to the ground. He circled around to the back of the building across the street where the second agent was hiding. He found a locked door but used the laser pistol at a low setting to burn through the deadbolt lock quietly and opened the door.

He stood in an entryway leading down a short hallway that bisected two unoccupied flats. He had marked the right flat as a target earlier.

He put his head against the door to listen. After a few minutes, he heard movement inside. Steps followed by the opening of an interior door. There was a short grunt and sigh of relief as the agent sat down on the toilet. Devang again quietly broke the locking mechanism on the door with his laser, quickly entered the flat, and silently padded over to the bathroom, where he jumped in front of the open door and shot point blank. The agent's body slumped to the right, awkwardly collapsing against the wall of the small bathroom.

Another piece off the board.

Devang checked the time on his PCD again and remained inside the flat with the dead agent watching through the front window. Fifteen minutes later, Ilse, Ekow, and the Dongs arrived and entered Auntie Dong's house across the street.

They should be safe for a while here.

Taking his PCD out of his pocket, he marked a spot on the map function's display, summoned his vehicle, and said, "Pick me up in two minutes."

Devang met the vehicle, got in, and said, "Take me to Ningbo Airport."

"Yes, sir."

"Darken the windows," he ordered.

As the high-rises of Ningbo passed, he pulled from his vest pocket a small, thin, hard-covered case about the size of a hand-held device. He carried it with him always. Devang opened the case and removed a folded coated paper containing a carefully produced self-adhesive mustache and goatee. Using the vehicle's mirror, he carefully applied the beard and mustache. He pulled out a small, rounded patch of lightweight material from his back pocket that unzipped to become a workman's cap.

Disguised, Devang left the taxi with instructions to remain within fifteen seconds of this drop-off point. He entered the airport through one of many sliding doors. Almost immediately, Devang spotted Black Dog agents, turned around, and left. He had not expected this large of a force. They had the entire airport covered.

I need to get them out of that house soon.

Once outside, he spoke into this PCD to summon his vehicle. "Pick up now. Take me back to the Ning Dong residence."

On the way back, Devang removed and carefully stowed his disguise. Once he reached Auntie Dong's neighborhood, he left his vehicle a few houses away and approached the house cautiously. He crept behind the one-story wooden home and carefully peeked into a common room. Leon and Jekyll Dong were having a discussion with Ning Dong on the couches, but there was no sign of Ilse or Ekow. Devang felt a strange pang of panic.

What if they were already headed to the airport?

Devang heard faint voices coming from the alley behind the house. He quietly moved around to the house, realizing an opportunity had been presented. Devang decided it was a good time for Ekow Aboah and Ilse Langstrom to meet their tracker. He drew his laser.

"Get into the Kia. Now," he ordered as he approached from the corner of the house.

Ekow and Ilse were standing next to the vehicle. They both jumped and then froze, staring at him like a deer in the headlights. Devang was struck by Ilse's presence in person. She frowned.

Devang plunged ahead, "Move. Now," He yanked open the door and shoved Ekow in. He gestured at Ilse with the gun to follow. "In."

She looked up at him with disgust but complied. "Who are you?" she asked as Devang got in.

Ekow chimed in, "Sir, I do not know who you are or what—"

"Save it, Aboah. I know who you are, why you're running, and what pursues you," he said calmly and professionally. "I'm here to help, and help is what you need. Tell the Kia to drive in a widening circular pattern."

Ekow and Ilse looked at one another in disbelief. Ilse looked at Devang and said, "You have a bizarre way of offering help. Who are you? Why did you kidnap us this way? Why should we believe you?"

"You should not trust me. You don't know me. But you have nothing to fear from me. You only made it out of Shanghai because of me. I know this will be a shock, but I was the Black Dog agent the Water Cabal initially sent after you. Do as I say and live."

Ekow and Ilse looked at each other again, neither knowing what to say.

Ekow sighed and said, "Ilse, this man came up behind us without a sound. By the looks of him, he is dangerous to say the least. I have a feeling if he had wanted to cause us harm, we would already be dead or captured." Turning to Devang, he asked, "You say "was" and "initially." What does that mean? What would you have us do?"

"Tell the car to drive in a widening circular pattern favoring the east side of Ningbo," Devang ordered.

"Kia, please do as this man says," Ekow complied reluctantly.

"Thank you." Devang acknowledged.

He watched the Dong home fade behind. He now had a mortal enemy in Ivan Damsky. He gave himself a fifty-fifty chance of surviving with Damsky alive and free.

"Okay, good. You're sensible," Devang began. "Like I said, I work, or worked until yesterday, for the Black Dog Security Company. I know how they think and have a contact at the World Police Force. I plan to deliver you both safely to the World Police Force, but you must follow my instructions without question. Please trust that I will know what's best in this situation."

"Why would you turn from your assignment to help us?" Ilse hid none of her skepticism.

He looked directly but not too deeply into Ilse's eyes. "Let's just say I've gotten tired of doing the devil's handiwork and thought it would be nice to be on the right side for a change. Aboah has something the world needs. The world should have it. I am your best hope of making that happen."

Ekow shrugged and looked at Ilse. "What choice do we have?"

"All right. Here's the situation," Devang went on. "If you had planned to go anywhere from the Ningbo Airport, you would have been toast. My former boss, a very accomplished operative, is already there with roughly thirty men. They are waiting for you."

Ekow blanched. Ilse's face drained of color. They would have walked right into it.

Devang continued, "While you have been creative and lucky, your luck has run out. Wherever you had planned to go next, there is a good chance Damsky already figured out where. He has virtually unlimited resources, which is how I found you so easily and why he is waiting for you at the airport. He and I know all about each of you. Your family, friends, coworkers, and even your former friends and colleagues. It's what we do.

"They have resources that can be deployed even to the most remote places you might go, so your next move must be to go to a place where you know no one and have never been. It's the only way to throw them off. More importantly, you cannot fly from Ningbo. You cannot travel in any vehicle tied to your real name or use the aliases you picked up in Faya-Largeau."

Ekow and Ilse looked at each other yet again, genuine fear in their eyes.

"I am thinking we have been arrogant to believe we could do this on our own," he said to Ilse. "Even Agizul's caution was not sufficient. Our aliases were uncovered in a day or two. I know we did not expect to be on the run very long, but it seems any length of time on our own will be fraught with more danger unless we can find an alternative."

Ilse's dismay turned to anger. "We weren't supposed to need a second set of identities," she snapped. "So what else do you know about us, Mister...? We don't even know your name. Our favorite color? Our preferences in music?"

Devang found he enjoyed how her eyes flashed when she was angry. "As a matter of fact, yes," he said more gently. "I know everything about you. The name is Devang. Devang Sen."

Ilse's anger abated somewhat as she continued to hold his gaze. She noticed the details of his face. His eyes, his cheekbones, the fullness of his lips.

What am I doing? Get a grip, Ilse!

He turned back to Ekow, breaking the moment. The Kia went three-quarters of the way around a roundabout and headed south on its circular route.

"Your only hope is to get help and set a trap. The only organization I know that could pull that off with Damsky on the other side is the World Police Force. I once knew the Commander of the World Police Force when I was working in the Middle East following the nuclear war there. I'm sure he'd love inside information about this Water Cabal. Your next destination was Guyana Vista in Venezuela. Ilse's best friend from university works in the oil fields there, which is very much out of the way. Under different circumstances, that might have been an excellent choice. But Damsky also knows about Anika Mortensen, and he will have agents watching her in case you show up. Of course, he can't know for sure until you move, but when you do, he will be very close behind and maybe ahead."

The more he spoke, the more Ilse knew they had no choice but to trust him. Surprised, she rather liked the idea. The Kia turned again. She decided they had to share what information they had. "We've already been in touch with the World Police Force but indirectly. My uncle, David Jacobs, my father, Bjorn Langstrom, and Ekow's mother brought our situation to their attention."

Ekow chimed in, somewhat caught up in the moment, "My mother, a tribal elder, assured me that the World Police Force would help us. I do believe help is on the way. I am just not sure they know where we are, and our method of making contact does not lend itself to swift action."

"Let me worry about that, Professor," responded Devang. "Your next move is for the two of you to fly to Atyrau, Kazakhstan, from Shanghai. I will join you there after making contact with Commander Yoshi. We both know the city, so it should not be difficult unless I cannot convince him. But first, you must return to Shanghai and fly from there. There will be one or two of Damsky's agents there, just in case you did double back. I will run interference for you and make sure at least one of them gets a message to Damsky about where you're headed. Don't worry. It will be long enough after your arrival that you won't be found."

"But what about Leon and Jekyll?" Ekow asked with genuine concern. "We will have disappeared outside their auntie's house."

"I believe they will be safe," Devang said. "Once they know you're on your way to Atyrau, there won't be time or a reason to pursue them. Mobilizing forces there should take Damsky some time, which helps us.

"The two of you need to go straight to whichever of the two international airports in Shanghai has flights with available seats to Atyrau first thing tomorrow. Once you get there, find a cheap hotel and text me the location using a burner device like this one you can buy at the airport."

"But what if you are apprehended?" Ekow asked, concerned. "We will have led these bad people straight to us!"

"If I don't respond within five minutes, leave. I will not be in a position to help. But that is very unlikely." Ilse said with a natural grace. "Devang, thank you for helping us. I don't know what we can do to repay you."

"Just promise you'll have a drink with me when all this is over. Oh, and come visit me in prison," he joked with a wry smile, "Because if this goes as planned, I'm pretty sure that's where I'll wind up. For a while anyway."

The Kia pulled up next to Devang's car, which had been following them since they left the Dongs. Devang got out of the Kia, turned back to them both, and said, "I know this is way outside your comfort zone, but just follow the plan. Don't try to get creative. There is a good chance this will work. See you tomorrow in Kazakhstan."

CHAPTER 18
ATYRAU

The sun shone brightly as Ilse's plane landed at the Atyrau International Airport. She wondered whether their decision to fly separately from Shanghai was a good one. When she and Ekow discussed it the previous day, it made sense. They agreed that separating might further throw off any pursuers. Devang wanted them to stay together but had not been with them when they made that call. Now, she was not sure the decision was a good one. She felt a foreboding when the plane touched down.

The mouthpiece that marred her teeth made her drool, and the padding that added twenty pounds was hot and uncomfortable. It was necessary to stay in character. Otherwise, they might make their pursuers suspicious.

Atyrau. Not a place she ever expected to be. Before her flight, she spent the day alone in a small hotel near the Shanghai Airport. Sleep has eluded her since, except for a few fitful naps. Part fear and part strange longing. She caught herself.

I need to be alert.

The flight to Atyrau had fascinated her. The plane resembled a rocket ship, and the seating was circular for the passengers and crew. It felt comfortable, seemed reusable, and safe. Even during takeoff, she experienced only mild pressure for a short time. The seat stabilizers quickly compensated. It was a one-hour giant hop into the atmosphere, after which she watched the ground rise to meet the hypersonic plane as it landed.

Ilse walked quickly and purposefully through the airport, her backpack her only baggage. She hailed the next available taxi, which pulled up outside the baggage claim area.

She got into the vehicle and ordered, "Take me to the Park Café. It's along the river on the Asian side, just north of the bridge. Stop and let me out two hundred yards before the restaurant."

Devang's instructions echoed in her mind. As he'd explained when they'd parted ways, "The Park Café should be a safe place for us to meet. Just hail a taxi and tell it to take you there. I will be right behind you."

The thought of him settled her. She was tired but excited for this nightmare to end. It would all stop soon, one way or another.

She sat up straighter in the taxi's back seat. Odd fantasies made her smile as she watched Atyrau pass by. After about twenty minutes, the vehicle pulled onto a road that ran along the Asian side of the Ural River. It went under the Central Road Bridge, connecting the Asian and European sides of the City Center, and continued to a pretty waterfront park with grass and trees lining the well-maintained paths. A bit farther on was the Park Café, the name spelled in English.

"We have arrived," intoned a mechanical-sounding voice.

Ilse got out of the taxi and paused for a moment to survey the area. People strolled along the waterfront, enjoying the fine weather. Everything looked ordinary even though she knew they were far from out of the woods. Indulging herself for a moment, she closed her eyes, drew in the tainted, slightly foul petroleum scents from the river.

As if in a waking dream, she opened her eyes and strolled toward the Park Café, enjoying the feeling of the sun on her skin. Devang's warnings buzzed in the back of her mind so she continued to look around the park for anything that might be dangerous. Ilse spotted Ekow in his disguise waiting on a bench opposite the main entrance when she was about one hundred yards from the restaurant. As she got closer, there seemed to be something peculiar about how he stood after rising from the bench that made her stop.

It was not Ekow.

She took a step back and turned to run, but hands grabbed her from behind, and before she could scream, someone put a wet, smelly cloth over her nose and mouth. They hustled her into a nearby vehicle on the waterfront road, stuffing her into the back seat.

As she lost consciousness, she heard one of the men say, "We've got the girl, sir."

Then all was black.

* * *

Devang watched Ilse and Ekow drive back toward Shanghai after a lengthy and somewhat contested discussion about where to go next and how to get there. The frustrating conversation echoed in his mind.

"I still do not understand why traveling separately is such a bad idea," Ekow had argued.

"It adds an additional layer of complexity to our plan without any appreciable benefit," Devang had patiently explained. He had not expected such stubbornness from the professor.

"I fail to see how a greater degree of unpredictability is not beneficial," Ekow had answered, unwilling to concede.

"Ekow, he has far more experience in these things than we do," Ilse had pointed out. "I think we have to follow his advice here. We don't have time to keep arguing."

"Thank you, Ilse." Devang had looked at her with appreciation. "Ekow, please trust me. I know it's hard, and traveling separately might make sense under other circumstances. But not here and not now. Please believe me."

"I have no real reason to trust you, but I will agree." Ekow had finally acquiesced.

After Ekow and Ilse left for Shanghai, he headed to a nearby private airport. It was getting late, and Devang needed to reach Iygal Yoshi quickly for his plan to work. Even if he could get through, convincing him would be a challenge. Though their time together had been short, it had been intense. He respected Iygal and hoped Iygal felt the same way.

He entered Iygal's old private line but got no answer.

No surprise there.

As his vehicle pulled up to the curb outside the private airport terminal, he had the vehicle connect him to the World Police Force's emergency hotline.

A confident, calm voice answered. "World Police Force. What is your emergency?"

Devang hesitated. This was the moment of truth. Was he really prepared to cash it all in? Ilse Langstrom's face flashed in his mind. There was no choice.

"This is Devang Sen," he began. "I am an old friend of Iygal Yoshi. I have urgent information regarding an ongoing investigation into the whereabouts of a Ghanaian scientist and a Swedish patent examiner. I need to speak with Commander Yoshi immediately."

"One moment, Mr. Sen," replied the intake officer seriously. The connection went silent for about thirty seconds before a different, more authoritative voice spoke.

"This is Lieutenant Schwartz, Mr. Sen. What information do you have?"

Devang expected to have to make his way through several layers of bureaucracy and hated it, but he was ready.

"I have been in direct contact with and know Ekow Aboah's and Ilse Langstrom's whereabouts. I am also a former employee of Black Dog Security, the firm hired by the North African Water Company to apprehend and/or kill these two individuals. In fact, until three days ago, I led the team pursuing them. Now, please put me through to Commander Yoshi."

"One moment, sir," Lieutenant Schwartz responded. Devang left the car and settled in the airport terminal lounge, a good distance from the few staff on duty at that late hour. This time, the wait was longer. The minutes felt like hours. He hoped his name and his paid-for special status would get him through. He smiled as a familiar voice came through his PCD.

"Devang Sen, what the hell are you doing involved with these people? Black Dog Security? The North African Water Company? I would have hoped you had better sense."

"It's nice to speak with you too, Iygal. It's a long and very sordid story. One I'll gladly share on my way to prison when this is over. But for now, we must prepare a strong trap for a dangerous Russian bear."

"Go on," Iygal said.

"But I need one favor in all of this. It's about Ilse Langstrom. She must not go to prison. Can you guarantee that?"

"At this point, Devang, be thankful I'm even speaking with you. Since you're involved with those chasing her and Ekow Aboah, anything you say will be considered false until proven otherwise. All I can promise is that I'll try not to shoot you if you are turning yourself in. You need to tell me what you know. We can take it from there."

"Fair enough for now. But the girl really cannot go to prison. I am going to insist on that. After you hear what I have to tell you now and the information I can provide later if I survive, you'll deem it well worth the trade. Let me get moving, and I'll contact you again in about fifteen minutes. What contact will get me through your buffer to reach you efficiently?"

Devang tried to be patient. He hoped Iygal trusted him enough to know his intelligence would be accurate and important. After a short pause that seemed much longer, Iygal said, "When you connect with the emergency hotline, use the code word *iron dome*. That will get you straight through to me. Just one quick question. We've been collecting a body count of Black Dog agents over the past few days. Does that have anything to do with you?"

"Let's just say I've had a change of heart," Devang responded, relieved but careful not to show it. "You'll have to discuss the rest with my lawyer when this is over. I'll reconnect shortly. Sen out."

Devang left the lounge and returned to the small terminal. He approached the rental counter, where an agent stood with a plastic smile.

"Welcome to Zhoushan Airport, sir."

"I need a fast, small plane for a jump to Beijing. What do you have available?" Devang asked.

"We have several Cessna X Class and one Rolls Royce C560," the rental agent announced, looking up at the big Indian with forced enthusiasm. "I presume you're credentialed for these planes?"

"Of course," Devang responded, handing him his pilot license. He watched the rental agent's eyes widen as he ran the license through the intake computer. Then Devang's credentials appeared on his tablet. "I'll take the Rolls. Have it fueled and ready to depart as soon as possible." Alongside the readout of Devang's credentials on his screen was a message, *AAA Service Member.*

"Right away, sir. No disrespect intended," the agent stammered. "The plane will be ready within the hour." Sweat suddenly beaded on the agent's forehead.

Devan watched with satisfaction as the airport's aircraft crew quickly began preparing the plane after the agent informed them who was renting it. He then brought out his PCD, sat in the nearest private communication booth, and reconnected to the World Police Force Emergency Hotline.

"World Police Force Emergency Hotline. What is your emergency?" a different receiving officer intoned, this time sounding slightly bored.

Iron Dome."

The bored undertone vanished. "Yes, sir. Right away, sir."

This time, Iygal only took a few seconds to get on the connection. "Okay, Devang. Let's have it. From a quick review of your more recent exploits for Black Dog, you have been a naughty boy. I'm surprised you would work for this kind of scum."

"Frankly, so am I. I'll explain myself later, but let's not waste time we don't have. You know me. Or I should say, you *knew* me. I was disillusioned. Deeply. It got worse. I'm not proud of what I've been doing. The money was good, and the perks were excellent. But I was able to stop a lot of the dirty work. I could lie to you and say it's about how this professor's technology can save the world, which is part of it. But the truth?" Devang hesitated but knew the only way Iygal would believe him was to be honest. It sounded preposterous as he said it. "I've been planning to bring down Ivan Damsky, Black Dog Security and his bosses for a long time. As soon as I understood who they were and what they had Black Dog doing, that was my mission."

There was silence on the connection for a solid twenty seconds. Then Iygal said, "Devang, in all the years I've been operating both covertly and overtly, I don't think I've ever heard a more outlandish lie or a more convincing confession. I don't know whether to congratulate you or cut the connection. But even if I did believe you, where does that get us? I need more intel. Without concrete facts, we can't help these two people or stop those pursuing them. I don't care what's motivating you."

Devang knew he'd hit the right tone. "I completely understand. I'm committed to doing exactly what you say. We need to meet tomorrow to plan the trap. Between now and then, I have to run interference so that Ilse and Aboah can make it to Atyrau. Let's meet there tomorrow afternoon. That is where they're going. I'll make sure Ivan Damsky knows it too."

"I suppose there's no way that you'll just lead us to Ilse and Ekow now rather than using them as leverage?" asked Iygal, knowing the answer.

"You know I can't do that," Devang answered. "The sharks have to be caught. I can't leave them out there to take revenge in their own time. This has to end now, and this is the only way."

"Against my better judgment, I agree," conceded Iygal. "The usual place?"

"The usual place. Sixteen-hundred hours. I need your word, though. I won't be taken out of the game until this is over. Ilse needs me. I need her. You don't have anyone better than me, and few are even close. You know this."

"I do know that," Iygal responded. "But you've turned your coat a few too many times. Skill is only one consideration. I will confer with my officers, and we'll settle it tomorrow. Good hunting."

"Thanks. That's all I can ask for at this point. Sen out."

Devang thought that went as well as expected. A short time later, the plane was ready, and he was off the ground on his way to Shanghai.

* * *

"Where are those fuckers?" snarled Damsky. "They should have been here by now. Contact Agent Koy."

"Yes, sir," responded his field assistant, recognizing his ever-fouler mood for the danger it was. He spoke into his PCD. "Agent Koy, report."

Silence.

"Agent Koy, report." the assistant repeated, getting more desperate.

More silence. The assistant began to sweat despite the cool, well-air-conditioned terminal. They were set up in the international terminal outside Security near the terminal's entrance.

"Agent Koy isn't responding, sir," the assistant fearfully informed Damsky.

"Goddammit," Damsky said quietly, seething. He didn't need to create a scene here. "Sen again."

Damsky grabbed the PCD from his assistant and connected with Olga Podelova.

"Where are they going, Olga?" he demanded when connected, not bothering with a greeting.

"I cannot be sure, General," she responded.

Well, find out, dammit!" This time, he did not restrain himself as he yelled into the PCD and then cut the connection.

Damsky paced back and forth between the rows of seats in the waiting area. Devang was proving an ever-growing cancer that needed to be cut out. It was fully dark when Olga's identifier appeared on his assistant's PCD.

"Speak," Damsky commanded after grabbing the device.

"It seems Devang Sen hired a small plane from a private airport not far from where you are, General," Olga reported. "The filed flight plan is to Beijing, but we must assume that is a diversion. I also found two reservations from Shanghai to Atyrau for each subject under their aliases, the Ghanaian departing on the 10:30 flight and the Swede on the 15:22 flight. We've got them, sir. If we set up in Atyrau, we can end this there."

"Good work, Olga," Damsky said in Russian. "We will discuss a nice bonus when I return to Greece."

"Thank you, General," Olga responded, also in Russian, with a smile Damsky saw on the PCD's small screen.

Damsky said to his relieved assistant, "Gather our forces. We leave for Atyrau by midnight."

* * *

As Devang guided the plane into the private airport next to Shanghai Pudong International, the sky began to lighten in the east with the promise of dawn. He considered his next steps. He did not expect a large force of Black Dog agents still at the international airport, but there would be at least two or more. Damsky was a pro, and would know by now that Devang had used company credit to hire a plane in Ningbo with a flight plan to Beijing. That he was coming in for a landing in Shanghai also surprised the Control Tower at the private airfield.

"This is Rolls Royce K134N requesting permission to land," Devang told air traffic control after the plane's operating system connected him.

"Please use Runway Four, Rolls Royce K134N. Be sure to check in with ground control upon landing. We don't have a flight plan for your plane's arrival here. We can't have unexpected planes showing up out of nowhere."

"Roger that, Control. My apologies. I did not mean to surprise you. I will report as instructed and explain. Rolls Royce K134N out."

Devang landed the plane without incident and taxied to the designated area indicated by ground control. He was met by the usual maintenance crew, both human and robot. He passed the plane's credentials to the human supervisor.

"Can you direct me to the administrative office?" he asked the human crew chief.

"First floor at the north end of the terminal, sir," the crew chief responded respectfully, seeing this pilot had elite status.

"Thank you."

Devang headed into the building, through the terminal, and out the main entrance to hail a taxi.

"Pudong International," he ordered the taxi's operating system in English. "International Terminal."

"Yes, sir," the operating system answered in English.

Devang watched people filter in for early flights as the sun rose higher in the sky. After one pass through the airport's terminals, he identified two Black Dog agents in disguise staking out the International Terminal. He kept out of the line of sight of the agent-janitor and the agent-passenger using pillars and people for cover. Devang made several more passes through the other terminals to make sure there were only the two. Ekow and Ilse were flying together on a flight scheduled for 10:30, so he expected Ekow and Ilse to appear about thirty minutes before the scheduled departure time to avoid spending any more time in public than was necessary. He had until 9:30.

Devang carefully observed the two agents' movements for two hours to determine their patterns. The agent-janitor made rounds every thirty minutes, pretending to empty trash bins and stopping in the restrooms as if to clean them. It was the perfect place for an ambush. Still, it could not happen too far before the flight's scheduled departure because the two agents checked in to Black Dog Control every thirty minutes.

The agent-passenger irregularly moved to new places around the international terminal each hour to avoid drawing attention. This was always timed to coincide with a scheduled check-in, so a potential gap between an agent going missing and Black Dog knowing about it was never more than thirty minutes. Standard operating procedure.

He decided on the agent-janitor first since he would not be out of the sight of his stationary colleague for much of the round. It was 9:12. He followed the agent-janitor to one of the restrooms he entered to "clean" no more than ten steps behind. Devang quietly came up behind the man and grabbed his head with both hands. He heard the snap when the man's neck gave out, ending his life, caught the collapsing body and hauled it onto a toilet in a locked stall. No one else was in the restroom at the time. His luck was holding.

One down and one to go.

Devang had sixteen minutes before they were due to check in at 9:30.

He watched as the agent-passenger got up and began his hourly move, and was surprised to see him move toward the restroom where he'd just left the agent-janitor.

This is too easy.

Devang watched the agent-passenger enter the restroom and followed.

Upon entering, he immediately sensed movement, and lunged back against the door as the blade scored his right side. The burn of the cut disappeared as instincts and training kicked in. The next blow came fast, but he was ready. Catching the descending forearm, he pivoted left, yanked the agent's arm viciously down, and flipped him onto his back. The knife scuttled across the floor as Devang landed a quick succession of devastating blows to the agent's throat, crushing his larynx.

A Chinese man washing his hands at the sink stood there stunned. Devang hadn't noticed him, having been so focused on dispatching the agent-passenger. They both stood there, the man with water dripping from his hands and Devang standing over the now-dead agent.

"Out. Now," Devang ordered in Chinese.

The man nodded and bowed several times, then raised his hands as he moved toward the bathroom exit.

"Silence," Devang mouthed in Chinese putting his finger to his lips.

Devang purposefully watched the man hurry from the room, looking for any sign of defiance and seeing none. The man would say nothing, at least long enough for it not to matter. He picked up the knife and, dragging the second agent into a stall, locked the stall door. As the adrenaline drained, his breathing returned to normal, and Devang felt the burn of the knife wound. Looking down, he saw a growing blood stain around a slit in his jacket. He was bleeding heavily from a deep cut that looked like it had scored a rib.

"Damn," he said aloud as he took off his jacket and shirt inside the stall with the dead agent. The cut was deep but clean. Probably six inches long. The weeping blood fell like a red veil across his right side. He used the bathroom's paper towels to staunch the wound but needed pressure to stop the bleeding. The blood had not stained his trousers, so he needed to find a shirt. The two dead agents were nowhere near his height or size, but he'd have to make do.

Devang stripped the undershirt off the corpse to use as a bandage. He used the man's belt to hold the bandage in place and hoped the pressure would stop the bleeding. He knew it needed stitches, but there was no time. The agents' check-in time was fast approaching. Ekow and Ilse should be at the airport any minute. He needed fresh clothes.

After ensuring the empty bathroom, he stripped off the agent-passenger's shirt and struggled into it. The fit was tight, at least two sizes too small, but nevertheless, he managed to squeeze into them and was pleasantly surprised that the tightness held the makeshift bandage in place. Hearing people in the bathroom outside the stall, he waited for silence before grabbing the dead man's identification and communicator. He set the lock on the stall door to lock automatically and stepped out, then left the restroom groaning quietly at the dull ache in his side.

At the appointed time, Devang reported to Control, mimicking the agent-passenger's English accent as best he could.

"This is Wei Nang reporting in for myself and Po Chung. We are maintaining our positions. There is no sign of targets or threats as yet."

"Roger that, Nang. You sound a bit different. Is everything all right?"

"Everything is fine," Devang lied. "I just ate something that did not agree with me."

"Roger that. Stay sharp. There's a trail of carnage from Cairo to Ningbo. Devang Sen is wreaking havoc. We are on high alert."

"Will do, Control," Devang said with a small smile. "I will report in again in thirty minutes."

"Control out."

Devang settled in to wait for Ekow and Ilse. He was confident that while Control might be suspicious, the receiving officer would wait until the next check-in before doing anything. He checked his wound to make sure it wasn't leaking and found the bleeding had stopped. Injury was an expected possibility, but this one was manageable. Things were going as planned.

At 9:40, Ekow Aboah entered the gate area for the flight to Atyrau. He was in disguise and didn't look too obvious. *Good*, Devang thought. He expected to see Ilse with him or right behind him. The communicator buzzed, but Devang ignored it. Time was up. Where was Ilse?

Ekow boarded the plane alone, and the gate closed. He didn't look like he expected Ilse to be there.

"Oh shit," he said out loud. "They've split up."

The people nearest him looked at him with surprise. Devang thought fast. They clearly understood English.

"The latest Hollywood scandal," he said in English as he moved off to get new clothes, deal with his wound, and regroup.

* * *

Damsky was furious.

"How the fuck did we lose them again?" he demanded angrily from his assistant. He and his forces had arrived in Atyrau before dawn and settled into an abandoned warehouse they took over.

"It seems Devang Sen has single-handedly dismantled our Shanghai Station. I did not know anyone could be this good," answered his new assistant, an experienced operative himself. "We need to set a trap."

"And get bait," Damsky snarled. "I think I know what's going on here."

Damsky forced himself to relax and think clearly. He had no eyes on the targets but was confident where they were going. Devang had removed a good number of his agents over the past few days. Impressed despite his anger, Damsky took deep breaths to maintain his calm. For all he knew, Devang was in communication with the World Police Force. His ire began to rise again.

"Sir, your orders?"

"It seems clear Sen is in contact with the targets, and they are acting in concert. Aboah is already here. We've lost contact with Chung and Nang, so we must presume they are dead. Is our agent booked on the afternoon flight? The girl will be on that flight, and we must expect Sen to also be on it."

"Yes, sir," answered the assistant. "Agent Fox is booked and fully briefed. He is nearly as good as Sen, sir. The element of surprise is in his favor, hopefully tipping the scales."

"Good," Damsky answered, deep in thought. After his initial outburst, he paid little attention to the activity around him.

"Could it be he fell for the girl?" he wondered aloud.

"Excuse me, sir?" asked the assistant.

"Nothing, Petranowych. I'm just thinking about our next steps." He then picked up his PCD, surprised it wasn't in pieces, given the many times he'd thrown it hard against a wall in frustration. He called Omar Gezi.

"North African Water Company. Omar Gezi's office. May I help you?" answered the receptionist.

"Get me Omar Gezi. This is Ivan Damsky. The matter is urgent."

"Please wait one moment," the pleasant voice from the other side said. Within thirty seconds, the receptionist was back on the connection. "Mr. Damsky, Mr. Gezi is not in his office today. We are trying to locate him. We will have him contact you as soon as we can deliver to him your message. I am very sorry."

"You will be if I don't hear from him within the hour. What is your name?"

"Fatima Sadat," she replied, fear creeping into her voice. "We will do everything we can, sir."

"Ms. Sadat, I expect you will."

* * *

Devang watched Ilse enter the international terminal to board the afternoon flight to Atyrau. While waiting, he had cleaned and stitched his wound and purchased fresh clothes at one of the airport's convenient clothing stores. His side ached. He boarded the plane in disguise with the last boarding group. He did not notice the nondescript European man boarding a few passengers behind him.

* * *

Ekow arrived in Atyrau without incident. The overnight drive back to Shanghai from Ningbo had been uneventful. There had been no time to contact Devang about their change of plans. He had hard time convincing Ilse.

"Ekow, I just don't understand why you refuse to follow Devang's instructions that we travel together," Ilse had argued that morning at the Shanghai hotel they'd booked for a few hours' rest. "He must have a good reason for wanting this."

"Maybe so," Ekow had answered. "But I still do not trust him entirely. This is a small deviation from his plan, which should be of no consequence."

"You don't know that," Ilse had continued to argue.

"Ilse, I understand your point." He'd looked at her meaningfully. "But we discussed it and agreed this was the best path."

Ilse had reluctantly agreed.

Ekow was glad they'd regained some control. He'd found a small hotel near the rendezvous point on the Asian side of the Ural River, which divided the city of Atyrau. Ilse's flight had arrived on time. He could see the entrance to the Park Cafe from his hiding place along the waterfront, and knew Devang would be on the same flight and expected them to come together. He saw Ilse walking alone toward the Park Café down the path leading under the Central Road Bridge. There was no sign of Devang. A moment later, he saw a black man get up from a bench in front of the restaurant dressed like he was looking in Ilse's direction. Then, two men appeared from behind trees on either side of the path, grabbed her, placed something over her face, and then carried her unresisting body to a vehicle on the Waterfront Road. Horrified, before he could so much as move, they put her in a Ford sedan and drove off. Just like that, she was gone.

Ekow sat down on a bench near the café in shock. It had happened so fast. A few minutes later, Devang sat down next to Ekow on the bench, clearly in pain, his hands bruised and blood staining his clothes.

Ekow, startled by his sudden appearance and injuries, asked, "Where have you been? I thought you would be on the same flight as Ilse."

"You two were supposed to travel together," Devang growled in an angry but controlled way. "I was jumped at the airport. Where is she?"

"They took her," Ekow said, the wind out of his sails. His face showed only devastation.

"I was afraid of that." Devang seethed. "Why did you not travel together? The early flight and the uncertainty of when you were going was intended to buy time for us to rendezvous with the World Police Force. By booking a later flight, you confirmed your destination and arrival time. That gave Black Dog time to set up their ambush of me at the airport and their abduction of Ilse. Now tell me what happened."

"I am very sorry, Devang." Ekow looked at his feet, embarrassed by his arrogance. "Two men grabbed her from behind, knocked her out with some sort of drug on a cloth, and drove away in a Ford sedan. I am afraid that is all I know. They left with her less than five minutes before you arrived."

Devang quickly got to his feet. "I know who took her, and I have an idea where. This was not the plan." He was angry. "We have to get her back."

Ekow looked up at the big mercenary. He was a mess. "I agree," Ekow said. "But first, you need to clean yourself up. My hotel is nearby."

"That would be lovely, but there isn't time. We were to meet Iygal Yoshi at 17:00 here so I could deliver the two of you into his custody and then set a trap for Ivan Damsky and his bosses. But now...?"

"This is my fault," Ekow said. "I insisted we travel separately. I did not understand the nuances of your plan."

Devang thought hard. His face resolved itself into a purposeful look. "For a genius professor, you can be very dense. I have to go after her. You must meet the World Police Force—you were going to, anyway. You need to explain what's going on to Iygal Yoshi. I'll need to contact Damsky within the next hour. You're lucky his agents missed you." With that, Devang strode away toward the center of the Eurasian city.

"Wait. How will I know him? What should I do?" pleaded Ekow.

Over his shoulder, Devang said, "Stay put, little man. He'll find you. Maybe this time you'll follow my instructions." And with that, he jogged away.

Ekow watched his receding back for a few moments. "Good hunting, Devang. I hope you find her in time," he said to himself out loud, nervously settling into doing the only thing he could, wait.

* * *

The ambush had been executed well, and Devang had to give them that. On the flight from Shanghai, he went over likely outcomes. He'd assessed the likelihood of Damsky's people figuring out their strategy and thwarting it at ten percent *before* Ekow and Ilse's decision to split up. That unexpected development raised that to better than forty percent. He was on edge. Even so, when the attack came, it was a surprise.

He'd been following Ilse from departing the plane in the Atyrau Airport through the terminal. Just after she got into her taxi, he was about to enter his own when he felt a gun barrel against his lower back.

"End of the line, Sen," the Black Dog agent said. "Let's get into this taxi you ordered us."

Devang froze for a split second, then reacted. As he raised his hands, he violently twisted to his left to sweep the gun aside as it went off. A bloom of pain flared on the left side of his abdomen as his attacker's bullet grazed him. He brought his right knee up into his assailant's chin with a stunning blow, nearly knocking him out. The other man, a local asset, stood behind the vehicle and slightly to the left of the open door. He drew his weapon, but Devang had ahold of the now-groggy first man and drove him back into the second. Avoiding the agent's body provided Devang an opening to get inside the second man's guard. They wrestled for the gun. His right rib burned, but he ignored the pain, pushing back the second agent before violently reversing direction to flip the man over his back. He took the gun in the same motion and shot him point blank. He quickly dispatched the agent groaning on the ground. Sirens were blaring due to multiple gunshots, which meant all vehicles were automatically shut down. Keeping the gun, he began to run. He had to get to the Park Café. He knew what would happen next if he was not there in time.

* * *

"We have the girl," the Black Dog agent informed Damsky. "She'sout cold. We are en route to the secure facility."

"Excellent. Finally, something goes our way," Damsky replied. "I suspect I'll be hearing from Devang Sen any moment."

The abandoned warehouse they chose lay outside the Center of Atyrau on the route north to the operating oil fields. Initially founded in the seventeenth century by a Russian fishing family, the city straddled the Ural River, its western side in Europe and its eastern side in Asia. It reached its economic peak in the last third of the twentieth century when it was the energy capital of Kazakhstan. A prosperous regional city at one time, the substantial number of empty industrial buildings suited Damsky's purposes. Upgraded pipelines kept the fossil fuel flowing even though the demand for renewable energy sources dominated by the late 2020s. Being on a major waterway close to the Caspian Sea kept Atyrau economically relevant, even without oil and gas.

Control signaled Damsky. "Sir, Devang Sen has requested to speak with you."

Damsky smiled. His suspicions were confirmed. "Put him through."

"Ivan." Devang's voice came through clearly. Breathing hard, he demanded. "Where is she?"

Damsky was going to enjoy this. "You're in no position to demand anything, Devang. I am supremely disappointed in you. I never thought you would betray me. You've mowed down an entire cohort of my agents. They are hard to find. I am not happy." Damsky felt himself growing warm with anger. He needed to keep calm and work this properly. He needed information from Devang.

"I'm sorry about that," replied Devang, catching his breath. "They were collateral damage. It was nothing personal. It was just business."

"Maybe, but that's not what you're about now, is it, my old friend?" Damsky asked. "I have the Swedish scientist. Obviously, you want her back. And I am willing to negotiate. After all, it *is* just business."

"Your terms," Devang responded without emotion in his deadliest voice.

"Simple. The Ghanaian for the girl. I have a mission to complete. I presume he is under your control. If not, he better be quickly. You've got four hours, or you will never see her again." Damsky cut the connection.

"Where is she?" Damsky asked his aide.

"She locked in a secure room, sir," the aide responded.

"Take me there."

CHAPTER 19
THE PLAN

Devang sat in Victory Park near the famous pedestrian bridge of Atyrau. The early summer growth around the river made the park green and pretty. The beauty of the park was lost on him as he considered the situation.

Nothing about Damsky's terms surprised him. There was a chance Damsky would want to exact revenge on him personally; still, Damsky would not jeopardize the job for a personal vendetta. No, he would save Devang for later. Devang knew he had become a marked man on the flight from Faya-Largeau to Cairo. He had to get Ilse back. And that meant he needed Ekow.

He started walking back toward the Central Road Bridge to find Ekow and possibly Iygal Yoshi. When he got to the Park Cafe, he carefully scanned the area. There was no sign of Ekow or the World Police Force.

> *Iygal must have found you and whisked you away into protective custody.*

That made the situation much more complicated. His plan was a simple handoff in Atyrau. Ekow and Ilse's improvisation might have cost Ilse her life.

> *I will save her. I must.*

* * *

Everywhere Ekow looked, he saw danger. The couple approaching from the north could be there for him. That man sitting outside the café seemed to look Ekow's way too frequently. He grew nervous sitting out in the open by himself. He missed Ilse. They had gone through so much together. He was worried for her. He wanted to do something to help. He did not understand why they had taken Ilse but not him. Their aliases were compromised. His disguise was not new.

My flight beat them here.

He realized what he had done by insisting they vary from Devang's instructions. The earlier flight would have gotten them all to Atyrau a few hours ahead of the Cabal's agents with time to spare. It was his fault Ilse had been taken.

As the minute hand on his watch reached the top of the dial, Ekow heard footsteps to his left. He looked up just as a young yet confident man dressed in trousers and a short-sleeved button-down shirt sat beside him on the bench.

"Ekow Aboah, my name is Alinur Karimov. I am with the World Police Force. We expected to see Devang Sen and Ilse Langstrom. Where are they?"

Ekow stood and backed away from the agent. "I wish I knew where Ilse was. Devang was just here. I do not know where he went. As for you, how can I know you are who you say you are?"

Karimov pressed his left forefinger just above the inside of his right wrist. The red, blue, yellow, and green World Police Force shield rose to the surface of his skin.

Ekow nodded. "I supposed that's difficult to fake."

"Just so," Karimov replied evenly. "We cannot stay here. It is not safe. We understood that you and Dr. Langstrom were to have arrived together, but you did not. You must decide now if you will come with me."

"I am the reason Ilse Langstrom and Devang Sen are not here. But there is nothing I can do about that now. I am ready to go."

"Good. This way, please."

Ekow and the agent walked across the short grassy space to the waterfront road and got into a waiting vehicle. As they drove off, Ekow glanced around the area to see if Devang had returned.

* * *

Damsky stood by the open door of the secure room where they were keeping Ilse Langstrom, who was asleep on a military cot. The room had a chair and a small table. She lay on her back but with her hips turned vertically toward the door. She really was something special. It was not just her beauty that attracted him. Damsky new about Devang's sister. Ilse had a similar history but survived. Damsky realized his mistake. Devang left the Indian Special Forces because he would not carry out missions for a government he viewed as corrupt. Damsky wanted his skill set but overestimated his greed while underestimating his conscience.

> *I have to be more careful with my future recruits.*
> *An expensive lesson.*

He closed and locked Ilse's cell and returned to the office, which served as command and control. He genuinely hoped Devang would be able to deliver the African. He was not heartless. If Devang survived, Damsky would give Devang six months to whatever it is he had in mind with her before eliminating them both.

* * *

Devang called the hotline once again.

"World Police Force," answered the agent. "What's your emergency?"

"Iron Dome," said Devang with some impatience.

"Yes, sir. Hold the line, sir," responded the agent.

Six seconds later, a familiar voice came on the line.

"Devang, we've been expecting to hear from you. We missed you at the rendezvous point. We have Ekow Aboah, so we are thankful you were able to deliver him," Iygal said without preamble.

"That's good to hear, Iygal. But I have a problem."

"Yes. We all have a problem. Professor Aboah tells us Ms. Langstrom has been abducted. Can you confirm?"

"I can. I've spoken to Damsky. He wants an exchange. I need Ekow."

"You know that will not happen. The professor has offered himself. An honorable man. I'm afraid we will have to do this the hard way."

Devang pulled the PDA away from his ear and howled silently at the sky. He needed to improve the odds of her rescue, and the only way to do that was for Ekow to cooperate. He brought his PDA back to his ear.

"Iygal, if he's willing, you can involve a civilian. It's the only reasonable chance she has, and you know it."

"I do know it. I am sorry. You're not the only person concerned. She has parents, friends and family. None of them want her harmed. But the professor is not on the table even if he *is* willing."

Devang examined his shoes but kept the PDA at his ear. There was a sliver of hope since Ekow wanted to help. But he would not have allowed it himself were he in Iygal's shoes. So, the hard way.

"What intel do you have, Iygal? Damsky's deadline gives us four hours to plan and execute her rescue. Where can we meet?"

"We will pick you up in five minutes at the north entrance to Victory Park." Iygal ended the call.

Devang's mind began running rescue scenarios as he approached the park entrance.

* * *

Ilse awoke groggily with a bad headache. She sat up on the edge of the narrow cot on hand, gingerly holding her head. She felt nauseous.

What did they do to me?

She lay back down to gather her thoughts and looked around the small room. There were no windows, and the walls seemed made of steel, though she wasn't sure. The door matched the walls, so no easy exit. A few minutes later, the nausea faded, and her headache became a dull throb at the base of her skull. She'd just hauled herself to a sitting position again when the door suddenly opened.

"So, you are awake," a large, older man said in English, the accent heavily Russian. "I regret the unfortunate circumstances under which you find yourself here. Hopefully, your stay uneventful. I can guarantee only one thing. Your time here will be short."

He shut and locked the door as the seal closed with a whisper.

She knew who had her. Devang had described him perfectly. Ivan Damsky. She just hoped Ekow was safe. It had always been about Ekow anyway. She was prepared to make whatever sacrifice necessary. The throbbing in her head eased after a drink of water from the small wash basin in the room.

What can I do to help from here?

The only thing she had was defiance. She sat at the desk, trying to think things through.

She gathered herself and shouted, "I know who you are, Ivan Damsky. The speaker in the upper corner of the cell buzzed. The Russian's now familiar voice said, "Of course I will.," he answered.

The lights went out. Ilse was in total darkness.

* * *

Devang exited the vehicle at a warehouse in northern Atyrau along the road to the oil fields. As the car moved off, he looked around the facility. From the outside, there was no unusual activity. Inside, he knew the building would be buzzing like a beehive. A moment later, a door opened, and an attractive blonde woman in plain clothes came out to greet him.

"It is nice to meet you, Mr. Sen," she put out her hand. "My name is Eva Kozlowska. Please come in."

Devang looked at her hand, surprised, then shook it. Ignoring the odd greeting, she turned and led him back inside the building.

Upon entering, Devang felt the hum. It was visceral. There was an energy in the air. As they got deeper into the building, nearly everyone was dressed in fatigues and alert. It felt right. They entered the warehouse's storage area and made their way around several tables piled with flak jackets and helmets to a command center on the far side of the building. It reminded him of his early days in the Indian Special Forces. Purpose, work ethic, pride, and confidence— all things that create excellence.

"Mr. Sen, please wait here." Eva motioned to a folding chair near the entrance to the command center area, which was cordoned off from the open floor plan. "I will inform the Commander you have arrived."

Devang inspected the command center carefully while he waited. It must have once been the headquarters of a prosperous import/export company, with its access to the Ural River out back and on an important commercial road. The command center looked like any well-run operation. Fatigue-clad soldiers studied hardened laptop computers and tablets. A different warehouse appeared on the wall behind the command center tables. A moment later, a fit thirty-something man came around one of the tables.

"Mr. Sen, I am Sargent Attila Matos. Please follow me." He led Devang through the open door into a corridor that led deeper into the building. After a few turns down a half-glass, half-metal hallway, Matos stopped before a door labeled "Conference Room 3." He opened it.

Devang entered a small room with a black conference table and seats for eight people. Each chair was padded and straight-backed. There were several people seated at the table who stood as he entered.

> *Two men, colonels both, three women, one a lieutenant, the other two majors. Two people missing.*

He moved to the opposite end of the table just as Iygal Yoshi, followed by an aide, entered the room.

"Devang!" Iygal shouted enthusiastically. "It is good to see you!" He approached Devang with his hand outstretched and brought him into a semi-hug.

Bemused, Devang replied, "And you, Iygal."

"Okay, let's get right to it," Iygal took over the room. "Ladies and gentlemen, this is Devang Sen, the man you've heard so much about over the last day or two.

"Make no mistake. Devang Sen is *the* consummate professional. Learn from him. This is a rare opportunity. His intel will be critical to the success of our assault. Devang, how much time do we have?"

It chilled Devang to think Ilse's demise was so near. His mission mask descended, taking him to that state of mind where he was trained and at his best.

"We have three hours and twenty-three minutes. Do you have a plan?"

"Thanks to you, we've tracked Damsky's movements and know where Black Dog is. We are eighty percent confident they do not know we are here and believe you are acting alone. We have the element of surprise, which would bode well for saving Dr. Langstrom. Attila, please bring up the holograph of the building Black Dog occupies."

A three-dimensional depiction of the other warehouse appeared above the table. The building lay only a few miles from where he stood. Rather than river access, the other warehouse opened to the salt marshes behind the property outside the city. Devang circled the display to get a better look at the rear of the enemy warehouse and the distance to the marshes.

> *That's where we have to hold them. They can't get away.*

"Iygal," Devang began. The room went silent as everyone looked at him. "Excuse me, Commander Yoshi." They all went back to their work. "Cutting off the escape route will require serious firepower. What did you bring with you?"

"Yes," Iygal agreed. "Fair question. We planned for a light-armed assault. That should be enough. We have standard-issue laser handguns and rifles, as well as small rocket launchers for demolition purposes. We have air support on call from the military air base outside Atyrau.

"Most importantly, we have the best-trained personnel available. Damsky diluted the quality of his forces with locals, who we believe are poorly trained. Our infrared satellite shows the new recruits are deployed outside the facility and in the halls and rooms nearer the road."

Sargent Matos enlarged the display of the Black Dog warehouse so that everyone could see the green dots toward the front of the warehouse representing the new recruits.

"The true strength of his force lies inside the facility with the operatives who traveled here with him. It's a classic but effective urban warfare strategy. Use the core of your strength to support outer defenses when needed. Damsky's core is in the storage areas closer to the salt flats."

Sargent Matos spoke into his PCD, and red dots appeared in the open area toward the back of the warehouse clustered near the rear entrance.

"That's good intel, Iygal," Devang said. "What is your assessment of the situation?"

"We don't think he's expecting a pitched battle. He has concentrated his forces in a way that would indicate he's expecting a minor assault from the salt flat side of the warehouse. He probably expects it from you. We are 97% certain that he doesn't know we're here. What can you tell us about Ivan Damsky that we don't already know?"

"Well"—Devang looked around the table as he spoke—"let's start by eliminating what you already know. Damsky recognizes his local recruits are just cannon fodder in the event of any real assault. I agree. He's not expecting any sizeable attack. No effective assault could come from the narrow alleys between the buildings, so they are lightly guarded. He'll have snipers on each corner of the roof. He'll keep his best people near him for personal protection."

Devang looked back at Iygal. "I also agree, to my amazement, that he doesn't seem to know you are here. However, the quality of his firepower will match anything you've got. He always travels with powerful but compact weapons. His favorites are the American heat-seeking mini-missiles designed for use inside large structures. He also has modified domestic robots into what Black Dog operatives call battle bots. Illegal under the AI laws promulgated in the New Hammurabi Code, but that never stops Damsky. No one wants to face those beasts. I've seen the carnage they can wreak." He shuddered.

"Last, the warehouse will be heavily booby-trapped. This is standard operating procedure for Black Dog. Highly sensitive sensors and targeted explosives make it quite the obstacle course unless you know how to navigate it."

Sargent Matos and Captain Kozlowska furiously tapped their tablets, inputting Devang's intel.

"Given where he's holding Ilse, it's unlikely it's booby-trapped, though it will be guarded. Damsky should be feeling confident at the moment."

"Thank you, Devang," Iygal said, taking Devang's pause as the end of his remarks. "Very helpful. We suspected much of what you shared, but these battle bots are new. They are not good news. We have encountered such things, and they can be particularly nasty in enclosed pitched battle situations like this one. It's no surprise that Damsky would flaunt the moral and legal imperative to never arm robots against humans. This man has no conscience."

Iygal took in the room. "We deal with Ivan Damsky. This is what the World Police Force was formed to do."

The World Police Force operatives nodded and sat straighter in their chairs. Again, Devang liked what he saw.

Iygal opened the floor. "Questions? Anyone."

Sargent Malos asked, "Mr. Sen, these battle bots, do you know how they're armed?"

"Typically, they have three levels of firepower. The first is high-powered laser guns mounted on four sides and on top of the robot's head. The second level consists of fifty mortar shells that launch more accurately than any human can do. Third is the heat-seeking mini-missiles that launch from its shoulders. A usual complement is ten of those rockets," Devang answered to low whistles from around the table.

"While all this firepower provides a battle bot with advantages, it also has weaknesses. Chief among them is a flaw in its outer shell armor plating. A well-aimed armor-piercing bullet can trigger an internal reaction that will blow the whole thing to pieces."

"We have a reasonable supply of armor-piercing munitions, Sir," Captain Kozlowska contributed. "What caliber would be the most effective against these abominations?"

Devang heard the underlying anxiety in her voice. Domestic robot use was commonplace, but there was an undeniable fear that humans would one day wake up to a world with robots in control. The New Hammurabi Code specifically outlawed using robots as weapons, and preventing that use was one of its founding principles.

"Fifty caliber should work," Devang answered. "And now that I have a better understanding of your resources, I have a plan."

"Let's hear it," Iygal encouraged.

"Okay. My plan won't vary too much from yours. First, we create a diversion on the road in front of the building with a frontal assault designed to draw the less experienced group to it. At the same time, a larger force would storm the warehouse from the salt flats to seal off any escape. This will engage the more capable forces, drawing them away from Ilse's cell and moving them to the back of the building and leave the side alleys lightly guarded and vulnerable. We don't expect the guards on the ground to be disciplined enough to remain in their positions once the assault begins."

"And what of Ilse Langstrom?" Iygal asked. "We'd considered a diversion strategy but not quite as you proposed."

"One person could enter the complex from a side alley after taking out the snipers on the roof after neutralizing the guards in the alley. The assault on the front and back of the warehouse should provide enough chaos that I could get in and out with Ilse unharmed."

Iygal instructed Captain Kozlowska, "Please incorporate Devang's plan into our own and run simulations to stress test the strategy."

He stood and addressed the room. "I want to hear from any of you with any ideas you might have. We aren't a go until we can raise the probability of Dr. Langstrom's survival to seventy percent. Before incorporating Devang's plan, that probability of survival stands at twenty percent."

Returning to Devang, Iygal said, "Let's see the stress test results and decide. Meanwhile, our assault should be just after dark. It will make all we do that much more effective, and we will still be an hour before your deadline. Let's reconvene in thirty minutes."

The World Police Force personnel gathered their tablets and exited the room. Before leaving, Iygal turned to Devang and said, "Why don't you get cleaned up? There's a restroom down the hall. Attila will take you there and help you throughout the operation. I have a few things to take care of, but we need to talk. Attila, please bring Mr. Sen to me once he's done."

Devang looked himself up and down. "Do you happen to have a change of clothes?"

"Attila, please find some clothes for Mr. Sen."

"Yes, sir." Sergeant Matos straightened and saluted. To Devang, she said, "What is your preferred size, sir?"

"Thank you, Commander," Devang said, relaying his sizes and lengths to the young officer as Iygal closed the door.

CHAPTER 20
SURVIVAL

Precisely thirty-three minutes later, Iygal returned to the conference room with an aide in tow. The other World Police Force officers were already there. Devang stood on the opposite side of the conference table, the three-dimensional depiction of the Black Dog warehouse between them. Devang had cleaned up and changed into camouflage fatigues. He acknowledged Iygal's entrance with a nod but continued stalking around the table, leaning in close to study the snipers' angle to the alley. He stepped back to watch the simulated assault and its expected effect on the Black Dog agents.

"Here," Devang said, pointing at a nondescript room in the projection.

"Yes," Iygal nodded. "Our intel confirmed that Dr. Langstrom is there." Iygal punched a couple of keys on his tablet, and a box in the rendering began to blink blue. It was part of a bank of executive offices near the salt flats entrance.

Devang looked across the spectral building at Iygal.

This could work.

"Commander, where are your people in planning the assault?" he asked urgently. "We are running out of time."

"They incorporated your intel into our plans. Unfortunately, it hasn't improved Dr. Langstrom's survival probability to more than thirty percent. We are considering offering Damsky and his people immunity and payment in exchange for Dr. Langstrom. He may be willing to negotiate once we have surrounded the complex and controlled the rooftop."

Devang understood Iygal's approach, which raised Ilse's chances of survival to nearly sixty percent. Unfortunately, his analysts did not know Damsky like Devang did.

Devang held Iygal's eyes as he moved further along the table, stopping when he could clearly see the salt flats' entrance.

"He will listen once surrounded by an undefeatable force, but he has higher gods to whom to answer than the World Police Force or the Global Attorney General. Omar Gezi is as ruthless as Damsky. But you know this."

Iygal nodded. "Nevertheless, according to our models, negotiating is the only path with a reasonable chance of success. I am open to other options, but as you say, we are running out of time."

Devang took Iygal's offer as an invitation. "Here is my option. There is a straight corridor from a hallway near the side entrance that parallels the back of the facility and leads directly to Ilse's cell. Even though it's near where Damsky will have set up command and control, if he genuinely doesn't know about the World Police Force presence, an unexpected two-front, simultaneous attack will get all his attention.

"We need to strike the Black Dog complex in the rear hard and quickly to draw Damsky's best forces away from where they're holding Ilse. That will give me two to three minutes to get to her."

"Captain Schwartz, everyone, may I have the room?"

It was not a request. Captain Schwarz rose and left quietly with the rest of the staff around the table.

Once they were alone, Devang dropped all pretense and took a seat. "I have to hand it to you, Iygal. This is an impressive bunch. Are there more of where these came from?"

"We've worked hard to bring in the best and the brightest," Iygal answered, relaxing and sitting opposite Devang. He turned off the image above the table. "The organization is excellent from top to bottom. We're not going to succeed as an institution with anything less. We have to be perfect. One slip-up and we could be in deep trouble. You cannot imagine how many people would love to return to the anarchy of before.

"But I digress. Devang, I cannot allow you to go on this mission." Iygal said simply.

Devang stood, his anger building.

"Sit. Please. Hear me out," Iygal quickly continued.

Devang sat back down. "Fine. Explain."

"I may be the only one on this task force who believes you've returned from the dark side. My officers, without exception, believe you should be in jail for your crimes. It's hard not to agree. We've gotten this far because I knew you would have excellent intelligence and would improve our plan for the assault. Having you part of the operation is unworkable." Iygal leaned forward with his hands on the conference table.

Devang recognized Iygal's signal. "I understand the issue, Iygal. I am prepared to face the consequences of my actions. But I will be part of this operation. I have no other option."

"I understand how you feel, my friend," Iygal responded.

"I do hope you can forgive me, Iygal," Devang said and reared up suddenly to chop Iygal across the neck. Iygal went down in a heap to the floor.

Within seconds, the alarm sounded as Iygal watched the blurry image of Devang leave the room quickly, his eyes barely open wide enough to see.

Good hunting.

Iygal made a silent wish for success after Devang as he remained on the floor, faking unconsciousness.

* * *

Devang encountered no opposition as he hurried out the front of the building. No one was on guard at any point along his escape route as he retraced his steps to the exit.

Thank you, Iygal.

He left the building and jogged to an all-purpose shop less than a mile down the road he'd spotted on his way to the World Police Force compound. It was the Kazak equivalent of a rural general store, selling everything from groceries to outdoor equipment, firearms, and rugged clothing.

> *I've got ninety minutes to take out those snipers and get inside.*

He knew the World Police Force assault would begin precisely one minute later. It would be a surprise attack to eliminate Damsky's outer defenses and lay siege to the Black Dog facility, followed by negotiation. Letting him escape had been a gamble. The World

Police Force model's prediction of Ilse's chance of survival to be nominal without someone infiltrating the Black Dog warehouse prior to the main assault. That made Devang Ilse's only true hope. The surprise attack should be enough to distract the Black Dog forces. It was the only way.

He quickly found a clerk working at the store and, in his halting Russian, said, "I need a laser gun, a 50-caliber magnum, an ankle mounts with a smaller laser gun, and a standard-issue military knife."

"Are you planning to storm a castle, my friend?" the clerk answered in good English.

"No, it's for a hot date," Devang smiled. He needed to seem matter of fact.

The clerk returned his smile. "Okay, my friend, whatever you want."

Devang paid with cash and took his purchases to Ekow's hotel room. He wanted to shower and clean up a bit more. Devang was going to see Ilse. As weird as it seemed, he cared how he looked.

Once groomed and dressed, he sorted the weapons on the bed. The laser handgun was powerful. He strapped the gun belt and holster with the laser snug on his left hip. The smaller gun strapped to his ankle gave him six extra bolts. He slung the 50-caliber magnum across his upper back just in case he had to deal with a battle bot. Finally, a military-issue battle knife. A nasty weapon when wielded properly. He was as prepared as he could be. He called Damsky.

"Dah, Sen," Damsky answered his call. "Where is the scientist? You have only two hours left before that lovely creature begins to suffer. I don't wish to damage such perfection, and I am prepared to let the two of you go on your way once I have the Ghanaian."

"I need more time," Devang demanded. "He isn't in the hotel we agreed. Ivan, I'm doing the best I can."

"*Nyet*," Damsky flat-lined the answer. "Your next contact better be that you have Ekow Aboah and are bringing him to me. If you ask for more time again, you'll get less."

Damsky cut the connection.

Well, that went as expected.

Devang thought through his plan. His main advantage was stealth. Damsky did not know where he was or what he was doing. Devang hoped the deception worked, but he was under no illusions.

I'm sure they'll be ready for me. At least the guys Damsky brought with him will be.

Black Dog's weakness was the local operatives. They knew nothing about him and rarely had the training the regular agents had.

Devang jumped out of the taxi three blocks from the Black Dog warehouse carrying a large canvas bag he bought for the weapons and quickly ducked behind the nearest building. He made his way methodically down the road, remaining out of sight, and confirmed the location of the sniper nests. He spotted two well-hidden camouflaged sniper nests on the corners of the Black Dog building facing the road and knew two more were on the other corners of the building.

I see you.

A casual observer probably wouldn't see them. Perhaps the locals were better trained than expected. He allowed the thought to settle as he kept himself out of sight.

Devang circled the facility to approach from the salt flat side. Hidden behind the corner of the building next door, he saw the gate set in a ten-foot cement wall that ran along the back of the property next to the salt flat. The gate was reinforced with steel girders and guarded by a stationary, high-caliber machine gun installed above and to the left of the entrance. There were two heavily armed men on foot outside the gate and several more inside. He wasn't sure how many but guessed another four.

Heavily fortified and guarded. No surprises yet.

As expected, snipers were on each corner of the building facing the salt flats.

This was his problem. The two snipers on the far side of the structure were Iygal's.

He marked the location of the sniper on the corner nearest the street again and the one nearest the salt flats before slipping away to circle back to the street side of the building.

You first.

Devang cautiously approached the Black Dog building from the corner of the next-door structure, carefully monitoring his first target. Agents patrolled on the ground inside the compound behind the building, but only two agents were in the alley.

I need to get on the roof without being seen.

The corner of the building was his best option. It was scalable and partially hidden from all three sets of eyes. A blind spot. As the sun began to lose some of its strength and the evening shadows made their way toward the Black Dog building, Devang waited until the guards on the ground were walking away from him, and the guards in the alley moved toward the street. He quickly scaled the ten-foot wall using the holds in the corner of the building that hid him and jumped across the gap to the corner of the Black Dog warehouse below the sniper's nest. He'd purchased special climbing gloves with retractable hooks commonly used by utility workers to climb stone, metal, or wooden poles and shoes with blades that flipped out of the insoles, allowing him to scale almost any vertical surface.

He crept up the wall below the sniper like a spider scurrying across its web to devour its prey. He grabbed the edge of the corner feature at the top and swung up and over to just behind the sniper. In the same motion, he sliced the sniper's throat as the sniper tried to rise, then lowered him to the ground as his lifeblood gushed from his throat. With a quick look back at the sniper on the nearest corner, Devang returned the dead sniper back to his nest with his gun looking much like he had a moment before. Then he set off in a low crouch, quietly scuttling across the roof to the next sniper overlooking the street. Like a big cat, Devang silently padded to the HVAC unit in the middle of the roof for cover. He watched the sniper near the salt flats studying his unmoving comrade and concluding something was wrong. As he reached for his PCD to call it in, Devang pounced, grabbed his face from behind and, with a violent twist with his big hands, broke the sniper's neck. He propped the dead man up in his nest, retreated to the HVAC, and sat with his back against the machine facing the alley.

Okay, Iygal, let's get things going.

It was ten minutes before Damsky's deadline, three minutes before the assault was to begin. He was going in no matter what.

* * *

Iygal got up off the floor of the conference room, feigning grogginess. He hoped he was believable.

"Report," he ordered Major Schwarz as he rubbed his neck.

"Devang Sen has escaped, Commander. We do not know where he went. Are you all right, sir?"

"Yes, I think so," Iygal responded, still rubbing his neck and straightening his spine. "I've had worse."

"If you say so, sir," Major Schwarz replied having played his part well. "The recording looked pretty nasty."

"Be that as it may, we have work to do." Iygal now appeared to be fully recovered. "Let's finalize our plans. I want our people in position within the next hour. Devang Sen will just have to fend for himself."

The World Police Force strike force flowed toward the Black Dog warehouse like a rising tide over an exposed reef. Most of the buildings on this street were abandoned, providing good cover. Iygal watched the live satellite footage of the local operatives milling around the front of the compound. He divided his forces into four teams. Two teams approached the front of the compound from both sides in a pincer movement. Likewise, two teams approached the back of the building following the same strategy to attack the fortified gate.

"Did you see that?" asked Major Schwarz, standing next to Iygal in the World Police Force's command and control center. "I thought I saw something toward the back of the warehouse on the roof."

Iygal smiled. "I didn't see it, but I can guess what it is. Are our teams in position?"

"Yes, sir," responded Major Schwarz.

"Then it is time to reach out to General Damsky," Iygal said grimly.

"Yes, sir." Major Schwarz entered the coordinates provided by Devang to reach Damsky.

"Who is this?" answered a gruff voice in English with a heavy Russian accent.

"This is Commander Iygal Yoshi of the World Police Force, General Damsky. Your location is surrounded. I came prepared to allow you and your men to depart if you release Ilse Langstrom unharmed. You have five minutes to comply, or we will come after her."

It was ten minutes until Damsky's deadline.

* * *

Damsky was stunned. Then, he muted his PCD.

"The World Police Force? Where in the seven hells did they come from?" he shouted at his aid. But then he knew. Devang Sen. "Incredible. Devang Sen has earned himself a very painful death."

"Alert everyone. We will be under attack momentarily," Damsky yelled again at his aide.

A loud *BOOM* shook the warehouse within seconds of his warning.

"Belay that! We are under attack!"

Devang's three minutes were up. He slid down the side of the building behind a large dumpster ten yards from the side door. The two guards in the alley faced the salt flats, listening intently to urgent orders coming through their PCDs. They looked in every direction at once. After a moment's discussion, one of the guards trotted off to the back of the building and around the corner. The remaining guard in the alley watched his companion head off to check on what was happening. Devang silently sprinted from his hiding place as the first guard rounded the corner and tackled the guard from behind. On the way to the ground, Devang slid behind the guard and slit his throat. He quickly hauled the dead man up and into the dumpster. He hurried to the sealed door.

At the door, he brought out the explosives.

> *No avoiding this noise. I just hope Iygal's got them occupied.*

He affixed the charges on strategic parts of the door, then backed off behind the heavy dumpster, crouched, and punched the icon on his PCD.

BANG!

The blast's force caused the side door to explode back out across the alley, crashing into the building next door. Devang felt the ground roll gently as the entire warehouse, rocked by the blast, settled back onto its foundation.

Here we go.

His mental clock was ticking.

Ten seconds to get in.

Devang sprinted down the hall toward the fortified room and Ilse. When he was halfway down the corridor, two loud explosions went off, one from the front and the other from the back. He moved faster, knowing the World Police Force assault had begun.

He made one zigzag turn down the corridor, then came around a corner to the fortified room.

Ilse.

There was a Black Dog agent guarding the door. He spotted Devang and unloaded his AK95 in a spray of heavy bullets.

Devang ducked back around the corner and paused for a split second before diving out across the corridor, side arm blasting. He neatly rolled across his right shoulder, coming up on one knee, shooting the entire time. The bullet-riddled agent fell in a bloody heap in front of the door.

Devang quickly surveyed the corridor for other guards before turning to the door.

"Ilse, are you in there?" he shouted.

"Devang? Is that you?" Ilse shouted back, her voice muffled by the thick door.

"Yes, I'm here. I'm getting you out. Stand back as far from the door as you can. I'm going to blow a hole through the lock."

Devang took a different set of charges from his backpack designed for more precise jobs. He placed four small charges around the steel plate housing the combination lock and the safe-like silver handles. He pressed the button on each charge and moved back around the corner.

"Here we go, Ilse!" Devang shouted.

He again pressed the detonate icon on his PCD. A powerful yet contained explosion punched a hole in the door where the star-shaped handles hung useless. Devang threw open the door to find a dim, windowless room filled with smoke and lit only by the hallway lights.

"Ilse, we have to go!" he shouted, shining his flashlight around the room landing on the most beautiful face he had ever seen.

She rushed into his arms, sobbing. "Thank God it's you. I thought I'd never get out." Detaching herself, she asked, "Now what?"

"Just follow me," Devang instructed. "Grab the straps on my backpack and hang on. If someone appears behind us, I may need to spin back and forth, so be ready to duck."

"Understood," she responded and took a deep breath. "Okay. I'm ready."

Devang led her back down the corridor toward the destroyed side door. They heard a steady stream of laser blasts, gunshots, and occasional explosions toward the salt-flat side of the warehouse. When they reached the ruined door, Devang turned them toward the back of the warehouse.

"How much farther, Devang?" asked Ilse, beginning to sound desperate.

"It's not far," Devang assured her. "There's a bolt hole in the floor of a room that leads out from under the warehouse. We're heading for that."

The bolt hole was their goal, but Devang had other objectives. They needed to end Damsky. Otherwise, they'd look over their shoulders for the rest of their days.

It ends here. Today. It must.

"Hang in there, Ilse," he encouraged as they carefully crept up the corridor toward the sound of heavy fighting. "The bolt hole will not be easy to reach."

"I don't understand. I don't think I can do this," Ilse said apologetically, sliding down a wall, shivering, her eyes wide.

"We can't stop here," Devang said, turning back to her. "It's too dangerous. You should know we're not the only ones looking for the exit. We need to beat them to it. Once out, then we'll rest."

He also knew that the World Police Force would cover escape routes, but he was counting on them to deliver Ilse safely and take him in if he survived. He had given his word.

Devang continued down the corridor with Ilse in tow. "We're almost there."

As he peeked around the next corner, three men came rushing toward them, trying to reach the back of the complex. They hadn't seen him, so he pushed Ilse back a few steps and into a nearby room, closing the door carefully putting his finger to his lips. After thirty seconds of not hearing a sound, Devang cautiously opened the door to peer out.

Shots rang out as bullets exploded close to his head. He ducked back into the room. "Damn," he swore. "There are five men in the corridor. There were only three a minute ago. They must have seen us come in here. Is there another way out? Look. Quickly."

"There's no way out," Ilse cried. "The window is covered with steel grating. There are no other doors. We're trapped!"

Ilse was not doing well under fire. He couldn't blame her.

"Okay. Here's what we're going to do. When I count to three, open the door. Then, be prepared to follow behind me, using my body as a shield. Are you ready?"

"No. I can't!"

Devang gazed into her eyes. "Trust me."

Ilse nodded and took a deep breath. "Okay. I'll try."

"One," Devang counted as he laid flat on the floor behind where the door would sweep as Ilse opened it. "Two," he said, looking up at her momentarily. "Three!"

Ilse pulled the door back hard and dove out of the way. Devang let fly with his hand laser, dropping three of the five men to the right of the door. He slid across the hall against the opposite wall as intense light beams cut grooves above his head. He returned fire, ending the remaining agents, leaving them in a heap to the left of the door.

"Now," yelled Devang as he rose to his feet.

Ilse ran to him, again hanging on to his pack's straps. Devang quickly returned to the corner of the corridor and peered around. It was clear.

"Ilse?" Devang paused and turned to face her.

"Yes?" She looked up into his face.

"Do you trust me?"

"I do," Ilse replied with a brief encouraging smile. "But are we going to make it out of here alive? Be honest."

"Yes," he answered defiantly.

"OK. Let's do this," she said with a hint of fire and humor.

"Right. We're out of here."

They set off down the corridor.

As they neared the room with the bolt hole, they heard a strange whirring sound ahead of them. A battle bot rounded the corner, a four-foot-high squat rounded machine on protected wheels festooned with weapons, and immediately opened fire. Devang grabbed Ilse and dove through the next open doorway.

"Stay in here and stay down," he instructed. He reached behind his back and drew the large 50-caliber rifle. In one fluid motion, he was ready to shoot. Ilse crouched behind a heavy metal desk at the far side of the room.

The battle bot scoured the corridor with bursts of laser fire as it moved down the hall. Devang stuck his head out of the room for a quick look only to see one of the mini missiles emerging from the bot's shoulder. They would not survive the blast, so he jumped out of the room into a somersault and came up kneeling on his right leg, ready to fire. He froze for a heartbeat before squeezing off five short blasts with the rifle and then dove back into the room.

Ilse began to rise, but Devang yelled, "Get back down. There's going to be an explosion."

The strange whirring stopped. As Devang reached Ilse, a loud explosion went off down the hall. The floor rocked as metal, concrete, and wood pieces flew past them. The walls between their hiding room and the corridor disintegrated into a billowing cloud of dust. The heavy metal desk shielded them from the pieces of the building raining down. After a few seconds, the rumble of falling concrete and steel faded to an eerie silence. The air was thick with floating debris making it hard to breathe.

Ilse looked down at Devang's smiling face, a smile which she returned until she saw his wounds.

"Devang, you've been shot!" she cried, kneeling to examine the injuries. There were a few minor burns on his neck and right arm, but the worst was the hole in his left calf, which was wholly cauterized by the laser that made it. There was no blood.

"Oh my god, Devang. Your leg. What should I do?"

"Devang, stop smiling. You're making me think you've lost your mind!" She tried hard not to smile back. "What do we do?"

Devang answered, replacing his smile with grim determination. "I can move. The wound is clean through and through. It's painful but manageable. Let's get to the room with the bolt hole. I expect Damsky to do the same. There were men behind the battle bot. This isn't over."

Devang emerged slowly from the room and limped carefully down what was left of the corridor. After about ten slow steps, three agents opened fire from the pile of debris left by the battle bot. It was Damsky and his two personal bodyguards. Devang and Ilse ducked behind a fallen internal wall, and Devang returned fire. Damsky's bodyguards began to advance. It was a mistake. Braving their fire, Devang squeezed off two blasts from his laser gun. Both men crumpled where they stood, but Devang was hit again, just below his right shoulder this time. His right arm hung useless at his side. He sat with his back against the fallen wall, breathing heavily.

"Ilse, I'm not sure I can go on," he gasped. "You have to get out. Take this and use it if you have to. You can't hesitate. If you do, we're both dead."

Ilse lost it. "Devang! No!" She refused to take the laser.

Damsky continued to shoot, and when no return fire came, he realized Devang must be down.

Damsky called out, "Dr. Langstrom, it appears you are in a bind. Unless I miss my guess, Devang Sen is badly wounded, maybe dead. I have a proposition for you."

"Go to hell!" she screamed, picking up Devang's laser gun.

"Come now, Dr. Langstrom. There's no reason to take any of this personally. We both want the same thing—to leave this building alive and free. I'm sure we can come to an arrangement. Otherwise, I will kill you and Devang if he lives here and now."

Ilse was terrified. What was she going to do? Devang was conscious despite the terrible pain he must be enduring.

"Don't believe a word he says," he gasped in a whisper. "Keep him talking. Get him to trust you. He has a weakness for beautiful women. You may be able to get him to expose himself close enough for you to take a shot."

"What?" She looked at him incredulously and whispered. "I can't shoot a person!"

"Yes. You can," Devang whispered back. "You must! Otherwise, we are done." The effort seemed to undo him.

Damsky called again, "Dr. Langstrom, please. I grow impatient. The World Police Force is closing in, and I do not wish to meet any of them. I will give you thirty more seconds to decide. We can both use the bolt hole to escape. Yes, I know why you're here."

Ilse did not know what to do. Devang lay bleeding and in terrible pain next to her. She heard a faint noise on the other side of the wall protecting them. As she turned around and raised Devang's laser pistol, Damsky emerged from behind the wall. They fired at the same time. Her shot scorched the right side of Damsky's chest and he fell back on the other side of the demolished wall. Devang's body jumped. Ilse dropped the gun, horrified. Devang had been shot again.

"Devang!" she cried as the new wound in the same leg, this time in this thigh, seeped blood.

"That was a great shot, Ilse. I'm not good, but you're okay. That's all that matters. Go!" he cried. "In the next room is the hatch and a ladder. You need to find it. Get in there and get down that ladder. It leads into the sewers, but there should be a contingent of World Police Force operatives waiting for us or any of Damsky's men trying to escape. I'm not sure I can move, let alone climb."

"Nonsense." Ilse began to cry. "You're coming with me."

Gunfire and occasional roars of larger munitions could be heard both in the front and back of the building. It seemed all the Black Dog forces were engaged at either end. Damsky and his personal guards lay dead in the debris.

"I'll try, but it's going to be rough," Devang warned her.

"I'm stronger than I look."

"I know," Devang said simply. "You're a survivor." He struggled to his feet, putting all his weight on his right leg, panting from the pain. She got under his good arm and, leaning on her, helped him limp around the bodies and clutter, looking for a submarine-like hatch. There was no sign of Damsky, but she found the hatch partially buried under pieces of concrete and a blasted door just a few yards from the fallen wall they'd used for cover.

I wonder where that bastard has gotten to.

Ilse helped Devang carefully sit on top of a pile of concrete. After pushing the concrete off, she moved the blasted door aside with difficulty. She knelt and tried to open the hatch. It hardly budged.

"I can't get it to move," cried Ilse. "What should I do? You're bleeding."

"I think I can help," Devang said through the pain. "Just get me close, and we'll pull together."

With Devang's help, Ilse unstuck the wheel and opened the hatch to a plume of nasty-smelling air. The ladder was there as promised. Ilse wasn't sure how she would get Devang down the ladder.

Then a light lit the ladder, and she heard, from just below, "Don't move, or I'll shoot. This is the World Police Force, and you're under arrest."

Ilse sat back in wonder as the World Police Force boiled up through the hatch and secured the ruined area before moving out into the complex. Devang sat lifeless, slumped against one of the still-standing walls, his fatigues dark red from his bleeding wounds.

Ilse yelled at them, "He's bleeding. Please help him."

CHAPTER 21
JUSTICE

Ilse sat on the edge of a couch with her father and David Jacobs, watching the wall unit show a live feed of the World Police Force "mopping up." Several groups of armored men with big, navy blue WPF across their backs surrounded the walls of what looked like a hilltop fortress in Greece.

"What are they waiting for?" she complained.

"A chance to end it without a fight," David answered. "Sen thought he might be able to reason with the remaining Black Dog agents."

"There's no reasoning with these types of people, Uncle David," Ilse responded. "They're animals."

"Maybe so," replied David. "But Iygal will give them a chance to surrender. With Ivan Damsky's disappearance, there is no one to command them. There are reasonable odds of avoiding bloodshed."

* * *

Devang sat as comfortably as he could in a halfway house, a place designed to be both a hospital and low security prison. He'd barely made it to the World Police Force medics in time. He'd lost a lot of blood in the Black Dog warehouse battle. He'd been extraordinarily lucky that the bullets he'd taken had missed major arteries and organs. The injury that bothered him the most was the hole in his upper right torso just below his shoulder. It had only been a few days, but he felt up to helping de-escalate the situation at the Black Dog headquarters if he could.

"Commander Yoshi, are your forces in position?" Devang asked wincing from the pain. He was impressed by the clear and expansive view of the Black Dog fortress provided by the headset he wore. He felt like he was hovering over the front gate. "This gadget is amazing. I just want to confirm."

"Roger that, Devang," Iygal responded. "You sure you're up for this? It's only been a few days since the Atyrau party."

"I'm fine, Commander," Devang assured him despite feeling the pain. The doctors would have him in bed. He needed to see this through to the end. Fortunately, Iygal had no time to worry about how he really felt.

"Okay. Let's begin," Iygal ordered. "Open the connection to the Black Dog building."

"Hello? Black Dog Security Company. How can I direct your call?" answered a synthetic voice.

"Direct me to whoever is in charge of this facility immediately," Iygal said firmly. "This is the World Police Force, and we have the compound locked down."

"Yes, sir. Right away, sir," it replied.

"*Da*. Who is this?" a voice asked in English with a heavy Russian accent. Devang recognized the voice.

"My name is Iygal Yoshi, Commander of the World Police Force. Your compound is under an Iron Dome Lid. If you resist, we will have no choice but to terminate. You have five minutes to comply."

"Fuck you!" Alarms began to sound from inside the compound walls.

"It looks like we're going to have to do this the hard way," Iygal said into his PCD.

"One moment, Commander," Devang broke protocol to speak up. "Igor Ivanovic, it's Devang Sen. I know I'm not your favorite guy right now, but I've always been a straight shooter. If you resist, you and your men will die. For what? If you open the front gate and cooperate, everyone will walk."

To Iygal, Devang asked, "Commander, can you confirm this?"

"I can. We never got beyond hello. Mr. Ivanovic, you have five minutes to comply."

Iygal cut the connection.

* * *

"Mr. Gezi? Sir?" his personal secretary tried to get his attention. "Our contact within the Global Attorney General's Office says the warrant for your arrest has been issued, and the World Police Force could be here to execute it at any time. It seems Ivan Damsky kept detailed records of every project assigned to Black Dog Security. Now the Global Attorney General's Office has them." The secretary wrung his hands. "What shall we do, sir?"

"Leave me," Gezi ordered in a calm, even tone.

"But sir…?"

"Go. Now," Gezi repeated with menace.

The secretary returned to his office across the hall and logged on to the camera secretly installed in Gezi's.

> *One never knows what valuable information might be available if one is open and ingenious enough to seek it.*

The secretary watched Gezi sitting at his desk, looking at nothing for several minutes. He showed no emotion, sat motionless and silent.

Abruptly, Gezi reached down to the lowest drawer in his desk and pulled out a small laser pistol. In one smooth move, Gezi brought the gun up to his temple and pulled the trigger. The feed showed the laser light exit the other side of his head before the body toppled to the floor.

* * *

As dawn approached, Iygal inspected his forces one more time. The World Police Force was arrayed around Lars Kunta's compound ready to attack. The sky was still a dark purple when he gave the order. Almost immediately he heard a loud explosion on the far side of the compound and watched the agents nearer him swarm up and over the six-foot concrete wall that effectively divided the small promontory from the surrounding area. The villa could be seen from the road that ran parallel to the wall interrupted only by a driveway that led to a well-fortified gate in the middle of the wall. The location offered an exceptional view of the sea around Cape Town. He'd counted six shots fired. Otherwise, it remained eerily quiet. His PCD came to life.

"Commander, the compound is secure. I repeat. Compound is secure. All hostiles are dead or captured. There are several wounded as well, sir."

"Roger that, Captain. I'm coming in," Iygal replied.

He'd flown by 'thopter the afternoon before approaching from the sea. His flight had taken him directly over the massive estate with its two large wings angling from the rectangular frontage opposite the driveway. It was built about two hundred feet from cliffs that fell away to turbulent water at their base. The formidable six-foot wall ran from one side of the rocky promontory to the other, completely sealing off the residence from the land. The only other way in was to fly or scale the cliffs.

He strode through the compound's central gate into a large oval driveway with a beautiful fountain in the center of a roundabout. He could feel his soldiers' tension ebbing and congratulated every person he encountered with a handshake or a pat on the shoulder.

"Job well done," he said. "The danger is passed."

He crossed the driveway to the main entrance of the house. Upon entering the foyer, he took in the extraordinary ocean view through the glass of the opposite wall.

What a shame all this beauty had to be stained.

Captain Busco approached.

"Captain, report!" Iygal commanded.

"Three dead, eleven captured, including Lars Kunta. Several wounded, again including Lars Kunta," Captain Busco recited. "Nothing but minor injuries to our folks. Lucky."

"Very good. Where is Kunta?" Iygal demanded as he surveyed the back lawn littered with dead and injured security guards as well as abundant scorch marks.

"We're holding the prisoners in the pool house, sir. I'll take you there," Captain Busco gestured for Iygal to precede him out of the house. The captain led him down the slope to a building that could not be seen from the main house above. On one side was an Olympic-sized pool. On the other, a tennis court. The pool house was at least three thousand square feet with three full-bedroom suites, a locker room, a sauna, and a steam room. A full bar occupied one corner of the open sitting area.

"Kunta is in a bedroom," Busco said." Please, sir. This way."

Captain Busco led Iygal to the nearest bedroom suite. When Iygal entered the room, he found an older, disheveled, but large man still bleeding from a gunshot wound in the abdomen lying on the bed, a WPF doctor by his side.

"Doctor, report," Iygal commanded.

"Yes, Commander," the doctor replied crisply. There was always a field doctor on every World Police Force field mission. "Mr. Kunta was shot trying to escape through a well-camouflaged escape hatch built into the ground under the house and driveway. When he refused to stop, our agents opened fire. As protocol dictates, the wound should not be fatal. I expect he'll recover after a few weeks."

"Thank you," Iygal said, appreciating the doctor's no-nonsense recitation. The doctor was pleased and went back to work on adjusting Lars Kunta's bandages.

Turning to Lars, Iygal frowned at the man.

"Lars Kunta, you are under arrest in the name of the United Nations, the Hammurabi Code of 2046, and all that's good and decent in this world."

Iygal walked away without looking back.

* * *

Bert Gheel sat in the study of his mansion in the Le Vivier d'Olce district of Brussels.

"They should be here within the next few minutes," Bert's lawyer said, glancing at the ornate clock adorning Bert's massive oak desk.

Three men sat around an exquisite antique coffee table in a large room lined with shelves full of books on three sides.

"Are you certain I have no other alternatives?" Bert asked his attorney for the hundredth time. "The spectacle of being taken into custody is worse than the prospect of prison."

"It's okay, Father," Henryk Gheel interrupted, trying to sound reassuring. "I'll support you to the end."

Bert looked at his useless son contemptuously. "Keep your mouth shut. I don't want you anywhere near me when this happens. Go to your rooms. Now!"

"But Father..." Henry pleaded.

"Pierre, get him out of my sight," he ordered his attorney as if he were a house servant. Pierre Houwer did not appreciate the treatment, but he did as he was asked.

"Come on, Henryk," Pierre said. "The press doesn't need to be reminded of the son when arresting the father. It's for the best."

"That's fine," Henryk sneered. "I know my dearest father always has my interest at heart. Especially when he put me into that retched psychiatric institution in Zurich for two years. I hope they lock you up and throw away the key."

Bert gazed at Henryk, wondering what demonic roll of the genetic dice could possibly have come up to produce such a creature. Considering all the likely probabilities, Henryk should be brilliant and well-adjusted.

"Henry, you never fail to disappoint." An unfamiliar pain welled up in his chest that bothered Bert. "You still don't understand the magnitude of what you did to that girl. You are a vicious, vacuous animal that must be caged. They're coming for you too. Ivan Damsky took care of your little problem and kept a record of that, along with all the other projects assigned to him. Now go."

Before Henryk could respond, there was a knock on the door to the study. The butler opened the door partway.

"They're here, sir," he announced.

Iygal Yoshi pushed the door open and stepped into the room, flanked by five fully armed agents.

"Bert Gheel, I am Iygal Yoshi, Commander of the World Police Force. You are under arrest for obstruction of justice and violating the articles of the Hammurabi Code of 2046." Iygal turned to Henryk. "I'm glad you're here. Henryk Gheel, you are under arrest for the aggravated sexual assault of Ilse Langstrom," he said to the stunned young man. "Put this creature in restraints."

"Mr. Gheel?" Iygal addressed Bert. "Stand up and turn around." To the closest agent, he ordered, "Cuff this man."

"But Commander, that was not the agreed arrangement," Pierre Houwer stood. "Please think about how this looks."

"That's exactly what I'm doing, Counselor. They are being arrested for being the dangerous criminals they both are."

* * *

Ilse and Devang walked hand in hand down a seaside street in Santa Margherita, gazing at the busy bay-full of boats of all shapes and sizes. They were just down the windy coastal road from Portofino, the better-known Italian fishing village. Four years had passed quickly.

"How are you feeling?" Devang could not help but be attentive. The trauma of the chase and the battle had taken a heavy toll on her.

"I felt better today," she answered honestly. "The best day this week."

"That's excellent!" Devang reassured her. "One step at a time."

Looking down at her upturned face, he saw a depth and maturity that made her even more luminous.

"But what about you, my love?" Ilse looked up into his dark face.

"I'll be fine," Devang answered. "I've been dealing with things like this for a long time. Just the last episode of a long-running show that's finally had its closing night."

She stopped and turned into his embrace. Despite trying to hide his pain, she saw it in his eyes. It was over.

"When is the next time you have to check in with your parole officer?" she asked, gently feeling his shoulder where he'd been badly injured two years before. Thinking of what had become known as the 'Black Dog Battle' had stopped sounding strange.

"I need to go to London next Wednesday. You?" replied Devang.

"Mine is at the end of the month," Ilse responded. "Maya Yardfeather did right by me. All I had to do was tell the truth. I expected prison. I am fine checking in with a parole officer."

"I was surprised you chose Geneva, though."

"Well, I had to go somewhere until you got out. It needed to be close to where you were, and Geneva is a short flight to London," she said, sounding completely reasonable. "I already had a place there and was interested in exploring the city, the lakes, and the mountains. It's very therapeutic. Who knew? It's a wonderful place to live."

Devang chuckled as she continued to smile at him. "But so much history for you there. Just surprised at the choice. That's all."

"I don't know," she agreed. "I guess I have unfinished business there. What news from Maya?" She still had trouble contemplating that she was on a first-name basis with the Global Attorney General.

"She and lygal have continued to lobby for a reduced sentence on my behalf. Ilse, we can't forget what I've done. My crimes were many and serious. While some were committed justifiably against Black Dog Security agents, innocents got hurt as well, and that cannot be forgiven so easily. I'm lucky to be out on parole as it is."

"And we get to be together in one of the most amazing places on earth." She gave him a thorough kiss.

"I'm not sure I would describe Parma, Italy, as one of the most amazing places, but the cheese is great, and it is near places like this," Devang offered once he could breathe again.

"It is the cheese, dear. I absolutely love the cheese," Ilse joked.

Devang held her tightly and gently said, "No matter how this turns out, I'm fine with it. Spending a little time with you is more than I ever expected out of life."

Ilse smiled at him. Devang caught his breath. He knew he'd never grow tired of it.

She held Devang tight. "You have no idea how happy hearing that makes me," she breathed. "I'm here. With you. Forever."

She nuzzled his shoulder as they continued down the quays side by side, holding hands.

"Let's stop for a coffee and enjoy the view of the harbor," she said as they strolled into the main piazza adjacent to a small cement harbor, sheltering a gaggle of fishing boats moored for the weekend. Devang took in the azure water, steep green hills spotted with cleverly constructed villas, some with private docks built down at the water's edge, and the wide variety of boats anchored in the protected cove. A passenger ferry chugged across the water, heading toward the Cinque Terre. They found a small café with an empty table and an umbrella to sit beneath. He sat back and continued enjoying the spectacular view.

"I love this coast," Ilse sighed. "You know that Ekow Aboah's weddings are coming up?"

"I was wondering when you would bring that up," Devang said, making a face. "I don't think he wants us there. We'll just remind him of those crazy few weeks, something I know I would like to forget. We're the creepy aunt and uncle that no one wants around, but you have to invite them because they're family. I'd rather not go."

"I don't understand why you feel this way. I know Ekow doesn't," Ilse countered.

"It's not Ekow I'm worried about, Ilse. It's Leon. The way she looks at me. I don't want any part of that."

"It just takes time, Devang. I felt the same way when I first met Leon, but she is intelligent and capable. I'm sure she won't look at you any different than she looks at me," Ilse said.

"That's exactly my point," Devang concluded.

"Okay. I know this man. Our time together was short but very intense. I consider him one of my best friends, and I know he feels the same way about both of us. I'm going. You should come too. Leon will be his wife. That changes things, I hope."

"Well, what can I say when you put it that way?" Devang replied. "Which one do you want to go to?"

"Both, of course," Ilse responded, smiling her most radiant smile.

Devang was defenseless. He quietly moaned as the waiter, who had just come up to the table, nearly dropped his tray. Startled, the spell was broken.

"Two cappuccinos," Devang ordered, shaking his head quickly. The waiter left, darting glances back whenever his walking direction permitted. It was something Devang was getting used to, and he loved it.

* * *

Ekow Aboah studied himself in the mirror. The tuxedo fit well, and the lion-skinned sash accented his formal attire nicely. He smiled and walked out of his bedroom and down the stairs to where his mother waited.

"You look handsome, my son," she cooed, brushing the fur of the lion sash and fussing over him. "This is going to be a great day for you."

"Thank you, Mother," Ekow answered, taking her hands gently off his shoulders and holding them. Minnie Aboah was in full tribal regalia with a giant, colored headdress, a finely made royal blue silk cloak, and jewelry. "It is time to go."

She gave him a fond peck on the cheek before they turned, walking arm in arm out of the front door and into the waiting white Rolls Royce.

"To the Assad Tribal Church, Idi," Ekow ordered.

The elegant limousine pulled around the resplendent water fountain that graced their circular driveway.

"I am still not believing we are having a second wedding," Ekow broke the comfortable silence.

"Yes, it has been a monumental hassle, but so few of your friends and relatives made it to Shanghai for the first," Minnie reminded him. "Everyone appreciates this. You are a good son and a wonderful man, not to mention world famous."

"Thank you," Ekow smiled at her with genuine appreciation. "It truly warms my heart to hear you say that, at least the first two."

"Did Leon's parents get settled? I heard they had some issues with their hotel."

"Yes, Mother. Not to worry. All they needed was an introduction to the local Chinese. They are fine. They were surprised by how many of their people had settled in Africa," Ekow observed wryly. "Sometimes I cannot quite believe I am seeing this day. Just two years ago, I was running for my life! Today, I am marrying the love of my life for the second time! How can this be?"

"Do you still have nightmares?" she asked, her furrowed brow showing her lingering concern.

"They are all but gone," Ekow replied. "I think Ilse had it much worse than I. And Devang. Who knows what that man has seen? Amazingly, he was able to maintain his moral compass."

"It is good to hear you are suffering no longer." Minnie did not believe him, but today was not the day for an argument. The ride to the church was short, and she hadn't had Ekow alone in days.

"When must you return to Shanghai?" she changed the topic again.

"Given how busy we both are, we can only get away for a week-long honeymoon. With Leon's job and my research into the use and consequences of the Waterfall Reagent, I am thankful we got a full week. Once things calm down, we are planning a more extended trip. I wish I knew when that was going to be. Mother, I cannot thank you enough for all of your help," Ekow added. "I do not know how I could have done it without you."

"You are very welcome, son," Minnie smiled, pleased by the appreciation. "It was a labor of love, dear."

* * *

Henryk Gheel hated his work in the laundry room. It was set apart from the main communal areas of the maximum-security prison on the Ilse of Malta.

> I can't believe I'm dealing with other people's shit!

He looked around furtively.

> I'm not sure how much more of this I can take.

He picked up a large laundry bag and turned around to empty it into the bin lined up for the next load. Suddenly, he was grabbed from behind.

EPILOGUE

David rose as Bjorn entered the upscale restaurant in Midtown Manhattan. The two men shook hands warmly.

"It is excellent to see you. Thank you so much for making the trip to New York," David greeted him.

"It's my pleasure. I enjoy New York. It's not too far, and it is still a unique city," Bjorn assured him. Clearly excited, he asked directly, "How is the deployment of Ekow's Waterfall Reagent going?"

"No small talk at all, eh?" David joked. He understood the excitement and felt the same way. Nothing like this had happened in modern memory. "It goes well. The driest places on Earth are dry no longer. The challenge is no longer whether there's enough water but how to use it. The United Nations Commission for Worldwide Water Management has become a reasonably well-run bureaucracy, well-intentioned and well-policed. The water industry is now scrambling to deal with this new paradigm."

"I'll bet they are," Bjorn said with conviction. "How did the Burry Water Company fare in the grab for the assets of those Water Cabal companies?"

"We did quite well, thank you," David smiled again. "A message has been sent to the corporate world. We are weathering the storm. It also doesn't hurt to have Ekow Aboah on the board and an excellent licensing arrangement for the rights to the Waterfall Reagent in the United States.

"However, the Rule of Unintended Consequences has reared its inevitable head. Ekow was the first to discover that we have crossed a heretofore unknown line. There is too much fresh water. There is a real worry that parts of the Earth's ocean conveyor belts are malfunctioning because the density of seawater globally has fallen significantly. For example, if the Gulf Stream stops circulating, the northern hemisphere will face weather five to ten degrees Celsius colder. Ekow and his team and several other institutions and universities are looking for solutions, but the rationing will continue."

'Fascinating!" exclaimed Bjorn. "Who would have ever thought the world would take this turn?"

"I just hope it's not a Pyrrhic Victory,'" David replied. "Replacing too little fresh water with too much is a real possibility. But of course, we had no choice. The Earth was parched."

"So, how is our friend, the professor?" Bjorn asked with a twinkle in his eye. David and Bjorn spent hours with Ekow after the Battle of Atyrau, as it had become known.

"About as happy as a man could be, I think," David said with a smile. "The African wedding was magnificent. It was a shame you had to miss it."

Before Bjorn could respond, the waiter came to the table and asked, "Gentlemen, would either of you like a drink?"

David ordered a glass of red California wine, his favorite, while Bjorn asked for a German lager beer.

"I'm planning on arriving the day before to get settled," Bjorn said. "I'm not sure about Ilse and Devang. She says Devang thinks going will trigger post-traumatic stress in everyone. Both of their doctors disagree. She's working on him. I hope they all find a way to normalcy before too long."

"I think she's made incredible progress," David said with conviction. "As you say, it's Devang. But I think she's worried for him. He made a lot of enemies. They're both in danger until Iygal catches Damsky and all of his mercenaries. That she's with Devang is what gives me comfort. Otherwise, I'd want her locked up in a castle until it's over."

"I think you've gotten dramatic. But certainly, it's better safe than sorry," Bjorn said. "You seem more worried for my daughter than I am."

"I don't know. Maybe because I never had any of my own. I've adopted her."

"That's quite all right. You've done wonders with her, David. I am forever in your debt."

Bjorn reached across the table to take his hand briefly.

"Okay, then," David said, slightly uncomfortable with Bjorn's unusual show of emotion. "Let's move on to something less dramatic. How is Katsumi's research going? When was the last time you spoke with him?"

Bjorn sat back and nodded, seeming to be making a decision.

"I just came from his lab at Columbia University. Ekow may have developed the Waterfall Reagent, but Katsumi may have surpassed him.

"Seriously?" David exclaimed excitedly. "Please share."

The End